KU-324-425

J. JEFFERSON FARJEON

The House Opposite

COLLINS
CRIME
CLUB

COLLINS CRIME CLUB

An imprint of HarperCollins*Publishers*
1 London Bridge Street
London SE1 9GF
www.harpercollins.co.uk

This paperback edition 2016

First published in Great Britain for The Crime Club Ltd
by W. Collins Sons & Co. Ltd 1931

Copyright © Estate of J. Jefferson Farjeon 1931

J. Jefferson Farjeon asserts the moral right
to be identified as the author of this work

A catalogue record for this book is
available from the British Library

ISBN 978-0-00-815586-5

Set in Sabon by Palimpsest Book Production Limited, Falkirk, Stirlingshire

Printed by Clays Ltd, St Ives plc

All rights reserved. No part of this publication may be reproduced,
stored in a retrieval system, or transmitted, in any form or by any means,
electronic, mechanical, photocopying, recording or otherwise, without
the prior written permission of the publishers.

MIX
Paper from
responsible sources
FSC C007454

FSC™ is a non-profit international organisation established to promote
the responsible management of the world's forests. Products carrying the
FSC label are independently certified to assure consumers that they come
from forests that are managed to meet the social, economic and
ecological needs of present and future generations,
and other controlled sources.

Find out more about HarperCollins and the environment at
www.harpercollins.co.uk/green

CONTENTS

PART I: NUMBER TWENTY-NINE

1. The Caller   3
2. Creaks   11
3. Ben Accepts a Job   19
4. At the Coffee Stall   27
5. The Contents of a Parcel   35
6. A Taste of Death   43
7. The Will of a Woman   51
8. Ben Finds New Quarters   59
9. The Seat   67
10. Back Again!   75
11. What You Can Do When You Matter   82
12. How Not to Kill an Indian   92
13. A Queer Association   100
14. Ben Sees a Murder   107
15. Ben Commits a Murder   117
16. Ben Takes the Plunge   121

PART II: NUMBER TWENTY-SIX

17. The Spider's Parlour   133
18. Cocktails in Jowle Street   143

19. Mr Clitheroe's Big Idea   150
20. Wheels Within Wheels   157
21. Little Hymns of Hate   165
22. The Friendly Surface   174
23. Midnight   183
24. Across the Roof   191
25. Nadine Goes In   199
26. Mahdi Takes Control   208
27. When Morning Came—   215
28. The Performance   226
29. The Terms of Silence   239
30. Ben Gets In   246
31. Outside the Cellar Door   255
32. The Conversation in the Hall   263
33. The Long Wooden Box   271
34. Into the Box   279
35. Out of the Box   285
36. And Life Goes On   296

PART I

Number Twenty-Nine

1

The Caller

'Gawd!' muttered the temporary tenant of No. 29 Jowle Street. 'That's done it!'

He was eating cheese. His dining-table was a soap box. His view was peeling wallpaper. And his knife, fork and spoon were eight fingers and two thumbs. Not, of course, that one needs a knife, fork and spoon for cheese. Eight fingers and a couple of thumbs are sufficient for anybody.

Despite his primitive accessories and his faded, dilapidated view, the temporary tenant of No. 29 Jowle Street had been quite content until this moment. He had lived in more empty houses than anyone else in the kingdom, and he knew a good one when he came across it. Beginning with No. 17, he had worked upwards and downwards, numerically, until his addresses had included every number under fifty. The usual method was to enter the houses slowly and to leave them quickly—and he had left the last one very quickly. But No. 29 had suggested a longer stay. Its peeling walls and rotting staircase had whispered comfortingly, 'No one has been here for years and years, and no one will want to come here for years and years.' This was the message of welcome one most appreciated . . .

But, now, this bell!

'I 'aven't 'eard it,' decided the diner. ''Cos why? It ain't rung, see?'

He continued with his cheese. The bell rang again. Again, the cheese halted.

'Wot's the good of 'is ringin' like that when nothink 'appens?' grumbled the diner. 'If 'e'd got any sense 'e'd go away and know there was nobody 'ere.'

The bell rang a third time. The diner concluded that Fate was not going to let him have it all his own way. When people rang thrice, you had to decide between the alternatives of letting them in or 'opping it.

You could 'op it, in this case, through an open window at the back. It would be quite easy. On the other hand, it was a nice house and a nasty night. Sometimes bold-ness pays.

The bell rang a fourth time. 'Gawd, ain't 'e a sticker?' thought the diner, and decided on the policy of boldness.

He had selected for his meal the front room on the second floor. He always liked to be high up, because it made you seem a long way off. Moreover, this was the only room in the house that was furnished. None of the other rooms had any soap boxes at all. Still, there was one disadvantage of being on the second floor. You had to go down two flights of creaking stairs to get to the ground floor, which you didn't exactly hanker after in the evening. And then, murders generally happened on second floors.

The temporary tenant of No. 29 Jowle Street faced the discomfort of the creaking stairs, however, because he felt he couldn't stand hearing the bell ring a fifth time, and he felt convinced that, unless he hurried his stumps, it would. He hurried his stumps rather loudly. No harm in being a bit impressive like, was there? He even cleared his throat a little truculently. The world takes you at your own valuation, so you must see it's more than tuppence.

Reaching the front door, he paused, and at the risk of his impressiveness called:

''Oo's there?'

The bell rang a fifth time. He fumbled hastily with the latch, and threw the door open.

He had vaguely expected an ogre or a fellow with a knife. Instead he found a pleasant-featured young man standing on the doorstep. For an instant they regarded each other fixedly. Then the pleasant-featured young man remarked:

'Say, you're a little streak of lightning, aren't you?'

'You bin ringin'?' blinked the little streak of lightning.

'Only five times,' answered the caller. 'Is that the necessary minimum in your country?'

The little streak of lightning didn't know what a necessary minimum was, but he was interested in the reference to his country. It suggested that it wasn't the caller's country. So did the caller's bronzed complexion. Still, this wasn't a moment for geography.

'Wotcher want?' asked the cockney. 'No one lives 'ere.'

'Don't *you* live here?' countered the visitor.

'Oh! Me?'

'Yes; you. Who are you?'

'Caretaker.'

'I see. You're taking care of the house.'

'Yus.'

'Well, why don't you do it better?'

'Wot's that?'

'Did you hear what I said?'

'Yus.'

'Then why did you say "Wot's that?"'

''Oo?'

The visitor took a breath, and tried again.

'Our conversational methods seem at some variance,' he said; 'but perhaps if we try to like each other a little more we may meet somewhere. When I asked why you didn't take care of the house better I was referring to its condition. It doesn't look as though anybody ever took care of it at all.'

'It ain't exactly Winsor Castle,' admitted the tenant.

'And then, you were the devil of a time answering the bell, weren't you?'

'P'r'aps it didn't ring proper?'

'I'm sure it rang proper!'

'Well, and now I'm 'ere proper, so wotcher worryin' abart?'

'To tell the truth, old son, I'm worrying about *you*,' answered the visitor. 'Rather queer, that, isn't it?'

'If yer like.'

'Who *are* you?'

'I tole yer.'

'I don't remember.'

'Caretaker.'

'Oh, yes! So you did! But what's your name?'

'Wotcher wanter know for?'

'Trot it out!'

'Ben—if that 'elps.'

'It helps immensely. Well, Ben—'

''Ere, gettin' fermilyer, ain't yer?' demanded the cockney. ''Oo's give you permishun ter call me by me fust name?'

6

'You haven't told me your last,' the visitor reminded him. 'What is it?'

'Moosolini.'

'Thank you. But I think I prefer Ben, if you don't mind. How long have you been the caretaker here?'

'Eh?'

'Who engaged you—?'

''Ow long 'ave I gotter stand 'ere answerin' questions?' retorted Ben. 'I'm goin' ter ask *you* one, fer a change. 'Oo are *you*? That's fair, ain't it?'

'Who am I?' murmured the visitor, and suddenly paused.

''E don't want me ter know,' reflected Ben. 'Fishy, the pair of us!'

The next moment he realised that there was another reason for the pause. A door had slammed across the street. The visitor had turned.

The door that had slammed was the front door of the house opposite. The number on it was '26'. For an instant Ben stared vaguely at the number, as the movement of a figure in front of it rendered it visible after a second of obscurity. A girl's figure; she appeared to be leaving hurriedly. But Ben found himself less interested in the girl on the doorstep of No. 26 than in the man on the door-step of No. 29, for the man suddenly left the doorstep and made for the pavement.

'Wot's that for?' wondered Ben. 'Wot's 'e arter?'

He appeared to be after the girl. The girl was hastening towards a corner, and the young man looked as though he were going to hasten after her.

'Lummy, '*e* don't waste no time!' thought Ben.

But if the young man's intention had been to follow the

girl he abruptly changed it when she had turned the corner and disappeared. Instead of following her, he veered round towards the house she had just left. No. 26 Jowle Street. Ben watched him from No. 29.

'Well, 'e's fergot me, any'ow,' reflected Ben. 'If 'e wants me 'e'll 'ave ter ring agin!'

He closed the door quickly and quietly. A bang might have brought the young man back. He waited a few seconds, just to make sure that the young man *wasn't* coming back again, and then began to ascend the stairs to resume his interrupted meal.

It has been said that Ben had lived in many empty houses. He had. But he had lived in them for reasons of economy rather than of affection, and it depressed him that he had not really and truly grown to love them. Perhaps this was because he had had a bad start. His first empty house, 'No. 17', had given him enough nightmares for life. But it must be admitted, and you had better know it at once, that Ben was not one of the world's heroes, and if there was one thing he couldn't stand it was creaks. 'Give me the fair shivers, so they does,' he confessed to his soul. (Ben had a soul—you had better know that, too, lest in what follows you may be tempted to be hard on him.) Yes, even in his able-bodied days he had hated the creaking of ships. Even when he had been surrounded by fellow-seamen. But all alone, in empty houses . . .

'In the langwidge o' them psicho-wotchercallems,' decided Ben, 'I got a creak compress.'

The creaks seemed rather worse going up the stairs than they had seemed coming down them. Somehow or other, the visit of that young man, his rather odd behaviour, and the sudden termination of the interview, had worried Ben more than he cared to admit. The shadows seemed deeper. The creaks louder. The subsequent silences uncannier.

But he reached the second floor without accident, and he found his room just as he had left it. There were no corpses about, and no one had been at his cheese. If he'd had a cup of tea, he could have soon got back to his condition of lethargic, vegetable comfort. Well, he'd have to get back just on cheese.

'P'r'aps I better 'ave a squint outer the winder fust,' he thought. ''E may be comin' back again.'

He crossed to the window. There, immediately opposite, was No. 26, growing moist in the drizzle. Looking down, he saw his late visitor on the doorstep. This rather surprised him. He'd been on the doorstep some while. By now, surely, he ought to be either in or out?

Ben stared. The front door was open—no, half-open—well, same thing—and a bit of an argument seemed to be going on. Couldn't see the fellow inside the house, but the fellow outside appeared to be very determined. He was taking something from his pocket. He was handing it to the fellow inside. A bit of a pause now. Who was going to win?

Then, all at once, Ben's eyes were attracted by a movement closer to him. Not in his own room—thank Gawd fer that!—but it, gave him a start, like. In the room immediately opposite. The second-floor front of No. 26. An old man had backed to the window, as though to get a better perspective of something he was gazing at. And what he was gazing at was a figure on the floor!

'That ain't nice,' thought Ben.

An instant later, however, the figure got up. The old man shook his head, and pointed to another part of the floor.

The figure lay down again. The old man nodded, and the figure got up again.

'Well, I'm blowed!' muttered the watcher.

He stared down at the front door. It was now closed. The young man had got in. At least—had he? Ben hadn't seen him go in. He might have left, of course, and be walking now towards the corner.

Ben twisted his head and stared towards the corner. If the young man had gone to the corner he had now vanished, as the girl had vanished; and in their place, regarding No. 26 with contemplative eyes, his dark skin rising incongruously above his European collar, was an Indian.

2

Creaks

Ben returned to his cheese. He possessed, in addition, a piece
of string, a box of matches, a cigarette, three candle ends,
a pencil stump, and sevenpence. These alone stood between
him and the drizzling evening and eternity.

He sat with his back to the window. He had seen all he
wanted until he had got a bit more cheese inside him. But
though he could shut sights out from his eyes, he could
not shut them out from his mind. Into the pattern of the
peeling wallpaper were woven a young man, an old man,
a figure leaping up and down on a floor, and an Indian.

'Well—wot *abart* them?' he demanded suddenly.

Why, nothing about them! If you got guessing about all
the people you saw, you'd never stop! The young man had
called to look over the house, the old man and the figure
on the floor had been doing a charade, and the Indian
was just one of them students or cricketers. Nothing to
it but that!

'It's not gettin' yer meals reg'lar wot does it,' decided
Ben. 'And this 'ere corf.'

By the time he had finished his cheese he was in a better frame of mind. After he had lit his solitary cigarette—almost a whole one, and cork-tipped—he was even able to rise from his soap box, turn round, and walk to the window again. Wonderful what a cigarette could do for you, even if it had been begun by somebody else!

The rain was falling faster now. A thin mist was curling through the gloaming. Never joyous at the best of times, Jowle Street looked at its worst just now, full of evil little glistenings as the damp night drew on. It was a forgotten road, and best forgotten. But the house opposite provided nothing especially sinister at the moment. The blind of the window of the second floor front was now drawn, presenting an expressionless face of opaque yellow. The doorstep was deserted. And there was no longer an Indian standing at the corner. The only movement visible in the street was that of a covered cart slowly jogging along through the slush.

Ben watched the cart idly. 'Well, I'd sooner be 'oo I am than that there 'orse,' he reflected. It was a poor, bony creature, a dismal relic of a noble race. Funny how some horses stirred and stimulated you, while the very sight of others almost made you lose your belief in the beneficence of Creation! 'Wot does 'orses do when they gits old?' wondered Ben. 'Sit dahn, like us?'

But a moment later he ceased to dwell on the hard lot of horses. The cart had stopped outside No. 26.

Well, why shouldn't it stop outside No. 26? Every day, millions of carts stopped outside millions of houses! Almost indignantly, Ben attempted to deride his interest. The interest held him, though. He could not tear himself away. He'd have to watch until he saw the cart move on again.

A man descended from the driver's seat. He moved towards the house, but almost immediately the front door opened, and a servant came out. At least, Ben deduced he must be a servant. A few words passed between the servant and the driver. Then they both went to the back of the cart, and were busy for a while drawing something out. The hood of the cart hid the something from Ben's view until the two men were actually carrying it towards the door. Then Ben saw it. It was a long object, covered with sacking.

About six feet long. About three feet wide. About three feet high.

Ben turned away. He didn't like it. And as he turned away, the front door bell rang again.

"Ere, wot's orl this abart?' he demanded of the uncommunicative walls. 'Wot's 'appenin'?'

As once before, he was faced with the alternative of the front door and the back window. This time he was even more tempted to choose the back window. He might have done so had not a sudden thought deterred him, a thought that abruptly changed the bell from a sinister to a welcome sound.

"Corse—it's on'y that young chap come back agin,' he cogitated, 'and 'e was bahnd ter come back some time or other, wasn't 'e? Blimy, if I don't ask 'im in and tell 'im orl abart it!'

Life is largely a matter of comparison. When first the young man had called he had been a nuisance. Now, contrasted with an old man's back, a contortionist, an Indian, and a long, six-foot object, he became a thing of beauty! And even without the advantage of these comparisons, Ben recalled that his face had been pleasant enough, and his voice amiable.

13

'Yes, that's wot I'll do!' muttered Ben, on his way to the passage. 'I'll 'ave 'im in, and arsk 'im wot 'e thinks.'

He slithered down the stairs. As he neared the bottom, the bell rang again. 'Orl right, orl right!' he called. 'I'm comin', ain't I?'

He opened the door. The Indian stood on the doorstep.

At some time or other your heart has probably missed a beat. Ben's heart missed five. Meanwhile, the Indian regarded him without speaking, as though to give him time to recover. Then the Indian said, in surprisingly good English:

'You live here?'

He spoke slowly and quietly, but with a strangely dominating accent. But for the dominating accent, Ben might have been a little longer in finding his voice.

'Yus,' he gulped.

'It is your house?' continued the Indian.

'No,' answered Ben.

He had tried to say another 'yus' but with the Indian's eyes piercing him he was unable to.

'You are, then, a tenant?'

This time Ben managed a 'yus.'

'And to whom do you pay your rent?' inquired the Indian.

The inflexion was slightly acid. Ben fought hard.

'That's my bizziness, ain't it?' he retorted.

'If you pay rent, it is your business,' agreed the Indian, with the faintest possible smile. 'But—if you do not?'

'Wotcher mean?'

'Then it would be—the police's business?'

Police, eh? Ben decided he was bungling it.

'Look 'ere!' he exclaimed. 'When I said I was a tenant, like you arst, I didn't know as 'ow you knew orl the words, see? Wot I meant was that I live 'ere, see?'

'But you pay no rent?'

'Corse I don't. Don't they 'ave no caretakers in your country? If you've come ter look over the 'ouse, say so, and I'll fetch a candle, but if you ain't, then I can't do nothing for you.'

The Indian considered the statement thoughtfully. Then he inquired:

'And who engages you, may I ask, to take care of this beautiful house?'

'No, yer mayn't arsk!'

'Pray oblige me. To whom do I write, to make an offer?'

Ben was bunkered.

'So we complete the circle,' said the Indian impassively. 'You live here, but you do not pay rent, and you fulfil no office. And it becomes, as I said, a matter of interest to the police. Do we understand each other, or must I speak more plainly?'

'P'r'aps I could do a bit o' pline speakin'!' muttered Ben.

'Yes?'

'Yus! P'r'aps I could arst yer 'oo yer are, and wot bizziness it is o' yours, any'ow? People comin' 'ere and torkin' ter me as if I was dirt—'

'People?' interposed the Indian, his thin eyebrows suddenly rising. 'Someone else, then, has been here—to inquire?'

'Nobody's bin 'ere,' lied Ben. He did not know why he lied. Perhaps it was instinct, or perhaps he disliked telling the truth to one who was so bent on drawing it from him. 'Nobody's bin 'ere. I was speakin'—gen'ral, like.' The Indian shrugged his shoulders, plainly unconvinced. 'And now I'll speak speshul, like. This ain't my 'ouse—but is it your'n?'

'It is not mine,' answered the Indian.

15

'Orl right, then! It's goin' ter be a nasty night, and I ain't takin' no horders from foreigners! See?'

Whatever the Indian felt, his face did not show it. He merely regarded Ben a little more intensely, while Ben struggled to maintain his Dutch courage.

The Indian did not speak for several seconds. Removing his eyes from Ben at last, he gazed at the hall and the staircase; then he brought his eyes back to Ben again.

'It is going to be a very nasty night,' he said, in an almost expressionless voice. 'And you, my friend, will get out of it as quickly as you can. I speak for your good.'

'Fer my good, eh?' queried Ben, 'Meanin' yer love me, cocky?'

Now something did enter the Indian's expression. A sudden flash, like the glint of a knife. But it was gone in an instant.

'You are nothing,' said the Indian.

'And so are you, with knobs on!' barked Ben, and slammed the door.

He had made a brave show, if not a wise one, but as soon as the door was closed he was seized with a fit of trembling. He backed to the stairs, and sat down on the bottom step. He wondered if the Indian was still standing outside, or whether he was walking away? He wondered whether he would really go for the police, and, if so, why? He wondered whether he had really shut him out? Indians were slippery customers, climbing up ropes that weren't there and what not, and perhaps this one knew a trick or two, and could duck into a house when the door was slammed on him! He might be in the shadows, now. He might have sprung by Ben, and have got on to the stairs. He might be behind Ben, at this moment, bending over him with a knife poised to prick his neck!

'Gawd!' gasped Ben, and leapt to his feet.

Nobody was on the staircase. Only shadows. It occurred to Ben that he had better go up himself, before his knees gave out. He went up, shakily. ''Ow I 'ate Injuns!' he muttered. When he got back to his room, he sat down on the soap box, and thought.

Of course, he had only been putting up a bluff. The wise thing to do would be to leave at once. Yes, even though the weather was getting worse and worse, and darkness was settling on the streets, choking out all their kindliness. Even though the wind was rising, still you didn't know whether it was the wind or a dog, and the creaking ran up and down your spine.

'Wot I can't mike out,' blinked Ben, 'is wot I come up orl these stairs agin for at all!'

Perhaps it was for his cap! Yes, one might as well keep one's cap. He took it from under him. He had used it as a cushion. Then, dissatisfied with himself, and life, and the whole of God's plan, he crept from the room and out into the passage.

'If on'y it wasn't fer that there creakin'!' he muttered.

Creak! Creak! The house seemed to have become populated with creaks! Perhaps he was making them himself? He paused, on the top stair. The creaks went on. Creak! Creak! Below him. And, once, a sort of slither. Like someone coming in through a window . . . A window! A back window! A back window that had been left open!

Ben had been standing on the top stair. Now he found himself sitting on it. His knees had given out.

There was no mistake about it! Someone *had* got in through the back window! Those creaks were not the mere complaint of a dying house. They were not just the moaning of bricks or the cracking up of decayed wood. Life was causing those creaks—life forming contact with death—movement outraging the static! In the more simple language that shames metaphor, someone was coming up.

''Ere—wotcher doin'?' gasped Ben to himself.

He caught hold of the rotting banister and heaved himself up. The banister just held. Then he sped back into his room, and waited.

He waited with his eyes on the door. The door was half-open, and he did not close it because, had he done so, he could only have followed the creaks in his imagination, and they could have ascended to the door without his knowing it. Now, at least, he could listen to them, in the hope that they would come no closer . . .

They came closer. Now they were on the lower stairs. Now a slight change in their character indicated the passage on the first floor. Hallo! They had stopped! What did that mean? Hallo; they hadn't stopped! Where were they? Something was wrong somewhere . . .

Something sounded immediately below him. First floor front! That's where they were! Gone in! To look for him!

Should he make a dash for it? If he was nippy he might get down the stairs, and then make a bunk for the back window below! Yes, if he was nippy . . .

He jerked himself towards the half-open door. Then he stopped. He was too late. The creaks had started again. They were now on the last staircase. Creak! Creak!

'I know!' thought Ben. 'I'll 'it 'im!'

He stood, galvanised. The creaks reached the landing. They reached the door. The door began to open . . .

3

Ben Accepts a Job

Shocks have an inconsiderate habit of getting you both ways. If you expect a parson and receive a cannibal, or if you expect an Indian and receive a beautiful girl, the world spins round, just the same. What you really need is a nice quiet life, with breakfast, dinner and tea, and ordinary things in between.

The beautiful girl who provided Ben with his present shock, and made him go all weak like, seemed quite as surprised to see Ben as he was to see her. There was, at least, equality of emotion, and that was something. Moreover, as he stared at her with mouth wide open (Ben never did his mouth by halves) and an exhibition of teeth that could not hold their own beside those she herself displayed, he began to discover certain other compensations in the situation. Item, her eyes. They really were rather a knock-out. The kind of eyes that made you feel sort of . . . Item, her hair. You couldn't see much of it because of the natty little helmet hat she was wearing, but what you could see was good. Item, her nose. Now there was a nose fit for

19

anybody! Item, her mouth, and the teeth that put Ben's incomplete army in the shade . . . Yes, as he stared at her and she, framed in the doorway, stared back, he realised that the world could spin quite agreeably.

Still, one couldn't stand staring all one's life! What was she doing here? But it was the girl who recovered first and opened the attack.

'Who are you?' she demanded.

Ben spent half his life telling inquisitive people who he was, and he had a large assortage of answers. He had confessed to being everybody under the sun, from Lloyd George to Tom Thumb. But he did not think in the present circumstances he could improve on the answer he had given to his two other callers, so he murmured: 'Caretaker, miss.' And hoped for the best.

'What—are you the caretaker of this house?' exclaimed the girl, with unflattering incredulity.

'That's right,' blinked Ben. 'No. 29 Jowle Street.'

He would prove he knew the number, anyway.

'I see—it's to let,' said the girl slowly.

'Yus,' nodded Ben solemnly. 'But you better not tike it.'

'Why not?'

'Carn't yer see? Comin' ter bits. Look at that there plarster!'

He pointed to the ceiling. The girl smiled. Yes, her teeth were winners, and no mistake! Like rows of little grave-stones. Noo ones, o' corse . . .

'If you're really the caretaker here,' she observed, 'you're not doing your duty very well. You oughtn't to run the place down.'

'It don't need me to,' retorted Ben. 'It does it itself.'

'I—I suppose you really *are* the caretaker?'

Ben looked uncomfortable. He hated having to repeat things.

'Why not?' he hedged. 'Come ter that, miss, one might arsk 'oo *you* was, comin' in like this?'

'One might,' she agreed, without hesitation.

'Yus—and torkin' o' that—'ow *did* yer come in?' inquired Ben suddenly.

'I came in through an open window at the back,' she responded. 'Like you.'

'Like me?'

'Yes.'

Ben capitulated.

'Oh, orl right,' he grunted. 'But it's fifty-fifty, so we ain't got nothin' on each hother.'

'No,' smiled the girl. 'We *both* came in to get out of the rain!'

'Oh rainin', is it?' murmured Ben. 'Well, that's an idea.'

Yes, it was an idea for him. But was it an idea for her? He regarded her dubiously, and an uneasy suspicion came into his mind that she wasn't playing fair. She had caught him up in a fib—made him admit it—and it looked as though she were fibbing herself!

Still, p'r'aps it didn't matter. It really wasn't Ben's affair, and there is something human about a fib, so long as it doesn't hurt you. What mattered was that she was here and he was here, and the sooner they both cleared out, the better.

'Well, tike my advice, miss,' said Ben, returning to first principles, 'and git aht agin, like I'm goin' ter.'

'But the rain—' she began.

Unceremoniously, he waved her down.

'Yus, I knows orl abart that, miss,' he interposed; 'but I knows somethin' helse, as well.'

'What?'

'Why, that fer orl the rine, yer more likely ter catch something' in 'ere than aht there.'

Now the girl frowned.

'I wish you wouldn't be so mysterious,' she exclaimed. 'Won't you tell me what you mean exactly?'

'Well,' answered Ben, after a pause, 'I don't wanter frighten yer, see, but this 'ouse ain't 'ealthy.'

'What makes you say that?' Her voice was interested.

'Creaks and things.' He was evading the issue. He really didn't want to frighten her. He knew what fright was. 'You know. On the stairs. Cupboards and that. You know.'

He wasn't doing it very well.

'I'm afraid I *don't* know,' replied the girl, her interest waning. 'Creaks don't worry me.' Ben looked incredulous. 'I don't believe in ghosts. Still, if you do, you'd better go. I won't keep you.'

What? Him go, and her stay? All the manhood in him— and he had a spoonful—rebelled against the suggestion. What would he feel like tomorrow morning when he read in the headlines:

EMPTY HOUSE MYSTERY
BEAUTIFUL GIRL FOUND WITH
THROAT CUT
AND HOARYENTAL KNIFE
IN CHEST

The words were bad enough as they stood up in his imagination. He knew that, if he had to face them in reality, cheese would never taste the same again.

'Orl right, miss, if yer will 'ave it,' he muttered. 'It ain't the creaks wot's sendin' me away. It's a blinkin' Injun.'

Now her interest flared up again, and Ben stared at her in amazement.

'Wot? Do you 'ate Injuns, too?' he asked sympathetically. 'Fair gits on *my* nerves, they does. And this 'un's the worst I hever come acrost, with 'is slimy manners, and sayin' good evenin' to yer in the sort o' perlite voice wot really means, "I'd like ter stick a knife in yer gizzard," if yer git me.'

'But—do you really mean,' she demanded, 'that an Indian has been *here*?'

'Yus.'

'In this house?'

'Ain't I tellin' yer? 'E comes 'ere, like as if 'e owned the blinkin' plice—the plice, that is—and tells me ter 'op it or somethin 'll 'appen to yer. 'Oo do yer think yer are? I ses. Oh, I give 'im a bit o' back chat. But—well, there y'are,' he ended up rather lamely. ''E kep' on as if 'e meant it. So yer see, miss, if it ain't safe fer me ter stop, it ain't no more fer you.'

But the girl made no sign of moving. Instead she looked into the bare room, beyond the packing case, to the window. And her eyes remained on the window.

'Have you any idea why he wanted you to go?' she asked.

'No, miss.'

'Or—where he is now?'

Ben looked a little uneasy.

'I thort fust as 'ow 'e was still 'ere,' he answered; 'but I reckon now 'e's gorn right enuff.'

'And you can't say where?' she repeated.

'Well, if 'e's gorn ter the 'ouse oppersit, where yer lookin' at, miss, 'e's a mug.'

23

She turned away from the window quickly, and her eyes were now on Ben again.

'Why should he have gone to the house opposite?' she demanded. 'And, if he has, why is he—a mug?'

'Look 'ere, miss,' said Ben seriously, 'orl this ain't got nothin' ter do with me and you, 'as it? I dunno where old Rangysinjy's gorn, orl I know is I 'ope it's a long way, and the reason I sed 'e'd be a mug ter go in the 'ouse oppersit is 'cos the 'ouse oppersit ain't much better'n this 'un, ter my thinkin', not with people pertendin' ter be dead—lyin' dahn, I seen 'em, and coffins bein' derlivered there in carts like stop-me-and-buy-one. And now, fer Gawd's sake, let's be goin', 'cos lummy I've 'ad enuff of it, that's a fack.'

He stopped to breathe. It was rather a long speech. The girl looked at him intently.

'I'm grateful to you for all your information,' she said; 'but if you want to go, I'm *still* not keeping you.'

'Yus, you are,' retorted Ben.

'How?'

'By not gettin' a move on. I ain't' goin' afore you do.'

'Why not?'

Ben's expression grew hurt.

'Well, p'r'aps I ain't much ter look at,' he murmured, 'but Napoleon wasn't seven foot!'

The remark, as well as the manner of it, made an impression. She regarded him more intently still.

'I believe I've been underrating you all this while, Napoleon,' she said, 'and I believe you underrate yourself.'

''Oo?' he blinked.

He wasn't quite sure of 'underrate', but he felt there was a compliment somewhere, and it confused him.

'I don't believe you're half as scared as you say you are,' she went on, simplifying it.

Ben considered the point. He tried to agree, but couldn't.

'There's times, miss,' he responded, with an outburst of frankness, 'when jellies ain't in it.' He misread her smile, and tried to save himself a little. 'Lorst me nerve, miss, in the war—thinkin' I was goin' ter be called up.'

'Just the same, I'm going to stick to my opinion, Napoleon,' she insisted, 'and, what's more, I'm going to test it. You say you won't go if I stay. *Will you stay if I go?*'

Ben's eyes became big.

'Wot's that?' he jerked.

'As *my* caretaker,' she added. 'Wages in advance.'

Ben's eyes became bigger as she opened her bag and laid a pound note on the packing case.

'Wot—is this *your* 'ouse?' he gasped.

'If you accept the offer, perhaps you could keep an eye on my view for me?' she suggested.

She returned to the window as she spoke. For a few seconds Ben gaped at her, and he had not found his voice before she suddenly darted back from the window again.

'I must go!' she exclaimed. Her voice was tense, and she was at the door in a flash. But at the door she paused for an instant, and her eyes grew worried. 'Don't accept my offer, Napoleon,' she said. 'It was thoughtless of me—I shouldn't have made it.'

Then she vanished. He heard her flying down the stairs. The rustle of her clothes grew more and more distant. A moment's utter silence. The slamming of a door. Utter silence again.

'Don't tike 'er hoffer, eh?' murmured Ben.

He removed his eyes from the doorway to the soap box,

on which lay the pound note. Then he removed his eyes from the soap box back to the doorway.

'Nobody couldn't tike this job from me,' he observed solemnly, 'not with a red-'ot poker!'

His words echoed out into the passage. And the passage seized them, turned them into hollow sounds, and sent them mockingly down the stairs.

4

At the Coffee Stall

Ben did not move for five minutes after the front door slammed and the dream had passed out of it, leaving only the nightmare behind. He wanted to try and work things out, and you could only do that when you kept quite still.

This girl, now, to begin with. What about her? She was a stunner, all right. Do for a queen anywhere, or p'r'aps more a princess like. The kind of girl he'd have liked *his* little kid to have growed up into, if she'd growed up at all . . . Just the same, there was something rum about her. First saying she'd come in to get out of the rain. And, afterwards, it being her house, all the time.

'Yus, but if it's 'er 'ouse, wot she wanter come in through the winder for?' wondered Ben. 'Don't they 'ave latch-keys?'

There you were, you see! There *was* something rum about her! You always got a latch-key with a house. Suppose it *wasn't* her house?

'Well, if it ain't 'er 'ouse, it don't mike no dif'rence,' Ben retorted to himself. 'I'll bet she ain't a wrong 'un, although I've knowed wrong uns afore wot couldn't 'elp it. Any'ow, there's 'er pahnd, and 'ere am I, and I've took on the job!'

So that was that. Next?

Next, the Indian. What about *him*? It was quite impossible to formulate any definite theory about him, either, but two points emerged uncomfortably from thought. First, would he come back to find out if Ben had left? Second, was he still here, waiting for Ben to go?

'Lummy!' murmured Ben, and decided to try and forget this for a moment or two. You see, when you started thinking about the Indian he got hold of your mind like an octopus and wouldn't let you think of anything else.

And there *were* other things to think about. That first chap who had called. What about him? And the funny going's on at No. 29. What about them? And . . .

Ben's eyes began to roam towards the window, and paused at the wooden case with the note still lying on it.

Yes—and the pound. What about *that*?

And now a wonderful idea dawned in Ben's mind, as the outcome of all these cogitations. If he was going to dig himself in here for the night, he would have to go out and buy a few things. It might even be a good idea to try and find a Lockhart's and stoke up. Why not use this occasion to fool the Indian, making him believe that Ben's temporary departure was a permanent one?

'Blimy, there's a clever idea!' thought Ben, rendered solemn by his own ingenuity. 'She called me Napoleon—I reckon she was right!'

He worked it all out carefully, just as Napoleon would have done. Say the Indian was away, but returned? He'd find the house empty, and would be satisfied. Say he wasn't away, but heard Ben leave? Same thing, wasn't it? Especially if Ben talked a bit to himself, to add a little local colour like?

Yes, that was the plan! Now to put it into operation! He stepped to the packing case, and secured the pound.

'Gawd—a pahnd!' he exclaimed suddenly. 'A 'ole blinkin' pahnd!'

It was the first time he had fully realised it. Turn that into cheese, and it'd take some carrying!

Yes, but suppose the girl returned, and found him gone? Him and the pound? What'd *she* think? Ben did not want to risk her bad opinion.

To avoid the risk he fished a scrap of paper from his pocket. It was a nice bit, the best bit he'd got. Only two thumb-marks. Still; she was worth it. From another pocket he fished out a pencil stump. This wasn't quite so impressive. They give you rotten pencils at the post office. Then, after thinking for a full minute of the best way to convey the idea on paper that he was coming back, he gave the lead a lick and wrote:

'COMIN BACK.'

He laid the paper on the wooden case, where the pound note had been. If she returned she'd be sure to find it . . .

'Yus, but if the Injun returns, 'e'll find it, too!' thought Ben, with a shock.

A bad mark for Napoleon, that! He sweated, to realise how nearly he had cooked his own goose. *What* a mug he was!

But the next instant he was smiling again. He needn't waste the paper. He'd use it to cheat the Indian further. He added a word to the message, and now it read:

'AINT COMIN BACK.'

He chuckled as he read the amended version, and continued to chuckle all the way out to the passage. Then the chuckling stopped abruptly.

'Yus, but s'pose, arter all, the Injun don't return, and the gal *does*?'

He turned and re-entered the room. He tore the paper to little bits, and threw them on the floor. Then he picked all the little bits up, and threw them out of the window. He realised that, after all, he wasn't quite cut out for a general.

Nevertheless, he did not scrap his entire plan of campaign, and when he reached the passage again and began to descend the stairs he remembered to pretend to be frightened, so that the Indian, if he were watching through any of the cracks, would believe he was being scared out of the house. He did not find the pretence in the least difficult. His first 'Ah' of simulated fear was so realistic that it sent him sliding down half a flight. It would have been a full flight but for a turn.

'Gawd!' muttered Ben, almost tearfully. 'I wish I 'ad 'old of the feller wot invented hechoes!'

He rose, and decided that his future demonstrations would be more quiet like. He began to mutter.

'Well, arter orl, wot's the good o' stayin'?' he asked. 'It's a rotten 'ouse, any'ow, and if the Injun wants it, 'e can 'ave it. *I've* 'ad enuff of it. I'm goin' away, and I ain't never comin' back, never, not so long as I live!'

That ought to do it. Still, just to make perfectly certain, he added:

'I reckon yer wouldn't git me back 'ere not if King George 'iself was ter come up ter me and ter say, "Ben, won't yer?"'

There! If the Indian didn't believe him after that, he must be a fool!

Satisfied with his effort, Ben reached the front door and opened it cautiously. It was not quite dark yet, but a vague drizzle still filled the air and merged into the indeterminate mist. Not at all pleasant outside. But then it wasn't at all pleasant inside, either. Life is largely a matter of comparisons, and the outside of No. 29 Jowle Street didn't have to exert itself seriously to secure the advantage.

Before leaving the doubtful sanctuary of No. 29, Ben looked across the road at No. 26. If anybody had popped out of No. 26 at that moment, he might have popped back into No. 29. No. 26 was already beginning to get upon his nerves and to exert an hypnotic influence over him. His mind was constantly drawn there. He hoped that his body would never be. But, happily, no one popped out at this particular moment, and, closing the door behind him, Ben slipped out into the road.

And now, for a few moments, he became a very different creature from the hesitating Ben we have known. He moved like lightning, having a remarkable ability in that direction when necessity arose. The necessity just now was simply the necessity of getting out of Jowle Street before Jowle Street saw him, as it were. That, and a sudden longing for the company of a cup of tea.

Already Jowle Street lay three streets away. You couldn't get back there by one move of the chess-board, not even if you were a knight. Ben breathed a little more freely. What about not going back at all? Yes, why go back? With a pound in his pocket to spend, and . . .

Ah, but was the pound his to spend if he didn't go back? There was the catch!

Three more corners; round two of them; and now a light streaked across the road. It came from the window of a shop outside which stood a stout man mechanically exhorting passers-by to purchase bacon before closing-time. 'Where bacon goes, cheese follers' was one of Ben's guides to existence. Ruth and Naomi were not more inseparable. He veered across to the stout man, and demanded cheddar.

The stout man cut him a slab, and held it out to him.

'Where's the piper?' demanded Ben.

'You don't want any paper,' answered the stout man, with a grin.

''Ow am I goin' ter write my letters ternight?' retorted Ben. 'Churchill's waitin' ter 'ear from me.'

The stout man laughed. He wasn't really unkind. He did the cheese up in a beautiful parcel, while Ben counted out his change, to make sure he hadn't received too many coins.

Along another street was a coffee stall. Ben made a bee-line for this when he spotted it, and life eased out.

'Cup o' tea,' he ordered. 'Big 'un!'

Then he nearly jumped out of his skin. The Indian was standing next to him.

'Good evening,' said the Indian.

Ben gulped. He wasn't quite ready for the courtesies.

But the Indian betrayed no annoyance over his lack of them. He continued amiably:

'You are out for a walk?'

Ben recovered himself, and answered:

'No. I'm surf-ridin'.'

The Indian smiled. So did the coffee stall keeper. The coffee stall keeper's smile was ever so much the nicer.

'Here's your tea, mate,' grinned the latter. 'Want anything to eat with it?'

32

'Yus, 'am sandwich,' replied Ben, 'and don't fergit the 'am.'

He drank the tea in one go, and shoved the cup across the counter for replenishment. The Indian watched him, still smiling. The coffee stall keeper took the cup, and turned away for a moment. Then the Indian bent forward suddenly, bringing his face within six inches of Ben's. It became magnified, like a close-up. The smile seemed to expand all round him.

'You are sensible,' said a voice in the middle of the enormous smile. 'See that you stay so!'

The coffee stall keeper turned back with the cup.

'Well, I'm blowed!' he exclaimed. 'Where's he gone?'

The Indian had vanished.

Ben rubbed his forehead. He felt as though the Indian's eyes were still upon him, and he wanted to get rid of them. He'd been through some nasty moments in his life; sometimes, indeed, he doubted whether there were any really nasty moments he hadn't been through; but the moment when the Indian had suddenly advanced his face and become a close-up was one of the very nastiest he could remember . . .

'Rum chaps, them Indians,' remarked the coffee stall keeper, breathing on a spoon and polishing it, 'but I like 'em.'

'I loves 'em,' replied Ben.

'Aunt of mine used to board 'em,' went on the coffee stall keeper, 'and she used to say nicer people she never met. But, of course, you get all kinds.' He leaned forward, and dropped his voice confidentially. 'Between you and me, mate,' he said, 'I wouldn't much care to sleep in a room next to *that* one!'

'That's right,' murmured Ben.

'If he was peckish, like as not he'd slice out your liver and have it for breakfast!'

He burst into guffaws at the joke. Ben did not join in. The coffee stall keeper looked disappointed, and tried something else.

'Fancy them findin' that old man in Bermondsey 'angin' upside down!'

''Ere, you're a little ray o' sunlight, ain't yer?' barked Ben.

He finished his second cup quickly, paid his account, and turned away.

Which direction should he take? Left—towards Jowle Street? Or right—towards peace? Suddenly he fished a coin from his pocket.

''Eads, it's Jowle Street,' he muttered, 'and tails it ain't!'

He tossed. The coin came down tails.

'It ain't,' he murmured.

And turned towards Jowle Street.

5

The Contents of a Parcel

Have you ever paused to realise the different mental attitudes of those who, superficially, appear to be engaged on business identical with your own? In a street, for instance, as you pass from one point to another?

To you a journey between two lamp-posts may be a forgotten incident, making no record in your mind. To the woman you overtake so carelessly it may be an eternity, though once her feet travelled as lightly and as fast as yours. To the young man who unconsciously keeps pace with you on the other side of the road it is a journey of breathless wonder, while each step brings him nearer to the whole meaning of existence waiting for him round the corner. To the elderly man, impelled to equal speed ten yards behind, it is a tragedy, with a doctor's house at the end of it.

Ben, on his way back to Jowle Street, was separated by similar gulfs from those he moved among, walking through a disturbing world of his own. It was not the world of the little whistling errand-boy he passed. It was a darker, grimmer place. A sort of tunnel, the sinister walls of which were closing in on him and pressing him forward. At the end of the tunnel were Indians with cynically smiling eyes, and a nasty old man gesticulating at a window—funny how that nasty old man stuck in Ben's mind!—and a chap hanging upside down. And towards all these things, despite the kindness of a tossed coin, Ben was moving. Why?

Yes—why? Ben stopped suddenly, and asked the question. There were loads of other ways, stretching to other points. Behind him, and on each side. Any one of them would be preferable to the particular way he was taking; any one of them would lead, if unpretentiously, to a peaceful night. For an instant he was out of the tunnel, and the walls ceased to press. 'I *did* come down tails, you know!' urged the coin in his pocket. 'Play fair!'

But he went on, with the question unanswered. You see, the answer was beyond the capacity of a bloke like Ben to fathom.

'Blinkin' Fate' was as near as he could get to it. He was quite unconscious that he himself had anything to do with the matter, and that, despite the coin's protest, the desire to play fair was very dominant in his cowardly little heart.

The drizzle had ceased, but the mist still wreathed through the murky thoroughfares, and the Indian wreathed through the mist. Of course, the Indian was just imagination. Ben admitted that. He hadn't quite got rid, even yet, of the nasty feeling on his forehead that the Indian had stamped there during that tense second while the coffee stall keeper's back was turned. Yes, that was it—*stamped* there. Like his photograph, like.

'Lummy, wish I could peel it orf!' muttered Ben . . .

Hallo, though! *Was* it all imagination? Ben suddenly ducked up a side street. Two large arms caught him.

'Now, then, my lad! What's up?'

It was a policeman's voice. You can always tell a policeman's voice. Solid and slow, and all right if *you're* all right.

'Beg yer pardon,' apologised Ben. 'Didn't see yer.'

'Of course, you didn't,' replied the policeman. 'You had your eyes shut.'

'Go on!' retorted Ben.

'Anybody after you?'

''Oo?'

'That's what I'm asking.'

'Yus. No. 'Ere, let go me arm. It's mine, ain't it?'

'Yes, your arm's yours,' admitted the policeman, though he still retained it; 'but can you say the same about that parcel you're carrying?'

'Eh?'

'That parcel?'

'Wot abart it?'

'Is it *yours*?'

'Corse it's mine!'

'You didn't take it from anybody?'

'Yus.'

'Who?'

'Cheesemonger.'

The policeman frowned.

'That's a pretty smart parcel, isn't it,' he remarked, suspiciously, 'for a bit of cheese?'

'Corse it is,' answered Ben. ''E knoo 'oo 'e was servin'. Smell it!'

He thrust the parcel abruptly under the policeman's nose. The policeman, unprepared for this sudden onslaught of cheddar, dropped Ben's arm. Escape was now easy, and effected.

Ben did not know, as he darted away, whether the policeman made any attempt to follow him. He hoped the test had proved his innocence, and would willingly have waited until the cheese had done its work; but the policeman was merely his second consideration, at the moment, for out of the corner of his eye he had spied somebody far more significant—somebody from whom it was infinitely more important to escape. There was no mistake about it this time. Ben had seen the Indian. Whether the Indian had also seen him he was less able to say.

Well, if the Indian had seen him, he mustn't see him any more! That was the one obvious thought in Ben's mind as he now began a definite policy of evasion. He turned away from Jowle Street. Then he angled towards it, then turned away again. Following a zigzag course, a course of which no crow could have conception, he utilised every corner and every alley and every by-street. Once he even ducked down a subway, coming up at the other end like a diver. He got hopelessly lost, but that didn't matter so long as he also lost his pursuer. And at length he decided that he had lost him, and he paused under a lamp-post to breathe.

'Gotter git back now,' he communed with himself. 'Wunner where I am?'

The lamp went up as he wondered. The sudden light illuminated some letters on the wall opposite the lamp-post. The letters spelt:

'JOWLE STREET.'

Only the letters weren't quite as distinct as you read them here. Years of dirt and depression had tried to wipe them out.

'Wot—can't I *never* get away from it?' blinked Ben.

It did seem, this time, as though Fate had taken a hand!

He peered cautiously along the road. He was at the 'No. 1' end of it. He'd only used the other end up till now, the end where there wasn't a lamp-post. That was why he hadn't recognised it. From the spot where he stood, No. 29 was on the left, and No. 26 was on the right. There was nobody about. He could nip along to No. 29, slip round to the back, and be in at the window in a couple of shakes. But, on the point of putting this simple plan into execution, he paused. No. 26 beckoned to him with almost equal insistence.

He stared at it. Like the Indian, it bore all the uncanniness of the unknown and its very mystery was hypnotic. He knew about No. 29. Well, about bits of it. But he didn't know anything about No. 26—he didn't know what it was like inside, or who lived there, or what happened when you got in. Would the person who opened the door ask you your name or seize you by the throat? Of course, it didn't matter. Ben had nothing to do with No. 26, really . . . But it was funny how that house seemed to face him everywhere. His thoughts as well as his eyes.

He decided to have one close view of it, just to make sure there were no bloodstains or anything, and then to 'go home'. Crossing the road to the even number side, he slithered along till the numbers climbed to 26. Then, at a blackened railing, he stopped. One—two—three—four—five stone steps. Same as his side. Mounting to a flat space before the front door. Same as his side. And then the front door itself. Again, same as his . . . Not, not quite the same as his side, this time. This door was a bit more solid like. And then the slit for the letters was higher up. A good deal higher up. Funny place for the slit, that. Shouldn't think the postman'd much care for it. He'd have to lift his arm more than shoulder high. Almost on a level with his eyes . . . his eyes . . . eyes . . .

'Criky!' muttered Ben, and backed suddenly.

He backed into something. Something that had come along quietly behind him. The collision was violent, and his parcel fell to the ground. Only by grabbing at the railing was Ben able to prevent himself from following the parcel. Then he swerved round, to see what the new trouble was.

He found it was the nasty old man.

The old man looked at him angrily. He, also, had dropped a parcel. He seemed very annoyed about it.

'Hey! What are you up to?' he cried.

Ben lurched down and regained his parcel, and the old man lurched down at the same time and regained his.

'Well, why don't you answer, my man?' rasped the indignant one. 'What were you doing on that doorstep?'

'Lookin' at the number,' replied Ben. It seemed a good idea. But the old man did not think it was such a good idea.

'What for?' he demanded.

'Ter see wot it was,' explained Ben.

'Yes, but what did you want to see what it was for?'

'So's I'd know it.'

The old man glared. Ben glared back. After all, there was no law against looking at house numbers, was there?

'Well, now you know it,' said the old man, 'what are you going to do about it?'

'Go away from it,' answered Ben, 'and never come back.'

The answer found favour. The old man actually smiled.

'Now, that's excellent news,' he remarked ironically. 'Our stormy little meeting ends happily for both of us, after all!' He turned, and mounted the steps. But, as he took out his latch-key, he turned again. 'By the way,' he inquired, 'what number *did* you want?'

''Undred an' eight,' returned Ben.

'I'm afraid you'll have some difficulty,' sighed the old man, as he inserted his key. 'They only go up to forty-two.'

He disappeared. So did Ben. But ten minutes later Ben reappeared in Jowle Street like a human rocket, fired horizontally, with a trajectory that ended abruptly through the window of No. 29. The conclusion was so violent that there were quite a few stars.

He waited a few moments to recover from the stars. He had known several thousands of stars in his time, so it didn't take long. Just shut your eyes, stand still, and they go. Then he crept round to the front hall, and called, 'Oi!' That was another good dodge he'd learned. If anybody answered your 'Oi' you replied, 'Nah, then, wot are you doin' 'ere?' If nobody answered you, then you yourself were safe from the question. Ben was no arch-sinner, but in the lesser omissions he could claim his share of proficiency.

Nobody answered his 'Oi.' Good! He ascended the first flight.

'Oi!' he called again.

Again nobody answered him. Again, good! He ascended the second flight.

'Oi!'

This was the most important 'Oi'. He was now outside his home quarters on the second floor front. But fortune continued to favour him—conscious, perhaps, of its coming desertion—and he shoved open the door with a contented mind. As contented a mind, at least, as is possible to anyone in a house that creaks.

The room was empty. Just as he had left it. There was

the closed window. There was the packing-case. There, even, were some familiar crumbs, including a bit of rind he remembered excommunicating to the corner. Each little sign that the room had not been entered during his absence gave him a reassuring sense of possession and of home.

Well, now it was time to start making a few *more* crumbs! He was sorry he had only got the cheese to make them with, because he had intended to buy a packet of biscuits and a bit of cake at the coffee stall; but the Indian, and then the stall keeper's conversation, had upset his plans, and he had come away with his shopping only half done. Never mind. The cheese was something. He mightn't even have had that.

'Aht comes me little parcel!' he murmured, fishing for it in a capacious pocket that was mainly hole.

Little parcel? Not so blinkin' little, neither! Had he bought all that cheese? As he opened the parcel he hoped the contents would not lie as heavy on his chest as they lay in the paper . . .

'Lord luvvaduck!' gasped Ben.

The cheese had turned into a revolver.

6

A Taste of Death

'Well, I'm blowed!' muttered Ben, in amazement. He had seen a rabbit turn into a Union Jack, but he had never seen a piece of cheese turn into a pistol. '*Now* wot 'appens?'

The next instant it occurred to him what would happen. The owner of the pistol would want his possession back. He was probably staring angrily at Ben's cheese at this very moment!

'Yus, 'e'll want it back, but 'ow's 'e goin' ter *git* it back?' reflected Ben.

Why, by coming across after it, of course.

'Yus, but 'e don't know I'm 'ere?'

Didn't he?

Well, Ben would soon find that out. If the old man knew that Ben was here—if he had seen him in that meteoric flight through Jowle Street, or if he had divined it by means of some sixth sense—then he would very soon pop across the road. Why, he might be on his way across *now*! Gawd! Wot a night!

Slipping the weapon into his pocket—it was a very small

one and went in easily—he crept to the window, keeping his head and body well below the level of the ledge. When he reached the window he discovered that one cannot see out of a window at such a meagre elevation. Grudgingly he increased the elevation till he was able to see more than sky and chimneys, and when he had increased it sufficiently to procure a view of the door of No. 26, he put himself swiftly into reverse and dropped down flat. For at that moment the old man had come flying out of the door, and his mood had not appeared pleasant.

In the most life-like guise of a pancake he could assume, Ben cogitated.

''E won't come 'ere, 'e'll go up the road,' ran his thoughts, 'but if 'e does come 'ere 'e won't git in, 'cos if 'e rings it won't 'elp 'im and 'e don't know there's a winder hopen at the back, and there ain't no hother way—well, is there?'

The slamming of the front door answered him.

'Golly! 'e's in!' gasped Ben. ''Ow the blazes—?'

But this was no time for theorising. The old man was certainly in, and just as certainly he was coming up!

''Ere—stop thinkin',' Ben rounded on himself, 'and *do* somethin'!'

What?

Well, you could stay where you were and hope—that was one thing. Or you could rush out with a roar, pretending you were a madman or a murderer—that was another. Or you could dart quickly up to the third floor—that was another—only you'd have to do that at once because the stairs at the top of the first flight were already creaking, which meant that in another moment the stairs at the bottom of the second flight would start, and when anyone got round the bend of the second flight they'd spot you.

Or you could say to yourself, 'Wot 'ave I done, any'ow? 'Oo's 'e, any'ow? Boo!' And wait, calm like.

Ben chose the last idea. He chose it largely because he was too late to choose most of the others, but even if the choice had been forced upon him by circumstances he came to the conclusion that it really was the best one. For, after all, what *was* he afraid of? The old man, if he possessed the right to warn him away, had not done so yet, and when it came to a direct battle of wits Ben's weren't so bad. Anyway, your brain worked better in the open than in a cupboard.

'Seven more, and 'e'll be 'ere,' Ben counted the steps. 'If 'e don't tread clear of No. Five 'e'll git a jump! . . . There she goes . . . Good, 'e's swearin' . . . Three more . . . One . . . Now 'e's up—'

The door was shoved open. A figure stood in the doorway.

It was the old man all right.

'So! You *are* here!' he cried, glaring.

'Well, I'm blowed!' answered Ben.

'What are you doing?'

'No 'arm.'

'I'll judge that, my man! Answer me! What are you doing?'

For the first time Ben had authority for saying that he was the caretaker, and for the first time he had no inclination to make the statement. He didn't mind lying himself, but he wasn't so ready to involve other people. If the old man had got in with a latch-key the house presumably belonged to him; and if the house belonged to him, then it couldn't belong to the girl; and if it didn't belong to the girl, then he couldn't really be her caretaker, could he? Well, there you were! . . .

'*Are* you going to answer me, or aren't you?' demanded the old man.

'Lummy, don't you '*urry* one?' retorted Ben. 'I'll tell you why I'm 'ere, guv'nor. I come in 'ere ter eat a bit o' cheese, and fahnd it rather 'ard.'

Now the old man looked at him sharply.

'Try speaking a little more clearly?' he suggested.

''Ow's this fer clear?' returned Ben, and brought the revolver from his pocket.

To Ben's disappointment the old man did not jump. Instead he darted forward with amazing nimbleness and snatched the weapon from Ben's hand.

'You rascal!' he barked.

'Go on,' responded Ben indignantly. 'You got my cheese. And, come ter that,' he added, 'I *want* it!'

'Bah!'

'Where is it?'

'Do you think I can worry about your bit of cheese, you fool? Clear out this minute, or I'll have the police after you.'

'Yus, but—'

'Do you hear? Or must *I* speak more plainly, too?'

Ben's indignation increased. Fair's fair! He had given the old man his pistol, and he wanted his cheese . . . But, all at once, his indignation began to yield to another emotion. What was the old man doing with the pistol?

'Nah, then!' muttered Ben. 'We don't want none o' that!'

'Don't we?' answered the old man, and raised the little weapon.

'I know it ain't loaded!' blustered Ben, now terrified.

'You know a lot,' replied the old man.

And fired.

Ben died promptly. He fell down, he was buried, and

he went to heaven. That he did insist on. As a matter of fact, there *was* a bit of an argument about the heaven, and just as he was explaining to a sort of Noah with wings that he had always kept his mother, and that one couldn't help one's face, the Noah with wings dropped him from a cloud and sent him hurtling back in an empty room he'd known years and years ago, and where he had once stood before an old man with a pistol . . . where he had once stood . . . before an old man with a pistol . . .

'And the *next* time,' said the old man with the pistol, 'I *will* hit you!'

Ben ran. There are moments when there is nothing else to do—when violent movement becomes the sole object of existence, as also the sole guarantee of its continuance. He had died once. He didn't want a second death so soon after the first. The memory was too horrible.

The old man was standing between Ben and the doorway. A mad position if the old man wanted Ben to get out through the doorway; and not even the revolver was going to make Ben choose the only other egress, the window! That would merely provide an alternative route to the winged Noah. But then the old man *was* mad, Ben was now convinced of it. So he closed his eyes and dashed past the madman with a roar and shot beyond him into the passage. By the time the old man turned, Ben was halfway down the flight.

The stairs assisted him down the second half. No escalator could have assisted him better. They seemed to join in the race and run with him. They rolled him across the few feet of passage at the bottom and deposited him on the next flight, and the next flight caught him and carried him on as though it were a relay race. Having won it, the stairs threw him away unceremoniously at the bottom. Then he paused, and startling, violent reaction set in.

His terror did not disappear. That had come to stay, and it may be stated here that, throughout all its risings and fallings during the succeeding hours, it never wholly went. It formed a solid, cold background to all he endured, advancing, receding, advancing. But into the terror other emotions entered, forming queer mixtures that produced astonishing actions, and one of these other emotions entered now. It was red anger. Anger, against the old man, anger against the world, anger against the Universe! Why had he, Ben, been marked for this sort of thing? What had he done? He hadn't *asked* to be born! As a matter of fact, if anybody had consulted him he would have answered very definitely, 'I don't think!' And he *had* been good to his old mother. For five years he had sent her three shillings a week, and once he'd sent her ten shillings when someone had told him he'd won a competition. If it had been true he'd have sent her another ten shillings and some cough mixture. And that little kid of his had seemed to like him a bit that night before she died . . . Wasn't he no good at all but to be frightened and chased, and shouted at?

'I'll beat 'im—I'll show 'im!' muttered Ben. 'I'll 'oodwink 'im!'

And, opening the front door swiftly, he closed it with a loud bang. But when it banged, Ben was still on the inside.

There! That'd do it! The old man would be down in a few seconds—Ben could hear him now—and when he got to the hall he would conclude that Ben had gone. But Ben wouldn't be gone. No, he would be waiting in a cupboard at the back of the hall. A nice, roomy cupboard, which

Ben had marked for an emergency. You could lie in it or stand up in it. The first thing you did in a house, if you had Ben's experience, was cupboards.

Here came the old man. Ben didn't wait. He dived for the cupboard, doubling back past the foot of the staircase and along the narrowing passage that ran alongside to the back quarters. He seized the knob of the cupboard just as the old man's footsteps sounded immediately above him. The cupboard was under the stairs. Chuckling, the old man, was he? Well, two could play at that game! In a moment Ben would be chuckling . . . What was the matter with the knob? . . . Yes, Ben would have, the laugh . . . Got stuck or something. Come on! Turn, won't you . . .

The cupboard was locked.

'Crumbs!' gasped Ben.

He plunged into the kitchen. He had not time to close the door behind him because, when he swung round to do so, having failed to perform the operation with his leg, the old man was already in the passage and might be looking his way. If he saw the door move, of course he'd smell a rat. So all Ben could do was to duck aside, ensuring that he at least was not within the old man's possible vision, and to wait between an open door and an open window for what might happen.

The old man was beyond the open door. Was anything beyond the open window? The thought induced complete rigidity.

Well, if you couldn't move, you couldn't. You just stood like a statcher. And, while you stood, and the moments went by, other thoughts came to you, to assist in the general merry-making. How had that cupboard come to be locked? It hadn't been locked when Ben had first entered

49

the house. Who had locked it? What was inside? And had
what was inside locked it?

'Yer know,' thought Ben, 'this is gettin' 'orrible.' A
moment later, he heard the front door slam.

'Thank Gawd!' he murmured.

But he wasn't going to take any undue risks, even yet.
Two might play at that door-slamming game!

He was out of the way, anyhow! Quickly Ben slithered
towards the passage, but in a flash he was back in the
kitchen again. The old man was still standing in the hall,
his silver-locked head slightly on one side, listening. Great
minds sometimes think alike.

Another two minutes of agony went by. Apparently, the
old man did not move from the door. He just stood and
waited, listening, with his revolver ready in his hand. Then
the door banged a second time . . .

You can't stand in a kitchen for ever. Presently Ben
tiptoed to the doorway again. This time, the hall was
empty. And—the cupboard?

7

The Will of a Woman

Back in his sanctuary on the second floor, Ben reviewed the situation. He did not review it as a detective would have reviewed it, building point upon point and forming question upon question; he reviewed it unscientifically and emotionally, the various problems revolving in the ample space of his mind like planets in a deranged solar system. But out of the chaos we, better fed and better equipped, may select material for constructive conjecture by seizing on the more important of the questions in transit, and letting the others go. As, for example:

"Oo locked that cupboard unner the stairs? Yus, and when did 'e do it'? Yus, and wot's in it? Or 'oo? Lummy! . . .

'That old feller! Is 'e mad? Lummy! . . .

'If the 'ouse is 'is—*if* mindjer—orl right! But it ain't the Injun's, too, can it? 'E tole me ter go, too! Sime as the old 'un did. Are they workin' tergether? Lummy! . . .

'If 'e thinks I've gorn—well, corse 'e must, wouldn't 'e, will 'e come back presen'ly and do wot 'e thinks I gorn for? Lummy! . . .

51

'Now this 'ere 'ouse can't be the gal's if it's 'is—*if*, mindjer. Orl right. If it isn't the gal's, wot she pay me ter stay 'ere for? Was it so's I'd be 'ere when 'e comes back ter do wot 'e's goin' ter do? Gawd! . . .

'And 'ere's a funny thing. 'E fires at me bang in the fice and misses me. Bang in the fice. And misses me! . . .

'Yes, and wot abart my cheese?'

To Ben's credit, he did not harp on the cheese. That thought merely came to him now and again in momentary pangs. He harped most on the bullet. He couldn't make that out at all. Think he didn't know when a revolver was pointing bang in his face?

'Well, if 'e didn't 'it me,' muttered Ben suddenly, still requiring documentary proof that he was alive, 'let's see where the bullet *did* 'it.'

He turned and gazed at the wall. He saw no evidence of a bullet mark. He walked to the spot where he had been when the old man had fired, and then he located the spot where the old man had been when he had fired, and then he drew an imaginary line between the two spots. He even traced the line with his finger along the floor, continuing it to the wall and up the wallpaper as far as the height of his face. Nowhere near his finger when it paused at the correct elevation was there any sign of a bullet's impact. There was no sign of it in the whole of the room.

'Well, if that don't beat a cat 'avin' chicks!' blinked Ben, in amazement. ''E fires at me. 'E don't 'it me. 'E don't 'it nuffin'!'

The only solution was that the bullet had suddenly stopped dead in the middle of space and had evaporated. 'P'r'aps it was disappointed like at missin' me and wouldn't go on,' thought Ben. But this thought was itself pulverising, so he reverted for relief to another problem—the problem of the cupboard under the stairs in the hall. It was, admittedly, a queer relief, but at least the cupboard presented a puzzle that *could* be solved, given a stout boot and a stouter heart. Ben possessed the former; it represented the best thing he'd ever found in a dust-bin; but he doubted whether he possessed the latter.

'And yet it's funny,' he cogitated. 'I done some brave things in my time. There was that toff 'oo was drahning that time. I was thinkin' o' savin' 'im jest afore that other chap done it. And once I 'it a copper.'

Could not those days of glory be revived? He went on cogitating. And suddenly, to his profound astonishment, he discovered himself in the passage, starting to go downstairs.

He was astonished because he believed he was being courageous. Actually, he could not survive the idea of spending the night in No. 29 Jowle Street with the secret of the cupboard unsolved. It would be too likely to work into his dreams.

'These stairs and me's gettin' ter know each other,' he murmured, half-way down. He liked to talk to himself. It was company. 'I could play a tune on 'em!'

As a matter of fact, he couldn't help playing a tune on them, and it wasn't exactly 'Home Sweet Home'. It might have been more aptly described as a nocturne in creak minor. Just round the corner to the left was the cupboard door. Oh, the difference!

But Ben had made up his mind, and when he made up his mind it sometimes remained made up. Swerving round the corner to the left and refusing to stop to think, he reached the cupboard door, gasped at it, and swung back his boot.

'Now fer it!' he thought, closing his eyes.

The boot thought differently, however. It remained swung back, and for exactly four seconds Ben became a statue of a blind man about to kick a goal. A taxi had stopped outside.

Four seconds was too long. He realised it during the fifth. A key was now being slipped into a lock of the front door, and the front door was beginning to open. He only had time to jump away from the cupboard and jerk himself round before the visitor appeared . . .

Once before in this house Ben had waited for an ogre and had received a vision. Now history repeated itself, although it was a different vision. The other had been a girl. This was a woman. A woman in evening dress, with a wonderful fur cloak, that half-concealed and half revealed an even more wonderful white throat. Ben didn't know they came so white. The whiteness of this woman's throat was dazzling. And yet, of course, he'd seen her kind at cinemas. Breathless close-ups, that advanced towards you enormously, outdoing reality. Yes—she'd make a close-up! She was difficult enough, even at six yards! Made your head swim . . . if you'd been through a bit of a time, you know, and felt emotional . . .

'So—you *are* still here,' said the ravishing woman.

Well, her tone was friendly, anyhow. She was smiling at him. Ben smirked back sheepishly, and swallowed.

'Do you know, I'm rather glad,' went on the woman, closing the door behind her. The taxi did not drive away. In the middle of his confusion Ben was still alert for details. 'Of course, it's very foolish of you, but I was rather hoping for a little chat.'

'Was yer, mum?' replied Ben.

The other had been miss. This was mum. Though, mind you, she was young. Young as blazes!

54

'Yes. You see, I admire bravery. I admire courage and character. And I can recognise it when I see it.'

'Ah,' blinked Ben, struggling against an increase of the sheepishness.

'Now, listen,' said the woman, opening a little evening bag and extracting a little cigarette-case. Gold. Or looked like it. 'I'm going to sit down on that uninviting bottom stair for two minutes, and I'm going to smoke half a cigarette. And by that time I hope we shall know each other and understand each other . . . Do you mind?'

'Eh? Corse not, mum,' answered Ben, wondering what difference it would have made if he'd said he had.

But, then, he wasn't sure that he did mind. A two minutes' chat with a dazzling creature like this? It did not often come within a poor sailor's experience. Just him and her, and the stairs! And the queer, tantalising scent she had on her! And the marvellous hair, as exact as a battleship. And that white throat of hers . . .

It may surprise you that Ben should have been affected by these things. You may consider it ridiculous, even presumptuous. But Ben, for all his dirt and his grime, his hunger and his ineffectiveness, was a bit of life, and the last thing that Life stamps out of us is the little spark of romance within us. When that is gone, we may as well go too.

About to sit on the stairs, the woman suddenly paused and held out her case.

'Won't you join me?' she asked.

Ben shook his head. That *might* be too presumptuous! But she continued to hold her case out, and he advanced in response to her urging and took a dainty, gold-tipped cigarette with fingers unprepared for the honour. Then his

55

spirit failed him again, and he slipped the cigarette into his pocket.

'Presen'ly, if yer don't mind, mum,' he mumbled.

She shrugged her shoulders. One shoulder actually peeped out for a moment from its warm nest of fur.

'As you like,' she said, lighting her own cigarette. 'But here is a match, ready?'

She bent forward with the match. The light glowed on her deliciously made-up cheeks, and her darkened lashes, and her very perfect lips. No man in her station could have refused the moment. But Ben again shook his head, hardly knowing why. Perhaps he was still struggling against presumption, even while she admitted it.

'Even in small things, I see you are consistently dogged!' She sighed, as the light went out, and with it, for the moment, her face. She seemed only a wonderful shadow now, with a little glow, first bright, then soft, before it. But her voice came from the stairs on which she sat, proving her substance. 'Well, that only increases my interest in you. The cigarette—that is nothing! But this house—that is another matter. Why are you dogged about *that*? Why won't you leave?'

So this was why she had called! This was what she wanted to talk to him about! . . . Of course, she'd already implied it . . .

'It's very foolish of you, Mr Strong Man, really it is,' her voice continued. Had a tinge of irony dropped into the voice now? 'It won't do you any good to stay in this house.'

Suddenly Ben faced her, and tackled matters squarely.

'Wot's wrong with the 'ouse?' he demanded.

'Wrong with it?' she repeated. Now the voice was perplexed. 'Nothing is wrong with it. Why should there be?' Ben was silent. 'The only thing that is wrong with it, if I may say so without offending you, is your own presence in it. That, of course, *is* wrong. But it's a wrong that can be so easily righted.'

'Can it?'

'Yes. And *must* be, before the little wrong becomes a big wrong. My father has a terrible temper, when he's roused.'

Ben stared at her.

'Yer father, mum?' he murmured.

'Yes, my father,' she nodded. 'You don't mind my having a father, do you? It seems we all have to have one. If you would like to get the position quite clear, this house belongs to my father, who lives opposite, and when I dropped in just now, on my way to a theatre, I found him in a frightful state. It seems he'd been trying to turn you out—forgive my gauche expressions—and that you had refused to go. I suggested a policeman—you mustn't mind, because you really *are* trespassing, you know—but he wouldn't hear of it. He prefers to deal with things himself, and I'm afraid he said, "Policeman be damned!" If you don't go at once, he'll get into one of his really, really bad states, and there may be murder done. So, you see,' she concluded, 'I decided to come here myself, because I knew I could persuade you, and could make you see reason. Was I right?'

It certainly seemed reasonable enough when she put it like that. But—was it *really* reason—or just her scent?

'Yes—but 'e tried ter shoot me!' blurted Ben, struggling against both her scent and her sense, and striving feebly to make out a case for himself.

She jumped up from the stairs, and seized his arm. Now her face was very close, and almost hypnotised him. A little wisp of hair was nearly touching his cheek.

'Tried to shoot you?' she cried, in alarm. 'Good heavens! He's in *that* condition! Don't you see, you must leave—you *must*! Now! This moment!'

Her fingers tightened convulsively on his sleeve. Unconsciously, he had strengthened her case instead of weakening it. He felt himself being impelled imperiously towards the door, while rich fur brushed against shabby cloth and Houbigant mingled with stale tobacco . . . Now the front door was wide. The damp street opened its misty arms . . . And now he was on the pavement, his mind in a whirl, being bundled into the taxi . . .

'Wot's this?' he protested.

'My taxi,' whispered the woman's voice in his ear. 'I'll get another, but you mustn't wait a second! I've told the man to drive you away, and I've paid him—'

He felt her final shove. The soft fingers could be hard and capable. The next instant the taxi began to move, and he was being driven away from Jowle Street.

His brain swam. He must steady it, and think. He groped for his cigarette.

8

Ben Finds New Quarters

There was no doubt about it, Ben needed a few soothing whiffs to regain his normal balance. Abruptly, within the space of a single minute, his little world had been uprooted and his immediate future changed; moreover, he was struggling to throw off the effects of the bemusing beauty that had entered the little world and had uprooted it. It had entered from a world much vaster than Ben's. It had enveloped him with almost sinister potency, and with all the cynicism of the unattainable; yet its design had been backed by ruthless logic, or else the semblance of it, and he could not put his finger on the flaw. A flaw there must be. But where was it? That was the problem Ben hoped, with the aid of his cigarette, to solve.

He little realised, as he inserted the dainty, gold-tipped thing, how definitely it was going to assist him in his search for the catch!

'I'll give meself a couple o' minits,' he thought. 'Just a couple, that's orl. Then I'll do something'.'

He struck a match, and lit the cigarette. The match-light

glowed on the back of the taximan. It was a broad back, and the end of an untidy moustache protruded beyond the curve of a cheek. It must be a big moustache, Ben reflected, because it was a big cheek. Funny how you liked some moustaches, and hated others!

The match went out. Now only the reflection of his cigarette glowed in the broad back of the taximan. Yes, it was soothing, all right! Just what he wanted. But only for a couple of minutes, mind! No longer . . .

Ben watched the little glow as he puffed. It expanded and dwindled. So did the back it shone in. Now the back was enormous. Now it was tiny. Now it was enormous again. Queer, that. You could puff a cigarette glow up and down, but could you puff a back?

'Wunner where 'e thinks 'e's takin' me,' thought Ben; ''cos wherever 'e thinks, 'e's wrong.'

But the next moment he was wondering about something else. The back was doing extraordinary things. It was swaying. First one side, then the other. Left—right— left—right! ''E'll fall off 'is seat in a minit,' thought Ben. But he didn't fall off his seat, and all at once Ben realised the reason, with a shock. The taximan *wasn't* swaying. Ben was swaying!

''Ere—wot's orl this?' murmured Ben. 'I'm comin' over orl funny!'

He puffed fiercely, and then suddenly raised his hand and snatched the cigarette from his mouth. His hand was like lead.

'Gawd—so *that* was 'er gime!' choked Ben.

He had struck the flaw in the logic. No really nice girl carries a drugged cigarette in her case!

Suppose he had smoked the cigarette when she had first

offered it to him? She had offered it, he recalled, before he had mentioned anything about the pistol shot. He would have been feeling *then* as he was feeling *now*. The hall would have swum, instead of the taxi. He would have become limp . . . he would have been carried out unconscious . . . into the taxi . . .

''Ere! Stop!' he bawled.

That was funny! Where was his voice? He didn't hear it! Nor, apparently, did the taximan, for he didn't stop.

'Police! Fire! 'Elp!' roared Ben.

But, again, it was a roar without a sound. His imagination raged, while his lips were mute. Two white arms went round him and held him. He sank into a sea of scent. A beautiful woman with a gleaming throat stood on the shore and laughed as he went under . . . Now, all was peaceful and velvet . . .

The sense of gliding—that remained. He had not smoked the whole cigarette. The body that could no longer function glided through the velvet, conscious of movement and of occasional incidents in the movement. Sometimes, for instance, the movement became a little jerky. Sometimes a cow squeaked through it. Sometimes it changed its direction abruptly, and took loops. Sometimes the velvet became speckled with little lights, or alleviated by a momentary big one, reminding one of the sensations of passing through stations on night journeys. And, as a sort of background to it all, there was a continuous, rhythmic throbbing, soft, and very close to the ears . . .

Now the movement became very jerky. Now the cow squeaked loudly, two squeaks at a time. And now the movement stopped, and the Universe paused in its transit. And now a new movement started—a heavy, formless, bumping kind of movement, that irritated one and made one vaguely rebellious. The gliding hadn't been so bad. You could sink into it, yield yourself to it, accept it. In fact, you had to. But you couldn't sink into this new form of locomotion through space. It shook you. It made you feel slighted. It caused your heavy arms to try and move with preventive intent, and your legs, equally heavy, to attempt kicks. But it wasn't any good. The bumping movement went on, up, along, up, along, up, along, this side, straight again, t'other side, straight again, now tipping, now swaying, now swinging, now jolting, now cursing, now grumbling—up, along, up, along—woosh—flop!

Ben's form became horizontal and inert again. Stretched out limply, it entered into its last stage of impassivity. When it began to emerge, the dim space around it started separating into sections, and each section formed into an object. An enormous oblong dwindled in size as it improved in focus, till it became a wardrobe. A block became a chest of drawers. A smaller block became a chair. A curious golden arrow became the light of a street lamp streaking in through a window.

''Ere—wot's orl this?' muttered Ben, sitting up suddenly. But he flopped back again almost immediately, because his movement had shifted the good work of the telescope, and the focused objects were beginning to lose their definition again. Once more he became inertly horizontal, but this time with a slowly-moving brain. 'Stop 'ere like this fer a minit,' advised the slowly-moving brain, 'and then try it agin more slow like.'

After the minute, Ben tried it again more slow like. It worked better. Now he was sitting up and the objects around him did not start running away. Even the object he was sitting up on stayed where it was, and proved to be a bed.

In a corner of the room he spotted something that spelt salvation. It was a jug in a basin. Keeping his eyes anchored upon it, he imagined a steadying rope joining himself to the jug. With the assistance of this rope he worked his legs over the side of the bed. When they touched the ground, the ground began to roll, but again the rope came to his aid and saved him from disaster. He waited for a few moments till the floor grew calmer, and then, glueing his eyes on the water jug, he made a sudden dive towards it. To his surprise, it was a bull's-eye, and the cool handle of the jug felt good in his hot hand.

'Nah fer a shower barth!' he thought. 'That'll do the trick!'

He raised the jug and inverted it over his head. He was rather surprised at the ease of the operation. He must be growing stronger! But the inverted jug produced no comfort. It was empty.

'There's a dirty trick!' muttered Ben.

He wanted to cry. He couldn't stand many more disappointments. But all at once he spotted a small water bottle on the wash-stand. It was full of water—probably last month's, but that didn't matter. Nor did it matter that the bottle had received its last rub before the war. He seized it avidly, and cascaded the contents all over him from his hair downwards. The chilly moisture made life worth living again, and battles worth fighting. Should we ever despair, when heaven itself may be contained in a filthy carafe?

As the water trickled down him and around him his blood responded immediately and began to flow freely again. His mind worked, his scant store of courage returned. And he needed all his courage for what was before him. Turning, he eyed the door. 'Aha!' he cried. It was the bark of the dog that has just emerged from the sea, though not, at this moment, a good-natured dog. Its desire was to bite as well as to bark. The person to be bitten was somewhere on the other side of the door.

Ben crossed to it. Yes, he found he could do so. A bit groggy still, of course, but he no longer needed an imaginary rope. 'Hi!' he shouted. 'Lemme out!' As he shouted, he kicked the door with his boot—his present from the dust-bin.

No one came. He went on shouting and kicking. The door held firm.

'Wotcher think yer doin' of?' roared Ben. ''Oojer think yer are? Lemme out, d'yer 'ear? Lemme out! If yer don't, by Gawd, I'll 'ave yer 'ouse dahn!' Hefty kick. 'D'yer 'ear?' Another hefty kick. 'Yer think I don't mean it?' Another hefty kick. 'Orl right, yer bit o' 'uman pulp with a bird's nest on yer lip, *I'll* show yer!'

Now he heard a tread upon the stairs.

'Yer better be quick,' bawled Ben, 'or the door'll come dahn on yer.'

It was a terrific kick this time. The door shook, and showed a little split.

'Now, then—stop that!' ordered a voice from outside.

'Yus, likely, ain't it?' retorted Ben, and went on kicking.

'*Stop it*. D'you 'ear?'

'Corse I don't 'ear? 'Ow can I? I'm lyin' on yer blinkin' bed drugged, ain't I?'

'You'll lie there again in a minute, if you're not careful!' threatened the voice. 'You'd better do as I tell you!'

'Yus, why shouldn't I do wot you tells me? Yer bin so nice ter me, ain't yer? Taken me fer a nice ride and ain't charged me nothin'. Why, I'm so fond o' yer I'll black yer boots fer yer—and then yer two eyes arterwards!'

It wasn't polished repartee, but it assisted the kicking, and evidently it worried the person outside. Someone joined him, and there was whispering.

'Yus, and 'ere's somethin' ter whisper abart!' bellowed Ben suddenly. 'Good-bye to yer 'appy 'ome!'

He staggered back to the water jug, seized it, and hurled it to the ground. It splintered with a crash. Then he seized the water bottle. There was another crash.

'Tinkle-tinkle!' cried Ben deliriously. There is a special form of delirium that accompanies the act of breaking things. 'Didyer 'ear it? Now listen agin! This is goin' ter be the soap dish. It's 'ole.' Smash! 'Now it ain't.'

Agitation grew in the passage. A chair followed the soap dish. 'Yer'll 'ave some nice firewood in the mornin',' cackled Ben; 'but I'm afraid yer'll 'ave ter buy a noo dressin'-table.'

The dressing table crashed over on its side. A leg splintered with a tearing sound. Ben seized another chair, and began to hammer the remains of the dressing table with it. Then he swung round . . .

The door was open. The taximan had entered, in a towering rage. Behind him, providing the light for his ferocious silhouette, stood a woman with a candle. Evidently Mrs Taximan.

Not another word was spoken. Deeds became the important matters, and the first deed came from Ben, with the raised chair. He hurled it across at the oncoming taximan.

It struck his adversary, but it did not stop him. He still came on. 'That's a pity,' thought Ben, and lunged. There was a long clinch. Its length might have rendered Albert

Hall indignant, but in a little room you cannot be really sporting. 'Well, if 'e's 'urtin' me I'm 'urtin' 'im,' thought Ben. They swayed and pummelled and jabbed. Then they rolled over, and the woman joined in.

That wasn't fair! Even for a little room! She had put down the candle near the door, and was kicking Ben. It is possible that she was doing so to preserve her husband's life, for Ben was conscious that the man he was wound round was writhing desperately. Still, two against one wasn't cricket, however you looked at it.

Something sharp touched Ben's hand. It gave him a nasty shock, for he thought at first a knife was being used on him. Then he realised that the cause was two half-rows of teeth. The woman was biting him.

He saw red. Not for the first time that day, or the last. He heaved himself up superhumanly, and shoved the woman away from him. It was odd, but even after she had bitten him he couldn't strike her. One day, the Noah-like old man with wings will have to remember that. He just shoved her, with the force of an enraged elephant, and she fell on to the broken dressing table. The next instant, Ben found himself erect, by the candle.

He blew it out. He staggered into the passage and slammed the door. He turned the key that had been turned on him. And, choking and gasping, he tottered down the stairs.

His one object was to gain the street before a little goblin with seventeen hundred and sixty bright eyes got hold of him, and swallowed him . . .

9

The Seat

For a brief moment we will leave Ben and take a peep into another world. The world of a good-looking young man and a more than good-looking young girl, who sat on a bottom stair and talked.

It was not the bottom stair to which the reader has already been introduced. It was so different, in fact, that it really ought to be designated by some other name. Perhaps one day in years to come, when the surrounding walls had fallen into decay and the wallpaper was peeling and the balustrade was rocky, this stair would creak its swan song and be as dismal and as neglected as the stairs of No. 29 Jowle Street. Houses, like humans, return to dust through processes not kind or gracious. But on this particular evening it was a stair of luxury and delight—soft-carpeted, soundless, and mellow with pleasant little memories.

From the bottom stair of No. 29 Jowle Street, you would at this instant have heard a window rattling in its loose frame, and a rat scuttling under a board. From this happier stair the young man and the girl heard dance music and rippling laughter. They were not very interested in either the music or the laughter, however, and they had actually sought their bottom stair in an effort to escape from them. The world we are momentarily peeping into comprised just their two selves, and they did not want to be reminded of any other personalities.

'Oh, for a desert!' sighed the young man.

'Or the North Pole!' added the girl.

'Or the moon,' suggested the young man. 'But, you know, I believe people would follow us even there! Why is it, Ruth, that when two persons want to be alone, the entire population of the globe insists on pursuing them?'

'Well, we're alone now,' the girl pointed out.

'So we are!' smiled the young man.

But before he could celebrate the fact a door opened, and more population poured towards them.

'Look here—I've an idea!' whispered the young man.

'It sounds splendid,' the girl whispered back.

'It *is* splendid,' said the young man. 'Are you game?'

'For anything!'

'Right! Then do you remember that seat where we had our first real chat?'

'Of course, I do,' she answered. 'We discussed the back-hand grip, didn't we?'

'*And* one or two other little things! It was on that seat, Ruth, that we arranged to go on the river, and it was on the river that we mooted Scotland, and it was in Scotland that your people asked me to this dance, and it was at this dance that I became the happiest man between here and Sirius.'

'And I the happiest girl,' she interposed.

'Very well, then! That jolly old seat isn't very far from here. What about going and thanking it?'

She hesitated, intrigued. It was a perfectly ridiculous suggestion. But, then, they were in a mood to do ridiculous things.

'It isn't June now,' she remarked.

'The seat is just five minutes away,' he retorted.

'And isn't there a mist?'

'As a matter of fact, I think it's only four minutes away!'

'Suppose we're wanted?'

'Wanted? My dear child! If anybody wants you henceforth they've got to ask *me* first, and if anybody wants me they've got to ask you. Objection overruled. Majority for the motion. Slip up and get your cloak, while I slip along and get my hat.'

She laughed. She had merely objected as a sort of conventional duty. They separated, and met a minute later at the front door.

'Glorious night,' he reported, opening the door. 'I told you so!'

'Glorious!' she agreed.

They went out into the mist. Again, not Ben's mist. It was a fairy mist, through which they walked very close together.

'I've just made a startling discovery,' said the young man. 'There's no such thing as unhappiness!'

'Never heard of it,' murmured the girl.

They laughed together. For three minutes they babbled nonsense. Then, all at once, the young man pointed to a clump of foliage by some railings.

'There's our seat!' he whispered.

'Yes, but what's on it?' she whispered back.

'Damn!' he muttered.

They stopped, and gazed at the blot upon their magic

picture. It was a queer-shaped blot. Five feet and a few inches of twisted humanity. It certainly didn't belong to their picture at all. It did not appear to belong to any picture, and perhaps it was that reflection that gradually softened indignation.

'Poor old bloke!' said the young man.

'Shall we go up to him?' asked the girl.

'It implied sympathy, not affection,' he answered, 'and half the sympathy is for the seat. To what base use, eh? Still,' he added, 'perhaps he would move off if we gave him a shilling, and the coin would do us both a good turn.'

They advanced a step or two closer. The short length of twisted humanity grew bigger and clearer. It was clutching the back rail, as though it had become frozen to it.

'Wonder if he's all right?' frowned the young man.

'Listen! He's talking!' exclaimed the girl.

'By Jove, so he is!' said the young man. 'Off his nut! I say—p'r'aps, after all, we'd better—'

They stood, hesitating. The huddled figure on the seat was undoubtedly talking. The girl drew nearer to her companion, and her companion wondered why on earth he did not lead her hastily away. The fellow was just an ordinary 'drunk', of course . . . But—*was* he? If only he'd raise his voice a little . . .

Then the fellow raised his voice.

'Lock me in a room, would yer?' he cried, with sudden and startling vehemence. 'Nah, then—git orf me! I'm goin' back—d'yer 'ear?'

'Yes, quite barmy,' sighed the young man. 'We'd better be going, Ruth.'

'What about that shilling?' she urged. 'I expect he hasn't had our luck.'

'You bet he hasn't!' responded the young man soberly. 'He doesn't look as if he's had any luck!'

He dived in his pocket and brought out a coin. The girl looked at him, and from him to the huddled figure on the seat. Philosophy was not her strong point, but little philosophy was needed to appreciate the contrast. The one in immaculate evening clothes and silk hat, with everything before him—the other in a torn and ragged coat and no hat, with surely nothing before him! Unaware of the theory of compensation, one might assume that Nature has no interest in equality.

'Here you are, old chap,' said the young man, holding out the shilling as though it were a bun.

'Git away!' answered the figure on the seat. 'I tole 'er I'd stick there, and nobody ain't goin' ter stop me!'

'Nobody ain't trying to stop you,' replied the young man gently, and turned to the girl. 'You know, he seems to have had a knock or something. I don't believe it's a case of drowning his sorrows. Shall I stick the bob on the seat, or give him a prod?'

'Give him a prod,' answered the girl. 'Just a tiny one. It may bring him round.'

It did bring him round. It brought him round so suddenly that the young man jumped back. The figure's arms were windmilling.

'Hey! Steady, old sport!' he cried.

'Wot's that?' muttered the human windmill, and opened its eyes.

The contrasts stared at each other.

''Oo are you?' blinked the less presentable.

'Thomas Medway,' smiled the more presentable. 'And who are you?'

71

'Gawd, if anybody asks me that agin ternight, I'll 'it 'im!' grunted the ragged fellow.

'Sorry, old chap,' said Thomas Medway; 'but I was only repeating your own question, you know.'

'Be careful, Tom!' warned the girl.

The ragged fellow transferred his eyes to the girl, seeing her for the first time. The sight banished his pugnacity.

'That's orl right, miss,' he mumbled. 'I ain't 'urting nobody.'

He rose from the seat as he spoke, then promptly sat down on it again. He didn't look as if he could hurt anybody.

'That's funny,' he said. 'Knees gorn wobbly.'

'Had a rough time, eh?' asked the young man sympathetically.

But the ragged fellow did not appear to hear the question. He was studying the seat.

''Ow did I git 'ere?' he inquired.

'I haven't a notion,' answered the young man. 'Is there anything I can do?'

'Yus,' replied the ragged fellow. ''Ow fur am I from Jowle Street?'

'Jowle Street?' repeated the young man. 'Never heard of it! Have you, Ruth?'

'No,' she answered. 'It sounds horrible!'

'It is 'orrible,' agreed the ragged fellow; 'but it's where I gotter git ter. Nummer twenty-nine.'

The young man and the girl exchanged glances. They had reached the stage in which they could understand each other without speaking. The young man dived into his pocket again, and this time produced a ten-shilling note.

'You don't look in much of a condition to walk,' he said. 'Take a taxi, will you, with our love.'

He held the note out.

'Go on!' said the ragged fellow.

'Don't be an ass,' replied the young man. 'Take it. And if there's anything over, drink our health. We're going to be married.'

The ragged man's hand went forward. His fingers closed over the note. At first slowly. Then, galvanically. A moment later, he was gone.

'Well, I'm blowed!' exclaimed the young man.

'His legs seemed all right *that* time!' commented the girl.

'Talk about lightning!' blinked the young man.

A soft sound behind them made them turn. Another figure stood before them, tall, lithe, and with the whites gleaming round his pupils. In the dimness he looked Oriental.

'Excuse,' said the new figure. 'But may I ask who was the person you were talking to?'

The young man frowned, and felt the girl's arm pressing his again.

'Why?' he demanded.

'I think I know him,' answered the newcomer.

'I'm afraid that's your misfortune,' replied the young man. 'He's my gardener, and I've this moment dismissed him for being drunk!'

'So? Your pardon,' said the Oriental.

And vanished.

'Why ever did you say that?' inquired the girl.

'I simply haven't a notion,' returned the young man; 'but I'm damned glad I did! I say, Ruth, rather a queer business, what?' He glanced towards the now empty seat. 'Has it spoiled a happy memory?'

'I don't think so, Tom,' she answered. 'But, if you're doubtful, shall we sit down on it for just a few seconds and win it back?'

They sat down, and he put his arm round her.

'Bit like, aren't you?' she commented, after a pause. 'What are you thinking of?'

'As a matter of fact, Ruth,' he confessed, 'I was thinking of Jowle Street.'

10

Back Again!

Ben ran a hundred yards, with eyes closed and such teeth as he possessed clenched. He ran in his own peculiar fashion, half-human, half-crustacean, and beat the zigzag record. When he couldn't go straight he went sideways, and he frequently had to go sideways because, when your eyes are closed, you keep on bumping into things. Normally, of course, you open your eyes when you bump into things, but Ben was not normal, and everything he bumped into seemed to be an Indian. That was an excellent reason for keeping his eyes closed.

At the end of the hundred yards his breath and his knees gave out. He had, therefore, to depend upon some other function for a continuation of existence. Since he couldn't move any more himself he had to find something else that would move for him, and the only way to find that something else was to look for it. So, risking all the evil of the Orient, he opened his eyes; and heaven sent him the sight of a taxi.

'Oi!' he gasped.

'Oi' is not the most effective way to stop a taxi, for

taxi-drivers have their pride. It was late, however. The theatre crowds had evaporated, and the dance crowds were not quite ready to follow. Therefore, the taxi stopped. Any fare in a storm.

Ben opened the door and lurched in. It was one of those new, comfortable taxis, and comfort purred around him like a narcotic. You couldn't do anything for a bit, but just lie back and think of bees and clover.

The taxi door opened. Ben straightened with a start.

'Where to?' demanded the taximan.

'Eh?' replied Ben.

The information was not sufficient. Nor, from the expression of the taximan, did the passenger appear to be. The taxi had pulled up in the darkest portion of the road, midway between lamp-posts, and the passenger had slipped in swiftly. This was the first time the taximan had got a proper view of the passenger, and he couldn't quite believe it.

'Bit of a toff travelling in a taxi, aren't you?' suggested the taximan.

'King's messenger,' answered Ben.

'Come off it!' retorted the taximan. 'Let's see your fare money!'

Ben held out the ten-shilling note. It had remained clutched in his hand ever since he had received it.

'Hallo! Rockfeller!' exclaimed the taximan. 'Where did you pick *that* up?'

Where had he picked it up? For a second Ben hardly knew. Then he recalled a young man in a glossy top hat and a girl in a bright yellow wrap. They formed part of a long string of memories, a string that was twisted. Had they been the last thing?

'Or p'r'aps you've been doing a bit of private socialism?' inquired the taximan suspiciously. 'Had I better drive you to a police station!'

'Shurrup!' growled Ben. 'You git a move on, and drive me ter—' He paused. He had been on the point of saying 'Jowle Street.' But suppose the Indian was waiting in a dark doorway, listening for the address? Better still zigzag for a while. 'Pickerdilly Circus,' he decided, aloud.

'Oh! Out for a spree, mate?' grinned the taximan.

'That's right,' answered Ben. 'I'm takin' Phyllis Dare out ter supper. So 'urry hup! She 'ates it when I'm late.'

The taximan chuckled, and climbed back into his seat. After all, he'd seen the ten-shilling note, and the rest wasn't his business.

Ben sank back again. This was a bit different from his last taxi ride! The taximan was taking him this time to where *he* wanted, and not to where the taximan wanted. And no drugged cigarette to fuddle the brain. It is not to be assumed, however, that Ben was happy. Piccadilly Circus was merely the first stop for Jowle Street, and he was quite convinced that Jowle Street was growing more and more unhealthy every hour. Nor can we deny the accuracy of his conviction.

For the umpteenth time he asked himself why he was going back. 'Reg'lar boomerang, that's wot I am!' he thought. Had the first girl of the many he had seen that night—no, the second girl; the first was the distressed girl on the doorstep of No. 26, wasn't it, the girl that Australian toff had gone after?—had this second girl, then—the really wonderful one—really got hold of him like this? Why, he'd only seen her for just a few minutes, yet in that time she had wound something round him he couldn't escape from.

Something elastic, that kept pulling him back to her, or to where he had last seen her. He couldn't make it out. No, he couldn't!

And there was something else too. A feeling that went even deeper than the wonderful girl—that went to something right beyond her. He couldn't explain this deeper feeling either. Whatever the cause of it, the effect of it in his emaciated person was a sense of *incompletion*. Something was waiting at No. 29 Jowle Street, something he had to do. It had been waiting ever since he had entered it. And he wouldn't be allowed to leave it finally, and to become complete again, until he had done it.

Yes; but what was it?

Lights grew more frequent. Shop windows, seeking night publicity, began to illuminate the way. The streets became more populated with their nocturnal inhabitants with painted women, pathetic in their callousness; elderly men, pathetic in their outlook; parties in evening dress; policemen; and beggars. Poverty and plenty, shoulder rubbing shoulder, while gulfs apart. And presently, to the reviving comprehension of the passenger in the taxi-cab, the streets assumed recognisable form. Oxford Street, Regent Street, Piccadilly . . .

'This do?' asked the taximan, opening the door and popping his head in with a grin.

'Yus,' answered Ben. 'Tike it out o' that, with a shillin' fer a drink.'

He thrust the note into the taximan's hand. The taximan glanced at the clock, and gave back the exact change.

'Kep' yer drink?' queried Ben, as he alighted.

'That's all right, mate,' replied the taximan. 'You have it.' And he sped off to gather up another fare.

Piccadilly Circus seemed immensely friendly. People everywhere. Policemen within call. Coffee and sandwiches, too. The ideal thing would be to pitch a tent on the big, flat island, and to sleep there surrounded by security. Then, if a hand suddenly clutched you, or a dark-skinned face were abruptly thrust towards your own, all you would have to do would be to holler.

But you mustn't pitch tents in Piccadilly, and even if you sit on doorsteps you are moved on. So what was the use of thinking? Besides, wasn't Jowle Street calling?

Ben looked round for another taxi. As he did so, his roving eye suddenly paused. A familiar figure was emerging from an hotel. The Piccadilly Hotel. For a moment Ben couldn't place her, though he was sure he had seen her somewhere recently. Then he recollected. It was the girl who had left No. 26, and who had been upset.

A young man was with her. He had a rather weak face, and his expression was worried. He seemed to be asking her questions which she couldn't answer. They stood on the pavement for a few moments, while a commissionaire procured their car. It was a private car. A Rolls. They got in and glided away.

'No bloomin' doubt abart 'it,' muttered Ben. 'I'm marked for it!'

For surely only Fate itself could have dealt him this reminder!

'Oi,' said Ben.

'Oi, yerself!' replied the taximan addressed.

He tried another method with the next.

''Ere! I wancher!' he called.

It was another blank. To get a taxi when you are in rags is an art.

But the third time proved lucky. A cab drew up beside him, a man got out, and Ben got in. As he got in, he said, 'Jowle Street,' and took the matter as settled.

The driver knew Jowle Street. He had driven a four-wheeler, and London was an open book to him. But he did want to know the number, and Ben kept in the shadow while he told him.

'Now we're really off,' thought Ben, as the taxi began to move. 'Next stop, 'Orror!'

He kept in the shadow for five minutes. Then he bent forward and looked out. Already the comfort of the West End was departing, the shops were less illuminated, and the policemen thinning out. Of course, ordinarily, policemen had their disadvantages, but they were desirable folk on a night like this. As the journey proceeded and grimness replaced gaiety, Ben's temporary happiness began to leave him, and his heart began to beat a little faster again. His respite was over.

'I orter've 'ad a bite,' he reflected, rubbing his forehead. 'This bump's makin' me barmy!'

Well, he was not going to stop for it now. The sooner you got there the sooner you'd get it over, and the sooner you got it over, the sooner you'd know whether you were dead or alive or not.

Towards the end of the journey he kept a sharp lookout upon the streets. He saw no ominous signs. Three corners from Jowle Street at a bridge that ran over a sluggish canal he poked his head out of the window.

'This'll do,' he said.

The taxi stopped. He slipped out quickly, and quickly paid his fare. The driver stared at him in astonishment. Was *this* what he'd been driving? The passenger did not wait to explain or to apologise. He left the taxi as swiftly as he had entered it, and the driver gazed after him. Well, whatever the passenger's appearance, he had paid his bill.

'Nearly 'ome!' muttered Ben.

The canal and the bridge were now behind him, and the three corners had become two.

'Wonder if anybody's waitin' up fer me?' muttered Ben.

The two corners became one.

'Gawd 'elp us!' muttered Ben.

Now he was in Jowle Street, slinking along its lugubrious length close to the palings. He was on the correct side. The odd number side. Across the way, becoming less and less distant, was No. 26. All still and dark there. And here, on this side, also becoming less and less distant, was No. 29. All still and dark, there too. Just a flat, black blodge, rising up into further blackness.

''Allo!' murmured Ben suddenly.

All still, yes. But—all dark? No, not quite all dark. A dim light flickered half-way up. It flickered from the second floor front . . . his room . . .

'I didn't see that afore!' he thought. ''Allo! Where's it gorn?'

Now, the second floor front was dark again.

'Blimy!' muttered Ben. 'Ain't life luvverly?'

11

What You Can Do When You Matter

There are times when it is best not to think. This, undoubtedly, was one of the times. Somebody was up in the second floor front who would hit Ben on the head if he entered the house. Therefore, if one thought, one wouldn't enter the house. And one had to enter the house—didn't one?

There was only one way to enter the house. It was to go round to the back and slip in through the open kitchen window. Of course, when you were in the kitchen, you could stop and take a breath, if you wanted to, and say a prayer, if you knew one. But it was no good breathing and praying first. That way thought lay.

So round to the back Ben slipped, trying hard to forget that he had just seen a dim light go out in the room that was his objective. Imaginary hands clawed at him as he passed through the narrow black alley. Imaginary knives stuck in his back. Imaginary creatures crawled around his feet, to trip him up . . .

Imaginary? Ben gave a leap. So did a big black cat.

'Lummy!' gasped Ben. 'There's a dirty trick!'

He glared at the two lamp-green eyes that glowed back at him. Ben's eyes were indignant. The cat's were reproachful. The cat made the first advances towards a better understanding. The lamp-green eyes glowed closer, and a soft body pressed against Ben's leg.

''Allo—wanter be friends, eh?' murmured Ben. 'Fergive and fergit!'

Well, any friend was better than none. He stooped and stroked the soft body. The spot he stroked was damp.

'That's funny,' reflected Ben. 'It ain't rainin'.' He raised his hand, which was now damp also. He held it close to his face. There were many dark portions of Ben's hand, but most of them were black. This new damp one was red.

Ben nearly gave way that time. He only just managed to hang on. It occurred to him that his prospects of seeing another sunrise weren't worth betting on.

He reached the kitchen window. The black cat followed him. The window was closed. The person who was up in the second floor front evidently didn't want to be disturbed.

Well, that was that! You couldn't get through a closed window. At least, not unless you broke it. And if you broke it, there'd be a noise . . .

'Well, wot abart it, King Coal?' Ben asked the cat.

King Coal did not respond. He had vanished.

Ben considered the new position. Then, all at once, a totally new idea occurred to him. It was rather an amazing idea, and intriguingly simple. The process at least was simple. The result might be less so.

'Why not go rahnd ter the front,' he pondered, 'and ring the bell, innercent like?'

The more he thought of it, the more he preferred it to the alternative of smashing glass. Perhaps its chief attraction was that it would delay matters for a few seconds. Yet, the idea had other virtues. He could pretend that he had left a pipe in the house. Or he could stand ready with a bit of loose railing in his hand. He remembered having seen a bit of loose railing . . .

He returned to the front. Yes, there was the bit of loose railing. It had got broken, just to keep in tune with the house itself, and the top portion was hanging insecurely from its enlarged time-eaten socket. He seized it and gave it a hard tug. It came away with the ease of a loose tooth, and he sat down on the pavement with it. But he didn't mind. He had got his weapon, and that was all he cared about.

He got up. His fall had ejected him towards another point of the compass, and now he found himself staring across the road at No. 26 opposite. A light went up in the top room. Well, why shouldn't it? He swung round nervily, and stared up at a more important window. There was no light there.

He mounted the few low steps. His left hand reached for the bell. His right was fully occupied, gripping the bit of iron railing. He found the bell, and pressed it. The bell sounded as loud as Big Ben. What a fool he was! Why hadn't he tried to ring it more softly?

He twisted his neck, for a final glance at the top room of No. 26. The light was out again. He gained the sensation that he was being watched from both houses.

'This ain't nice,' he thought.

He decided not to ring the bell again. If nobody came, he would go back to the kitchen window and smash it. He had an implement now for the purpose, and anything would be better than standing here with No. 26 behind him, like an enormous eye. An eye! That was it! The whole house was an eye, focusing on him . . .

Hallo! Somebody *was* coming, though! He could hear noises. Little creeping noises, coming downstairs. Faint, at first. Then getting louder. *Creak*. Gawd—he knew that stair! And a point of light too. Moving and dodging, like a will o' the wisp. His fingers tightened on his bit of railing.

Now the somebody was at the bottom of the stairs and had reached the hall. The light paused. It came on again. And, now, a little metallic sound. He knew that too. He had made it himself, when opening the door to others. An instant later, the door began to open to him. It receded slowly. A tiny slit of dim interior widened. He raised his bit of railing . . .

A hand shot out and grasped him. The light went out. He was pulled inside, and the door closed swiftly. He and the somebody stood facing each other in the pitch darkness.

'I'm goin' ter 'it yer,' said Ben idiotically.

'Sh!' came the response.

For a blinding moment the light dazzled full into his eyes, then was switched off again. Ben stood motionless. His ears were not sensitive to subtleties, saving in the case of stair noises, but something in that whispered 'Sh!' had arrested him.

''Oo are you?' he muttered.

The light answered him. This time, it illuminated the face of the person who held it. And, again, only for a moment.

'Lummy! It's you, miss!' gasped Ben.

'Hush!—upstairs—we'll talk there,' she whispered.

No longer antagonistic, they ascended. Only one thing was clear to Ben in the confusion of his mind. He had done right to come back. They mounted to the second floor without speaking. The door of his room—for so he thought of it—was open. They entered, and groped their way to the window. The soap box had been moved to a spot beside the window, and had been turned on its side to make a lower seat. From a pedestal, it had become a settee. They sat down upon it, without illumination.

'Now, tell me!' whispered the girl 'Why have you come back?'

'Why 'ave you?' answered Ben.

'Please answer my question first,' she said. 'Then I'll answer yours—perhaps. Why are you here?'

'Well—you tole me ter stop, didn't yer?' muttered Ben.

'I told you *not* to!'

'Yus, that was arter. But you left your pahnd.'

'So I did.'

'Well, then.'

There was a pause. Ben felt the girl's eyes boring him in the darkness. Lummy—wasn't she different from the other one—that one with the fur and the snaky evening dress . . .

'Do you mean, you decided to stay here, because of the pound?'

'I hexpeck that was one o' the reasons, miss.'

'One of the reasons?'

'Yus.'

'Was there another reason?'

'Well, yer see—if you was comin' back—like wot yer 'ave—it didn't seem exackly safe 'ere, like. See?'

'I think I do see,' murmured the girl. 'I say—you're rather a decent sort, aren't you?'

'Reg'lar boy stood on the burnin' deck,' replied Ben. 'But doncher worry, miss; I'll never grow one o' them 'aloes rahnd me 'ead.'

Nevertheless, he pocketed her compliment, in case old Noah ever needed to hear it.

'I don't still understand, though,' went on the girl, her voice soft and rich in the darkness. 'You must have gone away, to have come back again! How long did you stay after I went?'

'Lemmy think,' answered Ben.

How long had he stayed? It all seemed so far away he could hardly remember. He'd lived through a bit since their last meeting.

'Was you 'ere afore the old man, or was the old man 'ere afore you?' he asked.

'Old man?' she queried.

'Ah—now I got it,' said Ben. 'Arter you left I went aht ter git a bit o' cheese and a cup o' corfee, and it was when I was 'avin' the corfee that I come acrost 'im—no, not 'im, the Injun, that's it—and then I comes back and the old man comes hup and tries ter shoot me, and then I 'ides—well, 'oo wouldn't?—and then 'e goes, and then this hother woman she comes—'

'What other woman?' interposed the girl, attempting to stem the tide a little.

'Why, the old man's dorter, or so she ses, the one as gits me inter a taxi with one o' them drugged garspers, there's a dirty trick, and orf I'm took to a room where they locks me in, yus, it's a fack, but I starts smashin' up the 'appy 'ome, see, and that brings 'em in, and then I gives 'em a dose o' Sharkey—'

'They—?'

'Yus, the taxi bloke and 'is spoose, leastwise I hexpeck she was, nobody helse'd marry 'er, and arter I'd give 'em a bit o' wot-not I gits aht o' the 'ouse, see, and then

87

things went funny and I don't know wot 'appens fer a bit till I'm on a seat and a feller gives me ten bob, Gawd knows why, and I didn't wait ter ask 'cos the Injun, 'e's heverywhere, 'e is—'

'You saw the Indian—?'

'Yus, I'm tellin' yer, 'e's worse'n me shadder, but I give 'im the slip, too, and goes orl rahnd the world in a couple o' taxis—oh, I bin a nob orl right since I saw you larst, miss—and then I comes back 'ere, and I finds you 'ere, and—well, 'ere we are.'

He paused for breath. It has been a long speech, but a useful one. You gotter tork sometimes, or bust.

'Corse,' he added, 'there was a lot more, but that's jest the houtline.'

The girl rose from the case, and stood considering. She had rarely taken her eyes off the house opposite while Ben had been telling his story, and her gaze was still directed out of the window; but her focus had altered. She did not seem to be looking at the house now; she seemed to be looking far beyond it.

Ben waited. He wanted to hear *her* story. When she spoke, however, she still harped on his.

'Do you think the Indian knows you have come back here?' she asked.

'On'y if 'e's good at guessin',' replied Ben.

'And, of course, you can't say where *he* is?'

An idea occurred to Ben. She certainly harped on that Indian.

'Is 'e arter you, too, miss?' he whispered sepulchrally.

'Never mind about me,' she responded. 'Do you know where he is?'

'I don't know where 'e is,' said Ben, 'and I don't *wanter*

know where 'e is. Let sleepin' Injuns lie, that's my motter, miss. Wot I do wanter know is wot 'appened ter you?' He straightened himself a little. 'I'm 'ere ter 'elp yer like, ain't I? Well, then, 'ow am I goin' ter do it if I don't know nothin'?'

Now she turned her eyes away from the window, and fixed them on him.

'You've helped me a great deal,' she answered, and there was gratitude in her voice. 'Yes, more than you probably know. But there's nothing more you can do, and I'm going to repeat a request I made to you once before. Please go now. Believe me, it will be best—and wisest. I'm sincere.'

Ben could see that she was. Nevertheless, he shook his head.

'If it's a fack as 'ow I've 'elped yer,' he replied; 'well, it's a fack as 'ow I wouldn't 'ave 'elped yer if I'd took yer hadvice larst time and 'oofed it. That's right, isn't it?'

'Quite right. But now there's *nothing* you can do.'

'Sure o' that, miss?'

She nodded. Ben didn't believe her.

'S'pose the Injun comes back? Ain't yer scared of 'im?'

'No.'

Again Ben didn't believe her. He was working out a simple theory for himself. He believed that the Indian was after her, and that he wanted to kill her. He believed that the Indian *would* kill her if somebody didn't look after her. And he believed that if the Indian did kill her, he would kill the Indian. Whether he was right or wrong, it was an easy theory to hang on to. Let all the rest go hang.

'Well, miss,' he remarked solemnly, 'if you ain't scared of the Injun, I am. But I ain't goin', see?'

Something happened to the girl Ben didn't know what.

All he knew was that she suddenly seemed closer to him like. As a matter of fact, she really was closer, for she had drawn nearer and had laid her hand upon his arm. But he didn't mean only that way . . .

'Please! *Please*!' she begged. 'Don't you realise how dead in earnest I am? If anything happened to you—'

Her fingers tightened on his arm.

If anything happened to *him*? If anything happened to Ben? Somebody was minding, like.

'P'r'aps it won't matter the 'ell of a lot if somethin' does 'appen ter me, miss,' he muttered thickly. 'Gotter 'appen some time, ain't it? But *you* ain't marked fer it yet, see? So I'm sorry, miss, but I ain't goin'—Gawd! Wot's that?'

They turned towards the window again, their nerves tense.

'Didjer 'ear anythin'?' asked Ben hoarsely.

'I thought I heard a cry,' she answered.

'Yer did!' muttered Ben. Then suddenly added, 'Look 'ere, miss, ain't it time fer a policeman?'

'No, not yet!' she whispered sharply.

He looked at her in surprise. He noticed that now she wasn't staring at the house opposite. She was staring down the road. He followed her gaze. He gulped. The Indian was approaching swiftly.

The Indian was no longer the bland and sardonically subtle creature of Ben's memory. His swiftness and his attitude suggested definite purpose. The purpose, moreover, was connected with their own house, not with the house opposite. In a flash he was at the front door immediately below them. Now they could no longer see him; a projection above the door concealed him from view. But they could hear him. They could hear the tiny jangle of a key-chain, and of an inserted key . . .

'Where are you going?' asked the girl sharply.

Ben did not answer. He, too, could move swiftly, and he was out of the room before her question was complete. A second later, he had locked her in.

He was going to kill the Indian.

12

How Not to Kill an Indian

When you are going to kill an Indian you do not walk straight up to him to do it, even if you have a useful bit of rusty railing in your hand. You employ the Indian's own methods, and slink and slide and slither. In fact, you become almost Oriental yourself, forgetting the western rules of cricket, and plotting to surprise your victim suddenly in the back.

It was not any weakening of Ben's intention, therefore, that caused him to reduce his pace as soon as he had sped out of the door of the second floor front and locked it. It was tactics. He travelled at half-speed down the stairs to the first bend, and a quarter-speed down the remaining stairs of the first flight. On the landing he stopped and listened.

He did not hear a sound. Apparently the Indian was not coming up. Not yet, at any rate. He might be exploring the lower floor, to ascertain that it was empty, or he might be standing still by the front door, listening, as Ben was. The only certain things were that he was in the house, and that he had got to be killed.

Ben had not a murderous soul. That will already have

been gathered. But in his muddled state he was convinced that the Indian had a murderous soul, and that someone was undoubtedly going to cease existence within the next few minutes. And, of the three persons involved, he regarded the Indian as the one who would least be missed. In a criminal court a crime such as Ben now contemplated might form the subject of a week's intricate and expensive argument. The simple issue rarely interests the law.

The silence continued. Each seemed to be saying voicelessly to the other: 'You move first.' Rather surprisingly, the Indian moved first. A soft step fell upon Ben's strained ears.

Then another. Then another. And *still* not up the stairs! Ben located the steps along the passage towards the kitchen. Now the Indian would be reaching the cupboard. Now he would be passing it. No—not passing it! *Pausing* at it! The Indian was pausing at the cupboard.

Ben crept on a little. He reached the top of the second flight, and became conscious of a faint glimmer. Like the girl, the Indian had a torch.

Then a fresh sound fell upon Ben's ears. It was unmistakable. The Indian was opening the cupboard.

This was the moment! To hesitate now would be to lose a golden opportunity! The Indian would be standing facing the cupboard. There was a slight bend at the spot where the cupboard came, and a man facing the cupboard door would have his back half-turned to anyone who crept down the stairs and then twisted suddenly round towards him. A couple of yards, a quick leap, and a quick whack . . .

As Ben thought, he acted. He had scarcely formulated his plan before he was down the stairs and twisting round the balustrade at the bottom. By some miracle of memory, and assisted by his pace, he evaded the stairs that produced the worst creaks, and the Indian, when he veered round towards him, gave no sign that he had heard anything. He was standing, as Ben had visioned, before the cupboard door, and the cupboard door was open. Beyond the door loomed a black cavity, un-illuminated by the Indian's torch because the torch was pointing straight downwards, giving the Indian the effect of an erect shadow in a pond of light.

'Lummy, I've got 'im!' thought Ben, leaping forward with his bit of railing raised.

He felt a momentary sickness. He'd hit lots of people in his life, almost as many as had hit him, but he never really liked it. The sound of a crack on the boko was not real melody to him. A crack on the Indian's boko, however, might sound rather good. It would spell safety for the girl upstairs, and rid the world of most of its immediate horror.

Now he was right behind the Indian. Still the Indian stood motionless, peering into the black cavity of the cupboard. Ben closed his eyes, like a charging bull, and the railing came down with a swish. But it met nothing. The Indian had stepped aside, and the velocity of Ben's rush took him right into the cupboard. A gentle push from the Indian, now behind him, assisted the entrance.

And, just as Ben's railing had met nothing, Ben's feet met nothing. He lurched into blankness as well as blackness. It was as though he had been shoved into a dark lift without a bottom, while, above him, a door banged to.

As once before in this house of hideous happenings, Ben died, but this time he did not go up to heaven. He descended to the less soothing alternative, and discovered it damp and stagnant. Instead of Noah, he interviewed a slimy monster with one bright eye; and instead of begging to come in, he tried to argue himself out. 'Wot 'ave I done?'

he demanded. 'You've been a fool,' replied the monster, 'and all fools come down to me.'

'That's ridick'lous, you ain't got no tail,' retorted Ben; 'and, any'ow, there's a person up above wot don't think too bad o' me. 'Ere, stop shovin' me abart! Give us a floor! Wot's this? Water? It oughter be fire. Wot's this water doin'?' It was certainly queer about the water. The slimy monster with one eye laughed—a nasty, oozing, sucking laugh. 'Oh, tryin' ter drahn me, are yer?' exclaimed Ben. 'Well, yer can't drahn a sailor. Why, I bin orl rahnd the world, I 'ave. Sydney, Noo Zealand, Cape Town . . . It was in Cape Town I 'eard abart my little gal goin'. I'd 'ave bin back in three weeks. 'Ow was that fer bad luck? And she was a bit of orl right, that little gal was. Never knoo jest 'ow 'it 'appened. Yus, and *she* went up, and so *I'm* goin' up too. Why, that's wot I ses in Cape Town. "Never mind," I ses, to'er like, "I'll see yer later," I ses, yus, and I bin workin' for it, ain't I, and now yer tryin' ter git me dahn . . . Well, yer shan't . . . Gawd, ain't this water cold? . . . Oi! . . . Wot's 'appenin'? . . . It's up ter me knees . . . nah me waist . . . I ain't goin', I tell yer! . . . Oi! . . . Oi! . . .'

The moment of stunned inactivity was over—the moment that had embraced his second death and all its attendant thoughts. Now the cold water took effect, and his hands flew out. They touched rough brick. Moist, foul-smelling, and concave. One hand slid and scraped. The other, flung upwards as well as outwards, was luckier. It found a projection, and grasped it desperately. There was a great lurch. His shoulder seemed to be struggling to escape from its socket. But the hand held on, the water remained at his waist, and the descent was checked.

The check would have been merely temporary, and the

water would have mounted to his neck and head, if the other hand had not become busy. In trying to join its companion at the projection, it found an iron staple sticking a little way out from the brickwork. If Ben had struck this staple as he had dropped by, it would have written 'Finis' to his career; but by the grace of a few inches he had fallen clear of it, and now, instead of spelling his doom, it spelt his possible release. For he found that there was room for both hands to grasp it, and that, when one had hung on for a bit and regained a little breath, one could hoist oneself up a few inches.

This doubtful security would probably have been of very transitory value to you or me. To Ben, used to a ship's internals, the value was inestimable. The few inches led to a few more inches. Feet as well as hands came into play, and when once they had wriggled themselves out of the ooze they found niches in the brickwork, pressed into them, and levered up from them. The hands working upwards also, utilised every slightly protruding brick, every cleft, the very roughness of the wall itself. Inch by inch, Ben rose.

And, as he rose, hope began to glimmer again, though, it was still a very far-off glimmer, and his brain began to clear. He discovered, definitely, that he was not dead. The slimy one-eyed monster sank back into the dank water beneath him. The route to the nether regions became a vertical tunnel, a well-like drop that ended in a subterranean water-way. Probably the water-way connected with the local canal, to which it was designed he should have eventually found his way. But he had not found his way there, and no policeman or small boy would make a gruesome discovery from the canal bank on the morrow. He was finding his way up the vertical tunnel, the top of which was in a cupboard in No. 29 Jowle Street. And when he got to the top and battered a door down, somebody was going to hear something.

By now Ben's feet had contrived to reach the iron staple which his hands had gripped, and his hands were clawing at the brickwork higher up. Had the iron staple given way, Ben would have returned to the water, and the policeman or small boy would have eventually made his sensational discovery. Happily, however, the iron held, and was sufficiently firm to support Ben's full weight while his hands explored the darkness above him; and, when the exploration proved barren, the firmness of his support even permitted him to execute a series of jerky jumps, so that his fingers might explore a few inches higher.

The first of the jumps proved futile. So did the second and the third. Ben was afraid to jump too far up from his base, lest he should not return to it. But the fourth jump, a trifle more adventurous, gave one of his fingers the impression of an edge—an edge that might be gained if one's fifth jump were a little more adventurous still. The matter needed thought. To leap up with all one's might would be to leave the iron staple for ever. If the leap was lucky, he would have one chance in a thousand of descending again upon the iron staple, and one chance in ten thousand of maintaining his equilibrium even if he did descend upon it. Thus, it would be a final leap for life, with the life distinctly problematical. On the other hand, if you stand on an iron staple in a dark hole indefinitely, you will eventually starve, and meanwhile it will be exceedingly monotonous. There was no jam and honey either way.

And there was another thing. While he stood on the iron

staple and starved, an Indian would be killing a beautiful girl. Not only for Ben's own sake, therefore, but for the sake of the beautiful girl, must Ben call all his courage for this final effort!

So he decided to leap. And he bent down, to gain impetus. When he straightened himself, he found that he had not leapt. 'Funny!' he muttered, and bent down again.

He bent down and up six times before he worked up the necessary degree of pluck. Then he leapt. Darkness concealed the most terrified face since the Flood. It also concealed the most amazing spraying of limbs. No legs had ever kicked nothingness so hard before, no arms had ever slashed out on either side of a parent body with such velocity. By all the rules, they should have jerked themselves free of the body and attained a separate existence. Instead, they descended on damp, cold flatness, while the legs dangled beneath and tried to kick goals . . .

''Allo—I'm still 'ere!' thought Ben, astounded.

He was. For the damp, cold flatness came towards him on either side as far as each elbow, and when the legs grew still, he discovered himself hanging there as securely as a float.

He had executed the most amazing jump in history.

Where was he now? Six inches from the top or sixty yards? He was too limp to inquire, or to do anything for a long while but just hang. Seconds went by, or minutes, or hours. Again, he couldn't tell. Time was just as difficult to define as space. But suddenly he raised his drooping head. Voices! *Voices* . . .

'Oi!' he shouted.

No sound came from his throat. His voice seemed to have gone, like. He shouted again. Again, it was merely a loud thought. But the other voices droned on. A little way off. A little way above him.

One voice was that of the Indian. The other was that of the girl. They were talking together—doubtless, in the hall—and as Ben listened his eyes opened wide, and his mouth opened wider, and queer things happened to his heart.

13

A Queer Association

The Indian closed the cupboard door and regarded it reflectively.

He had just sent a fellow-being through the door into dank water, thereby carrying out the designs for which he had entered the house; he had known his victim would be in the house, having received proof of the man's queer tenacity, and it had become necessary to settle with him definitely and finally. But the Indian's expression betrayed neither satisfaction nor regret. Only the whites of his eyes gleamed a little more brilliantly than usual to record the fact that he had done what he had done, and that what he had done had to be done.

But, all at once, his inscrutable attitude changed. He turned sharply from the cupboard door and raised his head, extinguishing his torch at the same moment. A sound had fallen upon his quick ears. Somebody else was in the house—somebody else to be reckoned with!

He stole to the stairs. The sound was some way above him, and seemed to be connected with a key or a door-knob.

For an instant he hesitated. Then, deciding on his course of action, he flashed up the stairs without pausing until he gained the second floor. As he did so and switched on his light again, the key of a door was wriggled out of its hole and dropped with a little clatter on to the bare boards.

The Indian stood and regarded the key. It lay in the little arc of radiance produced by his torch. Then he raised his eyes and regarded the door from which it had fallen. Somebody on the other side of the door, having got the keyhole free, was now trying to manipulate the lock.

Off went the Indian's light again. In the darkness he drew a knife from the concealment of his sleeve, and stood waiting by the door. He waited nearly three minutes, while the person on the other side of the door continued the attempt to open it.

The Indian could have opened it, or could have rendered the attempt abortive by replacing the key in the keyhole and fixing it. He did neither, however. He wanted very much to know who was on the other side of the door, and he was far too intelligent to sacrifice the advantage of surprise. The twisting and scraping sounds continued. Then, at last, came the significant little click the Indian had been waiting for, and which marked the person on the other side of the door as a person of some skill. And now the Indian stepped back a little and gripped his knife firmly. The door began to open.

Then the Indian's torch flashed once more. It flashed full in the eyes of the person emerging from the room—full and blindingly. The person gasped. But the Indian's expression also registered surprise. The eyes that were momentarily dazzled and rendered useless by the torch's rays were the eyes of a girl.

101

'Nadine!' said the Indian, in a low voice.

The girl did not answer. She was leaning against the door frame, striving to regain her lost composure. The Indian regained his first.

'How are you here?' he demanded.

'Wait!' answered the girl. 'Let me get my breath!'

The Indian waited. Then he repeated his question, and there was a touch of impatience in his voice.

'I am here, because you are here,' replied the girl. 'Why are *you* here?'

'It was agreed you should ask no questions,' frowned the Indian.

'I am human,' said the girl.

'And that you should not follow me.'

'Even if you were followed?'

The Indian frowned more deeply, but there was a new quality in his frown.

'Who is following me?' he asked.

He saw her eyebrows go up.

'Don't you know—really?' she retorted. 'Haven't you met him?'

'Please!' said the Indian. 'It is I who request information.'

'But I don't like the look of your knife, Mahdi.'

'*You* need not fear it!'

'I know that. Still, put it away. Then we can talk. It makes me shudder!' He regarded his knife, and she drew a step closer to him, as though fascinated. 'I see you have not used it,' she remarked, staring at it also.

'You would not see if I had used it, Nadine,' he returned.

'Then—have you?'

'You insist on your questions?'

'I think I have earned the right!'

'How?'

'Why—by being here, Mahdi—for your protection!'

Now the Indian drew a step closer, and looked full in the girl's eyes.

'My protection?' he said slowly. 'You care so much, then?'

'Hasn't our friendship proved it?' she answered, turning her own eyes away.

'Friendship!' he exclaimed quickly. 'Yes, only that!'

'You are impatient.'

'What will patience bring?'

'And also crude, Mahdi, at times. How long have we known each other?'

'It is ten days since you passed me the salt in the restaurant in Soho,' he said.

'Ten days! And you think you are not impatient! My friend, we are in Europe, and friendship here does not move as quickly as your knife. Be satisfied that I came here for your protection—to warn you—and do not ask any more of me—yet.'

He considered the advice. Then he nodded slowly, and concealed his knife from view.

'Well, let it be so,' he answered. 'You came here to warn me. That I was being followed. And you still have not told me who this follower is.'

She shrugged her shoulders, and now her own voice reflected a little impatience.

'Why will you pretend to be dense?' she complained. 'Why do you persist in hiding your cleverness from me? The man who was following you is the man who locked me in this room, of course! Who else?'

'So—*he* locked you in.'

'Naturally.'

103

'He knew you had come to warn me?'

'Isn't that obvious? Why should he have locked me in otherwise?'

'And, after locking you in,' continued the Indian, thoughtfully, 'he came down—to me!'

'Yes.'

'Do you know why he did that?'

'I would like you to tell me.'

'You have no guess?'

'Oh, yes! I have a guess!'

'Let me hear it.'

'Well, then—he was a spy?'

'So?'

'In the disguise of a ragged fellow?'

'That is your guess, eh?'

'But why *should* he be a spy?' she exclaimed suddenly.

'Ah! Why?' nodded the Indian, and now he watched her very closely. 'I am waiting to know why *you* thought he was a spy?'

She hesitated. She knew he was watching her closely. She plunged.

'Ever since we have met, Mahdi,' she said, 'you have acted, in certain things, strangely. If you complain that I could give you more of my confidences, I might make the same complaint of you. Isn't it natural that—if our friendship is to lead anywhere—we must know all about each other? But what do I know about you? Nothing! And so—'

'Yes? And so?' he prompted.

'I have had to guess.'

'And your guess?'

Suddenly she laughed. 'It is a very romantic guess, Mahdi! You are the head of some secret organisation! You have enemies! But you are too big for them. And—might be bigger, still, if a woman's wits were added to yours! There! Now I have told you! How far am I right?'

He did not answer immediately. Instead, he continued to regard her fixedly. Then he moved to the door of the room outside which she was standing, and closed it.

'Come—we will go down,' he said. 'It is not good to be here. You will go home. It is my wish. You will obey it. And tomorrow—yes, tomorrow we will meet at the restaurant in Soho—and perhaps I will answer you there, Nadine.'

'And perhaps not!' she pouted.

'Perhaps not,' he agreed, smiling. 'That may depend on you.'

Without seeming to do so, he impelled her towards the stairs.

'And, meanwhile?' she asked.

'You leave this house, as I say, and you go home.'

'And that is all?'

He motioned to her. She was by the stairs, and she found herself descending ahead of him. Not till they had descended both flights and stood in the hall did he answer her; and a man hanging over dark water by his elbows heard the answer.

'You came here to help me, Nadine,' he said, 'and I am grateful. So I will tell you this much. The man who locked you in the room upstairs *was* a spy! And he came down here to kill me.'

'To kill you?' exclaimed the girl.

'With an iron bar. He stood behind me—almost where we are standing now. Yes, just as I now stand behind you. And he raised the bar, and he struck at me.'

The speaker paused. In a whisper came Nadine's entreaty.

'Yes! And then?'

'Then,' said the Indian, shrugging his shoulders, 'I stepped aside, and he toppled over. And, I picked him up and threw him out of the front door. He will not return. There is nothing for either of us to fear. We have got rid of him. And, now, no more of this talk. You must go!'

It seemed to the man hanging over the water that an eternity passed before she spoke again. And, when she did speak, her words were very ordinary.

'Yes, you're right,' she said. 'But please wait here a second. I left my bag upstairs.'

The man hanging over the water heard her feet above him. They grew fainter. They ceased. Then there was another silence. Then the feet returned.

'You have got your bag?' asked the Indian's voice.

'It was over a chair,' replied the girl's. 'Let's go quickly now—this house frightens me!'

The front door opened. Softly, it closed. The man, hanging over the water, made a sudden frantic movement. A loose brick dropped down into the water beneath him with a dull splash.

14

Ben Sees a Murder

A man once walked over a cliff in the dark. As he fell he managed to seize the edge of the cliff with his hands and to check his downward flight. He hung on till daylight, and when the sun rose he discovered that his feet were six inches above a wide, smooth plateau of soft grass.

Ben felt something like this man when, a few minutes after the Indian and the girl had departed, he had contrived by the last of seven different wriggling processes to bring his body completely out of the hole that had housed it for so long, and discovered himself on a bit of wooden flooring level with the bottom of the cupboard door. The flooring was to one side of the door, so would be missed by anybody stepping straight into the cupboard as Ben himself had stepped into it. Ben was convinced that the flooring of the cupboard had been complete when he had first examined it during his original tour of the house. Someone had since removed some of the boards.

But this was not the total sum of Ben's discovery, and it was the discovery immediately following that made him feel like the man who had hung from the cliff. When he raised his hand to battle with the door, he found there was not going to be any battle. The door came open easily. The Indian had either omitted to lock it through error when he had been diverted by the sound above him on the second floor, or else he had no longer considered it necessary. ''Cos, arter orl,' reflected Ben, as he wormed his weary body out, ''e thinks I'm dead, don't 'e? And I ain't dead. Leastways,' he added, in sudden doubt, 'I don't think I am.'

He had many times thought himself dead when he had been alive. It might be just as possible to think yourself alive when you were dead. Nothing was really certain in No. 29 Jowle Street.

Flopping out into the hall of this erroneously described 'desirable residence', and looking more like a walrus than a man, he sank down flat on to the floor for a few seconds. And then an astonishing thing happened. He fell asleep. Weary in every fibre, aching in every limb, he found the flat boards divine in their completeness, and discovered that their security was better than the finest spring mattress. Once, in a palatial shop window, Ben had stared at a mattress described as similar to one the King slept on. It was no better than the boards Ben lay on. You could relax here—you could let every muscle go—you could stay put. 'Ah-h-h-h!' breathed Ben, and slept.

It was not merely physical reaction that told upon him. It was also mental reaction. The most wonderful girl in the world was a friend of the most horrible man. It staggered one. It hurt one. It altered the shape of one's heart. One couldn't cope with it. So why resist the heaviness of one's eyelids and the lure of utter staticism? There was nothing to keep awake for . . . nothing to wake up for . . . nothing to climb up from the depths for . . .

''Allo!' said Ben, several hours later.

He sat up. He stared round. There was light about. Not torch light, but the light of day.

It was dismal light, because it was a dismal day, and perhaps of all the houses in Jowle Street, itself grudging of illumination, No. 29 let in the least. The windows were small and scarce. They had not been cleaned within living memory. One was not a window at all, but a bit of nailed boarding. Still, whatever the quality, daylight it was, and Ben blinked at the peeling walls with reproachful surprise.

What had happened during all these hours? Where was everybody? Were his recent memories close at hand, or had they flitted to China? But if Ben could not say what had happened, he could at least say that one thing had *not* happened, and he thanked his stars for the omission. Nobody had returned to No. 29 Jowle Street. Otherwise he would not have woken up so peacefully. Probably he would not have woken up at all!

'Wunner if it's orl hover?' reflected Ben, blissfully unconscious that it was just about to begin, 'Let's git this stright! Wot 'appened?'

He harped back. Yes; he remembered it all quite clearly. He had locked the girl in. He had come down to kill the Indian. The Indian had shoved him down the hole. He had got up out of the hole. But, before he had got out, he had heard the girl and the Indian chatting like old friends, and calling him a spy. And then they had left the house . . . left the house . . . left the house . . .

'Somethin' 'appened afore they left the 'ouse,' thought Ben. 'Wot was it?'

109

Something unimportant, he believed, yet it worried him. Some little incident—something that had made a tiny impression—well, it didn't matter . . .

'Ah, 'er bag!' muttered Ben. 'She went hup ter fetch it. That's orl.'

Nothing in that, was there?

She had gone up for her bag, and then she had come down again, and . . .

'Yus, but she said she'd lef' it hover a chair,' thought Ben, 'and there ain't no chair!'

Nothing in that, either, eh? Ben wondered. He wondered how she had come to leave the bag up in the room at all. He wondered whether, even if she had left the bag up in the room, she oughtn't to have thought of it before. But, mostly, he wondered about the chair, the chair that didn't exist. The chair . . .

Ben leapt to his feet. His heart was pounding.

'The Injun thort I was dead,' he muttered. 'But *she* didn't! 'E tole 'er 'e'd kicked me aht o' the 'ouse, the blamed liar, and if she thort I wasn't dead she knoo I'd git back some'ow, yus, she knoo that, and so up she goes ter the room when she knoo *I'd* go—'

Ben's mind was working. Now his feet worked too. He clambered up the stairs with the eagerness of a child trying to disprove the existence of the Bogey Man. Because, if he did not disprove the sincerity of the girl's friendship with the Indian—and he would know one way or the other when he reached the second floor front—the world would be entirely populated by Bogey Men, and the sooner one got out of it and tried another planet, the better.

I am not going to try and explain Ben to you. The simplest characters are sometimes the least explainable, and

110

the simplest impulses confound our subtle logic. I merely record that, as he raced up the stairs he almost cried, and that when he entered the second floor front and saw a little piece of paper lying on the soap box, tears did come into his eyes. For the sight of the little piece of paper gave him back his faith in the Universe.

He lurched forward and seized it, praying that there would be no long words. He read:

'My dear Friend,—If you return and find this note, as I believe you will, do nothing rash. I still advise you to go. There is great danger. But if you insist on remaining, then watch the windows of the house across the road— No. 26—and if you see me at one of them and I make a sign, it will mean, "Please go for the police." *But do not go for the police unless you get the sign.* I cannot say more now. One day I shall hope to thank you.'

There was no signature. None was needed. It was just a hurried scrawl, written by one who knew the person who read it would understand—an S.O.S., with trust behind it. 'One day I shall hope to thank you.' Ben required no greater thanks than the little piece of paper that bore these words.

So now she, too, was in the house opposite! Ben glued his eyes upon it—a house no longer in darkness, yet scarcely less forbidding in the misty morning light. He had no idea of the time. He had swopped his last watch for a drink after using it for a hammer. In this mist, it might be any time. Then, suddenly, he cursed himself. Why had he yielded to sleep? This paper must have lain here for hours, waiting for him! She had written it, of course, when she had run up for her bag, and while Ben was still in the hole in the cupboard. Then she had gone. Home, the Indian had commanded. But she would have double-crossed the Indian, as she had obviously been double-crossing him all along, and had found some way of getting into No. 26. And then what?

Ben's imagination came to a blank wall. The inside of No. 26, its aspect, its activities, and its significance, were beyond his power of visualisation. A closed book, though soon to open. All he could conjure up at this moment was a vision that gave him acute discomfort—a vision of the girl appearing at one of the windows and giving her signal, while he was still fast asleep on a hall floor! Suppose she *had* given her signal? And suppose the Indian, creeping up behind her, had seized her as she stood there, and pulled her back into the shadows.

And, at that instant, the Indian came along the road, a blurred but unmistakable figure in the increasing mist. The Indian who believed Ben was dead. The Indian who must continue to believe that Ben was dead! Hastily Ben ducked his head below the ledge of the window. And when, a few seconds later, he ventured to raise his head again, the front door of No. 26 was closing, and the Indian was no longer in sight.

'Lummy—'e's gorn in!' thought Ben.

Another figure came along the road. Ben was destined to see a long procession of shadowy forms that morning. The second figure was a fat policeman. He came along, contentedly and comfortably, trying to think of a vegetable of seven letters ending with 'i'.

'Wot abart givin' 'im a shout?' wondered Ben.

If he shouted, the dwellers within No. 26 would hear. If he slipped downstairs and ran after the policeman he might be too late to catch him. And even if he did catch him, what should he say to him? 'There's funny things 'appening in one o' these 'ouses, bobby—go in quick!' Ben pictured the bobby's face as he made the statement. No, it would have to be something a bit more startling than that to bring the bobby out of his cross-word. 'Oi! Gal bein' murdered in No. 26!' That would do it! But—was she being murdered? And, if she wasn't, did she want the policeman? *Do not go for the police unless you get the sign*!' Snakes, it was a puzzle . . .

'Brocoli!' murmured the policeman.

And passed out of Jowle Street.

As he disappeared, another figure came into view. This figure—the third of the procession—was far less comfortable and contented than the policeman. It paused, then came on again, then paused again.

'Well, I'm blowed!' murmured the watcher at the window. 'If it ain't the gal wot was cryin'!'

Yes, he recognised her now. The girl who had left No. 26 on the previous evening, and who had attracted the Australian chap away from No. 29. ('Yus, and I wunner where that Australian chap *is*?' thought Ben. He would have got a shock had he known.) The girl he had seen again later—round about midnight, wasn't it?—outside the Piccadilly Hotel, with a young man. And here she was again.

'Nah, then, young leddy,' muttered Ben, 'jest you keep on! Don't you stop and go in that there 'ouse! Lummy— she's doin' it!'

For, even as he had muttered his advice, she had suddenly run to the front door and rung the bell.

The door opened almost immediately. It seemed to have

been waiting for her. It closed. The street was deserted again.

A feeling of impotent desperation began to settle upon Ben. He ought to be doing something, and he hadn't an earthly idea what he ought to be doing. 'I ain't cut aht fer this,' he admitted, with humiliation. 'I wish I was a bit more like Sherlock 'Omes!'

Perhaps the best thing to do would be to stay and wait for the sign. The Indian had only just gone in, so the girl might not be in trouble yet. And, after all, that other girl had gone in too. You couldn't go far wrong, could you? not with a full house like that . . .

''Allo! 'Ere's another!' blinked Ben. 'Bloomin' number four!'

Number four was scarcely less interesting than number three had been. He arrived a few minutes later, and he was the weak-faced young man who had been outside the Piccadilly Hotel with the distressed girl. He, too, went into No. 26 Jowle Street.

'I know what I'll do,' thought Ben. 'I'll stick 'ere fer ten more minutes, and then if nothin' 'appens I'll—'

The ten minutes dragged by. Were they ten minutes? Ben couldn't say. Then, suddenly a light went up in the room immediately opposite.

It was certainly a morning for lights, as the mist was increasing every moment. Unfortunately, a lace curtain prevented Ben from seeing clearly into the room, but he was able to make out dim figures as they moved about, and he thought one of them was the old man. The old man who had shot at him . . .

He kept his eyes fixed on the window. The light was shaded, and not well fixed for his purpose of spying. He could only see the figures that were right by the window.

He could not see what they were doing, or who they were. Even the old man had disappeared now, and somebody else was hovering near the spot where he had been. Dim and blurred . . . now more distinct . . . now dim and blurred again . . . hallo . . . nailed him! It was the weak-faced young man . . . Number Four.

'Yus, that's the bloke,' concluded Ben. 'And good fer 'im! 'E's bumped back agin the curtain, and shoved it aside a bit. Nah p'r'aps—'

He strained his eyes till they almost left their sockets. There was a little patch of room he could see quite distinctly now—a sort of slit, like the enlarged eye of a needle. Someone appeared in the slit. Who? . . . Ah, nailed him too! It was the bloke who had lain down on the ground yesterday and then got up again. Nasty expression he'd got! Ben could see it, even though the man was some way off. Towards the back of the room somewhere . . . and turning his head as though talking to someone else beside him, but out of sight. Who was he talking to? . . . Hallo! The weak-faced young man by the window was getting excited, all of a sudden! Over the young man's shoulder, behind him, Ben could still see the other bloke, and the other bloke was still wearing that nasty expression . . . somebody was waving his arms . . . Hey! What was this? The weak-faced young man had seized a revolver from somewhere, and was pointing it at the bloke with the nasty expression . . . now the bloke had fallen . . .

'Gawd!' gasped Ben.

His forehead became pasty. He felt sick. Then, for an instant, the curtains parted more widely, and a face appeared. A face staring across the road directly at him. The face of the old man.

Ben had no time to move back out of sight. His nose had been pressed against the window, and he had forgotten caution in his excitement. He stood transfixed, immovable, while the curtains opposite were pulled quickly together again, and the old man's face vanished.

'I seen a murder done,' thought Ben, 'and they knows I seen it.'

He crept back into the middle of the room. The situation beat him. He felt his mind growing numb again. Numb with the horror of the sight he had just beheld, numb with the complications of his duty and his personal position, and numb with fatigue. It may be remembered that he had not had a square meal for over twenty-four hours.

And, being numb, he lost count of time. And he did not remember time again until the door of the room was pushed open, and he found himself face to face with the man he had just seen murdered.

15

Ben Commits a Murder

No two men, possibly, had ever faced each other before under such unusual conditions. Each, a few moments previously, had been convinced of the death of the other, yet here were their two living bodies to confound conviction. The rules of logic were turned topsyturvy.

Ben was the first to voice his indignation. He was entering a red tide that was to lead him to a terrible termination, but the first currents of the tide were merely a sort of stunned anger. He had seen a man killed. The sight had nauseated him. And here was the man before him!

'Why ain't you dead?' he demanded hoarsely.

It was a ridiculous question. The subject of it, however, did not appear to perceive its humour. He retorted, in kind:

'Why aren't *you*?'

The counter challenge increased Ben's indignation. He did not know it, but he was becoming dangerous. Had he known it, he might have exercised more caution. So might his antagonist.

'Why ain't *I* dead, eh?' exclaimed Ben, clenching his fist.

'Wot makes yer think I orter be? You 'aven't seen *me* shot, 'ave yer?'

'All worms like you ought to be dead,' said his antagonist.

'Oh, very clever, ain't yer?' retorted Ben. 'But it don't git past *me*. You think I orter be dead 'cos a durned Injun tole yer I was. And you're in with the durned Injun, and with a durned old man, and with a durned woman wot carries drugged gaspers, and Gawd knows 'oo helse! Well, I'll tell yer why I ain't dead, cocky! I ain't dead 'cos yer can't drahn a sailor, see? No! Yer can shove 'im dahn a well, but 'e climbs hup agin, and yer can lock 'im in a room, but 'e gits aht agin, and yer can kick 'im aht of a 'ouse, but 'e comes back agin, see? Orl right. Nah yer know. And nah we'll git back ter where we started from. Why aren't *you* dead?'

His antagonist regarded him thoughtfully.

'Yus, and I can see yer 'and goin' inter yer pocket,' added Ben; 'but bullets don't kill me no more'n they kill you. Git me?'

'Perhaps not precisely, at the moment,' answered his antagonist slowly; 'but I expect I shall get you before very long. So you saw someone shoot at me, you say?'

'Yus.'

'Did you happen to see who shot me?'

'Yus.'

'Who—if I may ask?'

'Bloke wot jest went inter yer 'ouse.'

'Oh! So you saw the bloke go inter the 'ouse—'

'Yus, and I saw a gal go inter the 'ouse afore 'im, and I saw the Injun go inter the 'ouse afore 'er, and I saw an Orstralian go in afore 'im, but I tell yer stright I don't care a twopenny pip abart none o' them 'cept that hother gal, and if *she's* in the 'ouse, too, I'm goin' ter git 'er aht, if I 'ave ter brike hevery bone in yer blinkin' body.'

His antagonist considered the statement. Then he moved a step nearer to Ben, as though to imply what he thought of it, and said:

'Now that's very interesting. But suppose we leave my blinking bones out of it? I don't really think you'd be able to break them, and, even if you did, it wouldn't help you. So what do you propose to do about it?'

The man's quiet sarcasm incensed Ben. So did that cool step forward. It was not a threat. It was an insult. Ben measured the decreasing distance between them, and replied:

'I'll tell yer wot I'm goin' ter do abart it. I'm not goin' ter stop 'ere torkin' ter you, which is wot yer want, ain't it? I'm goin' ter fetch the pleece, and you ain't goin' ter stop me!'

As he spoke, his fist flashed out, and sought his antagonist's chin. But the chin moved aside, and the fist was caught by stronger fingers than his own. Ben was flung off, and a revolver gleamed unpleasantly near his face.

'You damned fool!' growled his antagonist. 'If you'd been sensible you might have stood a chance, but it's gone now, and you've only yourself to blame for it. You've seen too much, and you've talked too much. Well, you're not going to see or to talk any more. God! Do you think a miserable, under-sized worm of a man like you can do anything against—*us*?'

'Mis'erble, am I—'

'Get over by that wall!'

'Worm, am I—'

'D'you hear?'

'Yus, I 'ear! And if yer let that thing orf, so'll the 'ole street!'

119

'Oh, no it won't. There won't be any sound. Just a little squeal—the last squeal of a squealer—and down you'll drop. And the *next* time you go down the well, my friend, you won't be in a condition to come up again, because you won't know anything about it. You'll be in the place where all contemptible snails go when they die—'

It all happened so quickly that Ben himself was confounded. The red tide caught him and swept him, as once before, but this time with even more dynamic force. He was a worm! He was a snail! Helpless, incompetent, scorned, and trodden on. And, because of that—because there was nothing in him that could ever rise above the mire—a girl in distress was appealing to him in vain! Where was his dormant power? Where was the might that was in every man who rose above the insects? He prayed for the miracle of Samson, and the answer flowed round, him in crimson. Everything was red. The walls. The floor. The ceiling. The jeering man in front of him. He, himself. The air through which he leapt. The head on which he battered. The hands he battered with . . . The pistol he seized and smashed with . . . Red! . . . Red! . . . Red! . . .

The hideous spasm passed. The red swept on and out of sight, and immediate things took on their natural hue. Trembling and shaken, Ben became a normal, fearful human being again. The walls returned to yellow. The ceiling to black. The floor to the negative colours of rotting wood.

But one thing remained red. It was the head on which Ben had battered. It lay close against the rotting wood, motionless, with eyes that no longer shrivelled one with sarcasm, and tongue that had lost its power to sting.

Death, this time, was real.

16

Ben Takes the Plunge

Ben had never killed a man before. He had hit men and kicked them, and scratched them and even bitten them, but he had never knocked a man down in such a fashion that the man would never rise again. He found it a shattering experience . . .

In his own mind, he had died a thousand deaths. He was not made of the heroic stuff that dies but once. Now he had dealt out death to another. He had become the spectre he himself so constantly feared. It was unbelievable, ironical. It cheapened death that he should be its instrument. Ben, the down-trodden, a murderer . . .

'Yus, but it was wotcher calls self-defence, like,' he told the judge who suddenly leapt into his imagination. ''E was thret'nin' me with a gun, 'e was, see? That mikes it orl right, see?'

Did it?

Then another loop-hole occurred to Ben. Perhaps the man was not dead, after all? Just a knock out, eh? Why, he'd seen dozens of chaps knocked out just like that! You'd think they were done to the wide, but five minutes later they were laughing and joking . . . One, two, three, four, five . . . Nothing doing . . . Six, seven, eight, nine . . . Nine, nine, nine . . . Ten.

'*That* ain't no good!' muttered Ben, 'Well, let's see if 'is 'eart's tickin'.'

He approached his late antagonist gingerly. Had this length of limpness ever been really threatening? It seemed impossible! He knelt down, and placed his hand over the left breast. No rhythm impressed itself upon the hand. Not the slightest flutter. He took the hand away, and replaced it by his ear. He listened hard. With all his might. There wasn't a sound . . . Yes, there was! Bing-bing! Bing-bing! Bing-bing!

'Gawd, it's me own,' murmured Ben.

He stood up again.

''Ow yer feelin', sonny?' he said loudly.

He nearly leapt to the ceiling. The dead man did not speak, but there was a sudden little movement somewhere. The next moment a small object slid out of a pocket, paused on a curve of the coat, and rolled on to the floor.

'Lummy!' gasped Ben. 'I'm comin' hover orl funny.'

The explanation of the small object's appearance was quite simple, however. When he had been bending over the form he had pressed on the pocket unconsciously, and had started a small sequence of movements in the creases and bulges of the cloth. The culminating movement of the little series had ejected the object, and the law of gravitation had done the rest.

Ben stooped again and picked up the object. It was a small button, half-red and half-green, fixed on a safety pin. It had evidently been pinned on the inside of the dead man's pocket, and had come unfastened in the struggle.

Queer thing to have on you. No one'd call it pretty? And, even if it had been pretty, what was the use of keeping it in your inside pocket?

Nevertheless, Ben slipped it in his own pocket. You never knew.

This brought him to the end of the immediate formalities. What came next? Yes, after you'd killed a fellow, what did you do?

The imaginary judge came next. He was wearing a black cap, and he suddenly filled the room. And, just outside the room, there was a gallows . . .

Ben found himself at the door. 'Steady!' he muttered. 'It won't 'elp yer ter run away!'

He wanted to run away badly. All this while he had been fighting against a creeping terror. The judge in the black cap was the terror, and a girl in a hat far prettier was the weapon he fought the judge with.

'Carn't go orf and leave 'er,' he told himself a hundred times. 'Well, can I?'

Of course he couldn't. He had got to help her. And he wasn't helping her! He was just standing there, doing nothing! The only way to help her was to take matters now into his own hands and to fetch the police. A pretty little story he had to tell the police!

Still it had to be done. Yes, and the sooner it was done the better. Down the stairs, out into the road, hook a bobby, and bring him back. Then the bobby could deal with Ben and the corpse, and the Indian and the old man, and the whole bang lot of 'em! . . .

Thirty seconds later, Ben was in the street of mist. He looked left and right, and saw no sign of official blue. He turned to the left, in pursuit of it.

'Hallo! Where you goin'?' inquired a voice.

It did not sound like a policeman's voice, but Ben stopped.

'Ter find a bobby,' he replied, barging straight to the point. Now that he had settled on his policy, an unnatural calm had settled on him. He couldn't quite understand it, and he didn't recognise it. It rather alarmed him.

'Bobby?' mused the voice.

'Yus,' answered Ben. ''Ave yer seen one?'

'Hun'reds an' hun'reds,' nodded the owner of the voice, and Ben discovered that the fellow was leaning against a lamp-post. 'But, lis'n, ol' lump of sweetness. I'm not drunk. Jes' happy, that's all. No need for a bobby.'

'The bobby ain't fer you,' said Ben.

'Oh, then I'm yours, to the las' fibre. Tha's funny word, isn't it? Fibre! And fancy rememb'ring it in my condish'n. Jolly good. Now, then le's get this straight. My name's Mr Eustace Moberley Hope. Wha's yours?'

'Shurrup!' growled Ben, and moved away.

But a long arm stretched after him, and pulled him back.

'Mustn't go, ol' lump o' sweetness,' reproved the tipsy one. 'I'm goin' to need you when I leave this lamp-post. Like hell I am. And what I want to know is, wha'do you want policeman for? I should have thought policeman would have wanted *you*.'

''Ere! Lemme go,' exclaimed Ben. 'I'm in a 'urry!'

'Ah, tha' sounds bad!' frowned Mr Eustace Moberley Hope. 'I don' like sound of that at all, little sunshine. Have you been killin' somebody?'

'S'pose I 'ave?'

The retort, coupled with the sudden desperation with which it was uttered, momentarily sobered the tipsy one. Mr Eustace Moberley Hope advanced his head several inches closer to the head of the man he was gripping, while the grip itself became tighter. An instant later, however, the tension passed, and Mr Hope smiled happily again.

'Well, so've I,' he said. 'I've just killed couple of nasty green tigers and a lalligator. What've *you* killed?'

'A bloke wot tried ter kill me,' cried Ben, wriggling; 'and nah yer *got* it! And if yer don't un'ook yerself, you'll be the nex'!'

The threat in no way depressed Mr Hope. On the contrary, his smile expanded.

'You know, I'm mos' beautifully drunk!' he confided. 'I never hatched anythin' s'good as you before. Oh, look! Here's some policemen! Lots an' lots of 'em. Hi, policemen! We want you. We've killed a bloke!'

A burly form grew out of the mist. Ben fought a sudden feeling of depression. Now he was for it!

'Now, then, what's all this?' demanded the policeman.

'We've killed a bloke,' repeated Mr Eustace Moberley Hope amiably, 'and we want you to arrest us.'

The policeman eyed the speaker with calm criticism.

'Bit early in the day to start this kind of game, isn't it?' he asked. 'Take my advice, sir, and get along home.'

'But you don' un'stan', sergeant,' retorted Mr Hope, pained. 'We're a couple o' killers.'

'Oh! And what have *you* killed?'

'I've killed two green tigers and a lalligator. Oh, an' a large tomato on wheels.' He turned to Ben apologetically. 'I forgot to mention the tomato on wheels. They're horrid!' He turned back to the policeman. 'And my dear frien' here—my little ray of sunshine—he's killed a bloke.'

The policeman looked at Ben, appearing to notice him for the first time.

'So you've killed a bloke, have you?' he observed. 'Well, hop it. *I'll* see to this little side show.'

'What? You're goin' to let him go?' exclaimed Mr Hope. 'Dang'rous man like that?'

'Dangerous, eh?' smiled the policeman tolerantly. Before joining the police force he'd been a bit of a sketch himself. 'Well, and where's this bloke you've killed?'

'Nummer twenty-nine Jowle Street,' answered Ben. 'Second floor front. Lyin' there nah.'

Once more Mr Moberley Hope looked interested. But he did not look nearly as interested as the policeman did.

'What's this?' he demanded sharply.

'Wot I ses,' replied Ben. ''E was goin' fer me with a pistol, so I 'it 'im.'

The policeman turned, and gazed up the road for a moment. Then he turned back to Ben and eyed him darkly and suspiciously.

'Let's hear a little more about this,' he said. 'Number twenty-nine Jowle Street's empty!'

'Yus.'

'Then what were you doing in it?'

'Watchin' the 'ouse hoppersit.'

'What for?'

''Cos of the things goin' hon there.'

'What sort of things?'

'Gawd know! I wancher ter go in and see.'

'Isn't he lovely, sergeant?' beamed Mr Moberley Hope. 'I swear I'll never touch anythin' but Cliquot again!'

'What sort of things?' repeated the policeman, frowning heavily. 'What's put all these ideas into your head?'

'Well, there's a gal,' answered Ben, 'she's the one you gotter git aht of it, and there's an Injun, 'e's arter the gal, see, leaseways that's 'ow I sizes it hup, 'cos 'e tries ter chuck me dahn a well or summit and drahn me, and then there's a old feller, 'e tries ter shoot, me—'

'I say, I *say*!' interposed Mr Moberley Hope, his eyes growing bigger and bigger, while the policeman's frown increased. 'What do *you* drink? I really mus' try it!'

But Ben wasn't interested in Mr Moberley Hope. Continuing to address the policeman, he went on, with a sort of desperate doggedness:

'And then there was a woman wot drugs me with a garsper, and then this hother feller wot I kills, but 'e tries ter git me fust, doncher fergit that—'

'Wait a bit, wait a bit!' interrupted the policeman. 'Ease down, old son! Do you say that this last chap tried to kill you, too?'

'Yus.'

'After the old man did?'

'And the Injun.'

'Yes, but *why*—?'

'Well, I'm tellin' yer, ain't I? 'E tries ter kill me 'cos I jest seen 'im shot at the 'ouse hoppersit—'

'*What?*'

'Oh, don' int'rup', don' int'rup'!' implored Mr Eustace Moberley Hope earnestly. 'He's the mos' beautiful creature God ever made! I've met whole heap, an' I know.'

'And seein' as 'ow I seen 'im killed, 'e comes acrost ter stop me marth, corse I dunno 'ow 'e come alive agin that's fer you ter find aht, but 'e's dead now orl right 'cos I puts me ear ter 'is chest an' it's quiet as a bust clock, but 'e don' matter, it's the gal wot matters, you gotter git 'er aht o' the hother 'ouse, yus, an' fer Gawd's sake look slippy or it'll be too late, and if yer'll tike my hadvice yer'll blow

127

yer whistle and git a lot more of yer, 'cos yer'll 'ave ter deal with a pack—'

'See here!' exclaimed the policeman warmly. 'I've heard quite enough to go on with, and if you don't mind I'll act on my *own* advice, not yours! We'll go and look at this corpse, of yours in No. 29 Jowle Street, and if I find you're playing a joke on me—'

'I tell, yer, 'e don't *matter*,' interrupted Ben. ''E's dead. It's the *gal* wot matters—'

'Be *quiet*!' cried the policeman. 'If you say another word I'll march you straight off to the police station! Be *quiet*, do you hear?'

'There! Now you've stopped him,' murmured Mr Moberley Hope sadly. 'I'm goin' to cry.'

'Yes, and I'll march *you* along there too!' rasped the policeman, rounding on him. 'If you think I'm going to waste the whole day over the pair of you, you're wrong. Now, then! Step lively! We'll be in No. 29 Jowle Street in a couple of minutes, and then we'll know where we stand!'

He took Ben's arm as he spoke, and thrust him forward. Ben realised that obedience, now, was his only course. Once the policeman had seen the grim spectacle in No. 29 with bis own eyes, he would need no further prompting.

The little procession proceeded in silence. Ben and the policeman led. Mr Eustace Moberley Hope lurched behind. He had not been definitely invited to join the procession, but he had not been forbidden to do so. Apparently he regarded himself as a privileged member of the party.

The policeman regulated the pace. It was a sort of compromise between dignity and efficiency. If Ben had told him the truth, no one should say afterwards that the policeman had been too slow. If Ben had lied to him, no one should say afterwards that he had rushed into the hoax. Thus, while Ben strove to increase the pace, and Mr Eustace Moberley Hope strove to lessen it, the correct official speed was faithfully maintained.

They reached No. 29 in just under the predicted two minutes. The door was ajar, as Ben had left it. The policeman commented on the fact.

'You left the door open, I see,' he observed.

'Corse I lef it hopen,' retorted Ben. ''Ow was we goin' ter git in agin if it was shut? A deader don't answer bells.'

'Was it open when you first went in?' queried the constable.

'No,' answered Ben. 'I used a winder.'

They entered the house. The complacency of Mr Hope began to fade.

'What a lot of stairs!' he murmured.

The constable and Ben began to mount the stairs. Mr Hope brightened a little under the impetus of an idea.

'*I* know,' he said. 'I'll jus' sit here an' wait. An' when you come down you can tell me *all* about it!'

He sat down on the bottom stair, while Ben and the constable rounded the bend above him and disappeared from sight.

'House,' murmured Mr Hope. 'I don' like you.'

Ben and the constable continued their ascent. They reached the first floor, and the second floor. On the second landing the constable paused.

'Which room?' asked the constable.

Ben pointed. The constable entered. He came out again. His eyes were thoughtful.

He stood for several seconds, regarding Ben, and Ben could see that a lot was going through his mind. At last he said what was in his mind.

'Now, listen,' said the constable. 'I could get you into serious trouble, if I liked. I could take you to the station and clap you in a cell. That's what I *ought* to do, you know. No doubt at all about it. But you look to me as if you'd had a peck of trouble, and you've either got delusions or that tipsy chap downstairs has paid you to back him up in a silly joke. My own idea is that the chap downstairs is at the bottom of it. If he is, you can hoof it. If he isn't—well, p'r'aps you can hoof it, just the same. But don't think you'll get off so light a second time. And, take my tip—*keep off the drink*.'

'Wotcher—torkin' abart?' gasped Ben.

He lurched into the room. Then he lurched out again, and, his mind in a daze, followed the policeman down.

When they reached the bottom they found the hall empty.

'Where's he gone?' cried the policeman.

He ran out into the mist. Ben stood still for a moment, holding on to the rickety balustrade for support.

Something pricked his chest as he breathed. He clapped his hand over his chest in a new panic, and as he did so, the pricking increased. He thrust his hand in his pocket. He brought out the little red and green button. The pin had pierced his one layer of clothing and had scratched his skin.

He stared at it. He turned, and stared up the flight. He turned again, and stared at the open front door.

Then he went out of the front door, crossed the road, and rang the bell of No. 26 Jowle Street.

PART II

Number Twenty-Six

17

The Spider's Parlour

Presently we shall follow Ben into No. 26 Jowle Street and endure with him (if we are still interested in his fate) the worst of his experiences. But for a while we will leave him to wait on the doorstep—as he himself was destined to wait—and enter the House of Happenings with others who had preceded him. With the Australian, for instance, who entered some fifteen hours earlier and who first aroused Ben's curiosity as to what lay on the other side of the door.

The Australian's own curiosity, it will be recalled, was inspired by the sight of a distressed girl who was leaving the house. The sight of this girl diverted him from the queer creature he was interviewing at No. 29, creating a more magnetic interest. "*E* don't waste no time!' Ben had commented, but the comment had not been entirely just. The Australian appreciated pretty faces; he did not, however, spend his life chasing them. Otherwise he might have followed the distressed girl farther than the corner instead of changing his mind and returning to the door step she had just left.

He rang the bell. The person whose duty it was to answer bells was either asleep, deaf, dead, or unwilling. The Australian rang a second time, smiling rather ironically as he did so. Apparently bells were not popular in England. He had had to make five efforts, he recalled, before he had got anyone to answer the bell of No. 29!

Twice was enough for No. 26, although when the door did open he again received no encouragement. Indeed, it is scarcely truthful to say that the door really opened at all. Something clicked, and the side of the door nearest the click receded a few inches, while in the grudging crack of space was faintly materialised a nose. Not a nice nose. A nose that gleamed palely, more like its own ghost than the reality, about four feet from the ground, its proximity to earth implying an anxiously bent body somewhere in the dimness behind it. Its shape was not as God had designed it, if God had ever designed it at all, which was doubtful. One side of the nose went in, and the other went out. It seemed to have grown against a heavy wind that had blown constantly from the left, billowing it, like washing on a breezy day, into a permanently curved fixture. But the blow that had really sent the nose out of the fairway was a blow of another sort.

'Say, where did you learn to be so darned quick?' asked the Australian.

'What's that?' replied the nose.

'See here,' retorted the Australian. 'Don't people in this country ever answer anything but "What's that?" I asked you where you'd learned your excessive speed? I suppose you know I had to ring twice?'

'Oh! Did you?' said the owner of the nose. 'Well, you see, there ain't no one in.'

'I saw a lady go out, but isn't there anybody else in the house?'

'Lidy? Oh, yus, that's right. But she don't live 'ere.'

'No?'

The nose wagged sideways.

'Then may I ask who does?' pursued the Australian.

'I tell you, there's nobody *in*,' repeated the owner of the nose, and tried to close the door.

But the Australian anticipated the move, and inserted his boot.

'Say, that sort of stuff won't wash!' he exclaimed, frowning. 'How do you know I don't want to leave a message or a card?'

'Wot's the message?' grunted the other. 'Or where's the card?'

'The message is that whoever *does* live here had better dismiss you for incompetence and impertinence, and—here is the card.'

He drew out a letter-case as he spoke, and presented a little piece of pasteboard. The nose advanced towards it. Thick lips materialised below the nose, and small, suspicious eyes above.

'Jack 'Obart,' mumbled the thick lips.

'No, Hobart,' corrected the Australian. 'And now, if you don't mind, I'm coming in!'

He shoved forward as he spoke, and the incompetence and the impertinence fell back, revealed completely now as a furtive, under-sized man.

''Ere!' exclaimed the under-sized man indignantly. 'What are you doing?'

'I am anticipating your tardy courtesy, old son, by entering the hall of this Palace of Welcome, and taking a seat while you convey that card to your master, or mistress, or whoever runs you.'

'But there ain't nobody *in*,' insisted the under-sized man again desperately. 'I've *told* yer! We ain't *receiving* visitors!'

'I'm not a visitor,' replied Hobart. 'I'm the owner of this house.'

The information impressed the under-sized man. He stared at the Australian with startled eyes, and his whole attitude changed.

'What—the boss?' he murmured.

'If a house owner is called the boss in this country, then I am the boss,' nodded Hobart, smiling slightly; 'but it's the first I've heard of it. Say, how much longer are you going to stand there gaping? How do you know I don't want to go to a film tonight?'

Then, suddenly, the Australian turned and glanced towards the staircase. An old man was descending.

The old man from the look of him, was seventy, but by the movement of him he was considerably younger. He came down the stairs at an agile pace, which decreased rather abruptly, however, the moment Hobart turned and saw him.

'Good evening,' said the old man promptly. 'What can I do for you?'

Released from the necessity of further argument, Hobart smiled good-naturedly.

'Well, sir,' he responded, 'you can inform your servant here that I am a nice, law-abiding gentleman, and that it isn't in the least necessary to tell me fibs. Not even pretty little white ones.'

'Fibs?' queried the old man.

'He told me nobody was at home,' the Australian

pointed out. His pleasantness in no way interfered with his determination, and the old man was quicker to read the determination than his servant had been. 'Was that really necessary?'

'Since you are a nice, law-abiding gentleman,' replied the old man, 'I can't think, that it was at all necessary. You can go, Flitt, I'll speak to you later.'

The last five words were uttered with an underlying tenseness not lost upon Flitt, who disappeared furtively into the shadows. Then the old man continued:

'I'm quite sure, sir, that you are nice and law-abiding, but may I know who else you are, besides?'

'Why, certainly,' answered the Australian. 'My name is on a card your servant has taken away with him. Jack Hobart. And may I know, sir, who I am addressing?'

'My name is Clitheroe.'

'Thank you, Mr Clitheroe.'

'And I am the tenant of this house.'

'Then I'm tickled to meet you, because *I* am the owner of this house, and this is the first news I've had that the house is let.'

Mr Clitheroe advanced from the foot of the stairs, and regarded the visitor with increased interest.

'Excuse me, Mr—Hobart, did you say?' he observed. 'But is this house really and truly yours?'

'Sure thing!'

'And you did not know—you say—that it was let to me?'

'The pleasant knowledge has been withheld from me, Mr Clitheroe. So now I hope you'll forgive me for calling on you.'

'Of course,' murmured the old man thoughtfully. 'Naturally. But may I have a little more information?'

'I reckon you may, sir. We're both seeking it, aren't we?'

'Exactly. What I am really wondering, Mr Hobart, is this. How comes it that—'

'Being the owner of this house, I don't know more of its affairs?' interposed Hobart.

'You have taken the words from my mouth,' smiled the old man.

'Well, that's easily explained, sir. I only landed in England today. Steamship *Aristhenes*. Left my luggage in a cloak-room—that what you call 'em here?—and came along to have a look at two bits of property an obliging grand-parent left me some time ago—but which so far haven't brought me in a penny. And there you are! All quite clear and simple, isn't it?'

'*Two* bits of property?' queried Mr Clitheroe, who had followed the story with close attention.

'Yes,' answered Hobart. 'Nos. 29 and 26. And, say, if you want to make me an offer for the pair don't hesitate! I've a notion I'll sell them cheap. But, meanwhile, there ought to be a spot of rent, you know. May I ask where it goes?'

'Where? . . . Oh, you mean, who do I pay my rent to?' said Mr Clitheroe. 'Yes, of course. I settle with the agent through whom I took this house. By the way, did you say you had only arrived in England this morning?'

'That's right. Who's the agent?'

'But, I take it, this is not your first visit to England?'

'Sure!'

'Then you have no friends here? No relatives?'

Jack Hobart looked a trifle puzzled.

'No, I haven't,' he answered, 'though I don't quite see what that has got to do with—'

'I asked merely because I was wondering who was

looking after your affairs,' interposed Mr Clitheroe quickly. 'Of course—if there's no one here to interest themselves in your concerns—'

'No one.'

Now Mr Clitheroe regarded his visitor more intently than ever. The visitor frowned. He wasn't sure that he liked being regarded as intently as all this.

'Say, is anything the matter here?' he demanded, with sudden bluntness.

He was not quite sure why he asked the question. It might have been something in the old man's atmosphere. It might have been something in the atmosphere of the house itself. Or it might have been the momentary appearance, on the stairs, of a hesitating and obviously curious figure. At a sign from Mr Clitheroe, the figure had vanished from sight as abruptly as it had appeared.

'Matter?' Mr Clitheroe observed, after a pause. 'What makes you think anything is the matter?'

'I didn't say I thought there was anything the matter,' retorted the Australian, fencing for no reason that he could definitely establish. 'I asked if anything *was*?'

'Dear me, I apologise,' answered Mr Clitheroe. 'How careless my phraseology is becoming! Let me amend the question. Why do you *ask* if anything is the matter?'

Jack Hobart shrugged his shoulders.

'Not sure that I know,' he admitted unwillingly. 'P'r'aps a girl I saw leaving the house started me on the track.'

'A girl?'

'Yes. She seemed pretty upset, I thought.'

'Pretty upset,' murmured the old man. 'H'm. Yes. She would be. She had—er—just been dismissed for—theft.'

'What—that child?' exclaimed Hobart, incredulously.

Mr Clitheroe shook his head sadly.

'I fear you have little knowledge of human nature, Mr Hobart,' he said. 'Or perhaps human nature is different in your country? Canada, I think you said?'

'I didn't say anywhere,' granted Hobart; 'but it happens to be Australia.'

'Oh Australia! . . . Well, perhaps in Australia pretty maids never disappoint one. But in England they can be terribly deceitful. That very girl you saw, for instance. I caught her in the act of taking five pounds from my pocket-book. I had left it on a table in my study. Never judge by faces, Mr Hobart. That girl whose face looked so innocent to you will spend most of her life in prison. The unprepossessing fellow who opened the door to you is a teetotaller and keeps a lame sister. Behind the squint may lie a warm heart, and behind the smile a disposition to murder, eh? Why, Mr Hobart, people have called me kindly, but how can you judge from my amiable countenance whether I may one day poison you or not—till the day dawns, eh, and you know me better?' He laughed. 'Or how do *I* know that, in spite of your own equally amiable countenance, you may not have come here with some unfriendly purpose—till I know *you* better? Eh?'

He laughed again. Jack Hobart did not join him. He wrenched the conversation back to a point from which it had strayed.

'I've explained my purpose,' he said shortly, 'and I reckon it'll be attained just as soon as you tell me the name of the agent to whom you pay your rent. It's quite likely I *shall* be unfriendly to *him*!'

'You will visit him?'

'There won't be any time wasted!'

'Quite right. He appears to be a rascal.'

'I'm asking the name of the rascal.'

'His name. Yes. It is—Wainwright.'

'Wainwright. Good. And does he pocket the rent?'

'I assumed, till now, that he passed it on.'

'Did he say who to?'

'I believe I have the owner's name—the alleged owner's name—in my desk somewhere, but, to be truthful, it never interested me. Perhaps you would come into my study while I look? You must forgive me for having kept you standing so long. Dear me, I have been very discourteous! Yes, yes, and of course you must have a drink, too.'

'I won't trouble you as far as that, sir—'

'Nonsense! Nonsense! If not for my sake, Mr Hobart, then for England's. The memory of your first call at an English home must not be marred by an impression of inhospitality. This way, if you please!'

He opened a door.

Hobart hesitated. Once more, he could not understand his hesitation. He did not like Mr Clitheroe. That he told himself quite candidly. But if Mr Clitheroe were trying to be a good advertisement for England, then Mr Hobart must not make himself a bad advertisement for Australia. Therefore, the hesitation passed, and Hobart entered the room into which the old man had invited him.

Mr Clitheroe entered behind him, moved towards a desk, then suddenly paused, and snapped his fingers.

'The drinks!' he exclaimed. 'Pleasure first, eh, Mr Hobart? I will fetch them!'

He turned and darted from the room, closing the door behind him. Alone, Jack Hobart frowned. He was wondering why the devil his host could not have rung?

141

A moment later, a new wonder disturbed him. Beneath the desk was a small cupboard, and one of the cupboard doors was half open. Clearly visible through the aperture was a decanter of whisky.

'I'm damned!' he muttered.

Impulsively, he swung round, and ran to the door. It was locked.

18

Cocktails in Jowle Street

The usual impulse, after discovering that you have been locked in a room, is to demonstrate your indignation by making a noise. You either kick the door or you shout. But after his first angry exclamation Jack Hobart realised the folly of such policy. If he had been locked in deliberately and not in a fit of senile absent-mindedness—the latter theory did actually enter his mind, since old men occasionally did queer things and Mr Clitheroe was both old and queer—it was not likely that shouting would serve any helpful purpose. Mr Clitheroe presumably ran the establishment, and his will would prevail. By remaining quiet, on the other hand, Hobart might profit by an unrevealed knowledge of his predicament.

So, instead of kicking the door or shouting, the prisoner utilised the next two minutes by surveying the room and taking his bearings.

There was one window. It was not a large window, and the desk, a very massive piece of furniture with a high back, was pushed up against it and blocked most of it. The desk was not impossible to shift; the operation, however, would involve some effort, and even when the window behind the desk had been won and opened there would be an eight-foot drop into a back area to be negotiated—an area that did not necessarily lead to security and that was probably in view of some other lower window. If necessary, of course, the desk would have to be shifted and the eight-foot drop would have to be performed, but Hobart decided that the necessity had yet to arise. He had a distinct objection to running away, and his fist was quite a useful one. It had knocked out more than one tough on the other side of the world.

At the end of the aforementioned two minutes a sound outside the door heralded the next move in the odd drama. The key was turned, and Hobart stepped close to the door. His nerves were steeled. The useful fist was ready for swift action.

It was not the old man, however, who faced Jack Hobart a moment later. It was a remarkably attractive woman. She was in evening dress, and the whiteness of her throat was accentuated by the glinting green of her gown, which in itself gained vividness from the contrasting auburn of her hair. Altogether, Hobart confessed to himself, a most desirable creature, and a very considerable advance on anything he had so far met in No. 26 Jowle Street.

Words are often seen on lips before they are heard, and the woman's lips suggested that she had entered the room with the intention of speaking immediately. A second passed, however, before the lips responded to their impulse and the words were spoken, and during that second they stared at each other in unconcealed surprise. Hobart was surprised that the sound outside the door should have materialised so alluringly. Her surprise appeared equally complimentary. The eyes that stared into Jack Hobart's, momentarily usurping the prerogative of the lips, said: 'I expected some old tramp or other—never a man like you!'

Then the second passed, and the attractive woman broke the pregnant little silence.

'I've come to apologise!' she exclaimed. 'I hardly know what to say! Please tell me what has happened. Has my father gone off his head?'

'I don't believe I'm much wiser than you are,' replied Hobart, recovering quickly, and with rather a grim smile. 'If the—the old gentleman who has just left me is your father—'

'He is,' she interposed, 'though at this moment I'm not too happy to claim him! I am Miss Clitheroe.'

'Thank you. Well, Miss Clitheroe, your father locked me in here, but I'm quite in the dark as to the reason.'

She turned her head and glanced towards the door, now invitingly open. Her foot was tapping the floor impatiently.

'My father is growing old, and I'm afraid he sometimes suffers from an old man's delusions,' she answered, turning back to Hobart. 'That is not an excuse. It's just an explanation. I do hope, when *I* grow old, I'll make a better fight against the years!'

Hobart repelled an absurd impulse to retort that such a woman as she could never grow old. Infinite is human faith when confronted with beauty and youth! She may have read his thought, for a vague little smile suddenly flitted across her face while her lips ran on:

'Do you know, he frightened the milkman away only yesterday morning? There was a terrible bother. And now you, I suppose, are his latest victim!'

'It seems like it,' said Hobart.

145

'But what *started* it?' she exclaimed. 'What set him off? This locking people in rooms is quite a new idea! Can you give me any hint why he has acted in this way to you? You must remember that I don't know who you are, or what you came to see him about.'

'Well, I can soon set that straight,' he answered her. 'My name is Hobart—Jack Hobart—and I came here because—well, because I happen to be the owner of this house.'

'You—the owner?' she responded, surprise in her voice.

'Yes, Miss Clitheroe,' he nodded. 'The house we're standing in is mine, although I've never clapped eyes on it before today. You see I only arrived from Australia this morning. I'm quite a stranger here, and perhaps—not being up to all your conventional ways yet—I worried your father by suddenly turning up like this. I ought to have written and made an appointment, eh?'

'It's nice of you to try and find excuses for my father,' said the attractive person; 'but it's not at all necessary. Do you mean that he locked you in this room because the house was yours? It isn't a crime to own a house, is it?'

'No, it wasn't quite that way. I reckon he didn't believe that I owned the house.'

'Why not?'

'Well, Miss Clitheroe, it looks as if there's been some funny business with the agent. The scamp's evidently pocketed the rent. So, you see,' he went on, 'the whole thing may have got on your father's nerves, and he may have thought I was blaming him. Well, if he did, you can assure him he's mistaken. It isn't Mr Clitheroe's fault that things have got a bit off the track.'

Hobart was not really convinced that the old man deserved a clean bill, but one naturally tries to make matters smooth for a charming woman with glinting auburn hair, particularly when she draws near enough for you to become conscious of the fragrance of the hair.

'It's nice of you to put it like that,' replied Miss Clitheroe. 'If anybody treated *me* as you've been treated, I'd make the dickens of a row.'

'I'll wager you wouldn't!' returned Jack Hobart. 'By the way, may I know where your father is now? You haven't locked *him* in a room, have you, as a punishment?'

'He'd deserve it if I had!' she laughed.

'He was going to tell me the name of the alleged owner of this house, you know, though the actual reason he left me was supposed to be a drink.'

'Then I'll make good both his omissions, Mr Hobart,' said Mr Clitheroe's substitute, 'because I can supply you with the name *and* the drink. The drink is in the little cupboard under the desk. Will you bring it out? And the name of the alleged owner of this house is Parton. A. H. Parton, The Grange, Stowmarket.'

'That's fine!' smiled Hobart. 'Now I can go to the agent and ask to meet this Mr Parton! The agent's name is Wainwright, isn't it? What's his address?'

'I'll give it to you in a minute,' answered Miss Clitheroe; 'but I'm not going to give you anything more until I've given you your drink.'

'I don't think that matters—'

'Not if *I* want one too?'

'Well, of course, in that case—'

He walked to the cupboard she had indicated. As he did so the attractive woman turned towards the door, looked out into the passage, and closed the door.

'You'll find that rather a prolific little cupboard,' she said, now drawing closer to him again. 'Whisky, sherry, Martini, orange bitters, angostura—even a cocktail shaker. Do they drink cocktails in your country, Mr Hobart?'

'Anything wet,' he replied. 'What are *you* going to have?'

'I rather like my own cocktails.'

'Say, you know how to mix them?'

'Would you like to test me?'

He laughed, and handed her the bottles. As she began manipulating them, he had to admit her dexterity. She was patently no novice at the job. In the middle of the operation she paused, and looked at him.

'Bitters?' he queried.

'No—the door!' she answered, dropping her voice. He regarded her sharply.

'What about the door?' he asked.

'Perhaps—nothing. But I thought I heard my father.'

'Would it matter?' he frowned.

'Not if he were frank and came right in,' she replied. 'Would you go and see?'

He went to the door and opened it. There was no one outside. When he came back, she was continuing with her task.

'You've cheated me!' he complained. 'I was learning this wonderful cocktail of yours. What was the last thing you added?'

'My secret!' she smiled. 'The kick!'

'But why a secret?'

'The conjurer must keep *one* trick up his sleeve, or nobody will patronise him.'

'That's true enough! And I'll wager yours *was* a trick too! I believe you sent me to the door just now to get my back turned!'

'I did!' she confessed. 'Now for the shake. *Et—voilà!*'

She poured her triumph into two glasses. The glasses had long stems, and black cocks were painted on the bowls. The cocks, open-beaked, were laughing.

'Well judged, Miss Clitheroe.' He applauded her as she concluded the pouring. 'Two doses exactly!'

'I hope you'll praise the mixture as well as the measure,' she returned.

'Sure, I praise it in advance!' he exclaimed.

He took his glass and raised it. She raised hers.

'Right down!' she ordered. 'No heel-taps!'

'Right down!' he answered, obeying.

Just as she was about to follow his example, her eyes turned away from her glass.

'That's funny!' she murmured, 'I'm *sure* it was father, that time.'

She laid her glass down, and ran to the door.

'Say—this—strong,' murmured Jack Hobart.

A minute later, Mr Clitheroe and the attractive lady who knew how to mix a good cocktail were standing by him again. But he was quite unconscious of the fact.

19

Mr Clitheroe's Big Idea

'Well, there he is,' said the attractive woman. 'And now what are you going to do with him?'

'That, as Hamlet observed,' answered Mr Clitheroe, 'is the question. I am not quite sure, Jessica, *what* I am going to do with him.'

'But you've got some idea at the back of your head, Mr Clitheroe,' she retorted. 'And this is the time to explain it to me.'

Had Jack Hobart, lying inert in his chair, been in a condition to hear her retort, he would have been interested in the fact that she addressed her assumed father by his surname. But if he had been in a condition to hear, she would have continued to adopt the daughterly attitude which she now very definitely shed.

'I explain things at my own time,' snapped the old man. If she was not daughterly, neither was he paternal.

'No, at Mahdi's time,' she corrected spitefully. 'I suppose you know he's not far off?'

'I am quite aware that he is not far off,' barked the old

man, more testily than ever. 'Is it likely that he would be far off? Is it likely that he will take himself off at all until we've carried this through? And am I going to carry it through unless I have absolute and unquestioned obedience?'

'Obedience?' exclaimed Jessica. 'I say, are you being funny? In the space of three minutes you tell me to send a man I've never seen to sleep. In five minutes I have done it—'

'Eight and a half minutes, my dear,' corrected Mr Clitheroe, with a cynical smile.

'Don't be irritating! I've done what you asked me to do—'

'Told you to do!'

'If you like! What's it matter? And now you prattle about obedience! What would you do if I became disobedient, for a change?'

'I would make the change complete,' replied Mr Clitheroe. 'It would be a change from a charming evening frock, and charming furs, and charming jewellery, to the kind of fashion in vogue at Brixton or Holloway.'

'Well, I'm not pretending that I'd like it,' she responded shrewdly; 'but at least I would have the satisfaction of knowing that your own beauty would be in the very latest Dartmoor style! You've often complained that I'm over-curious. Perhaps I am. I'm a woman, and it's my prerogative! But *you're* over-secretive, and unless you unbutton your tongue a bit more, maybe you'll land us *all* in the soup!'

'Unbutton my tongue? In the soup? What horrid phrases!' murmured Mr Clitheroe. 'Well, well, if you insist on increasing your personal risk by sharing dangerous knowledge, I will tell you one of my ideas concerning our friend Mr Hobart. It is to kill him.'

'I'm out of that!' she muttered quickly.

'Oh, no, you are not,' he answered. 'You are in it. Right up to the neck, my dear. The only way to get out of it is to go to a policeman and tell him that you fear for the life of a man you have just drugged. In certain ways, Jessica, you are the cleverest woman I know. If I were twenty years younger, you might even bring off one of your clever tricks on me. White skin means nothing to me now, however . . . But, yes, in other ways, Jessica, you are a fool. You drive me to tell you things which it would be far healthier for you not to know. You drive me to tell you that, before long, I may kill Mr Hobart. Now, who but a fool would want to know that?'

She tapped her foot impatiently. If she felt any sympathy for Mr Hobart, she did not betray it. Her antagonism towards Mr Clitheroe appeared to be based on other considerations.

'The fool continues her folly,' she responded, 'and now wants you to tell her *why* you may kill Mr Hobart?'

Mr Clitheroe considered the question thoughtfully. Then he turned towards the subject under consideration, and regarded him silently for several seconds.

'Mr Hobart came into this house out of the void,' he said, almost as though he were thinking aloud. 'Would anyone be the wiser if he departed back into the void? He has no relatives or friends in England. He has never been in England before. He landed in England only this morning, and does not even seem to have interviewed a hotel manager yet. Out of the void, I said. I am not sure that he has not come to me straight out of heaven.' He smiled acidly. 'Why not return the gift?'

'Somebody on earth might inquire for Mr Hobart in time,' she suggested.

'And might find that some other person—not necessarily Mr Clitheroe—had killed Mr Hobart.'

'I dare say. You're clever enough. But I'm still waiting to hear the reason for Mr Hobart's death, if it is really and truly to occur?'

'If it is really and truly to occur,' murmured the old man. 'If it is really and truly—well, I will tell you one reason. Mr Hobart owns this house. He is a man who could be very pertinacious about his property. He could, in fact—what was your own rather pretty expression just now?—land us all in the soup. Do you know, Jessica, that he seems worried about a certain young lady who left this house a little while ago in tears? He is susceptible, as well as pertinacious, and those are two dangerous qualities when allied against you—'

'Excepting when you want to give the susceptible one a cocktail,' interposed Jessica. 'Well, that's one reason for the proposed death of Mr Hobart. What's the other?'

'Have I another?'

'Yes. And, if I'm any judge, a damn sight better one.'

'It is,' nodded Mr Clitheroe. 'A damn sight better one. Presently, my dear, you may know all about the damn sight better reason for abruptly shortening the existence of Mr Jack Hobart, late of Australia, late of the world, but for the moment all I am going to tell you is this. If I give Mr Hobart a stiffer dose than you have given him, or if I make a little bullet hole in him in a vital spot, it will be because my action will perfect a plan, which, at the moment, seems to have a little flaw. Yes,' he added, with a sudden little chuckle, 'and here comes the flaw. Well, Wharton, what is it *this* time?'

His eyes were towards the door, which had opened

unceremoniously. In the doorway stood the man who had begun to descend to the hall when Mr Clitheroe had been talking to Hobart, and who had been waved back.

'Mr Wharton is as curious as you are, Jessica,' observed Mr Clitheroe, while the newcomer stood and stared. 'Now, you'll see, *he* will start asking questions!'

'By God, yes!' exclaimed Wharton. 'What's happened here?'

'A man named Wharton has entered my study without knocking,' replied Mr Clitheroe smoothly, 'and if he does it again he will be bumped off.'

'I didn't know a private interview was on,' retorted Wharton. 'Look here, suppose we cut out the repartee? That chap there—have you bumped *him* off?'

'Not yet,' answered Mr Clitheroe.

'Just doped, eh?'

'Just doped.'

'What's the big idea?'

'A *very* big idea, Wharton, believe me,' Mr Clitheroe assured him. 'In fact, quite an enormous idea. Stand still for a moment, Wharton. About five feet ten, aren't you?'

'Why the deuce—'

'And our friend here is about five ten. And you've both got dark hair, and you're both clean-shaven. It's a pity you're so pale, Wharton, but a touch of Bronzo could remedy that, and if you wore a similar suit, and the light were not too good—'

'Look here, what the devil are you talking about?'

'I am talking about big ideas, Wharton,' said Mr Clitheroe, 'and now let me hear your voice on smaller ones. What are you here for?'

'To tell you that the van has just stopped outside.'

The front door bell rang as he spoke. Mr Clitheroe's eyes lit up.

'But how opportune!' he cried. 'The van! The van that is delivering something just a few inches longer than five feet ten. Go to the door, Wharton, and help Flitt bring it in.'

'Where are we to put it?'

'In the back room on the second floor,' responded Mr Clitheroe. 'And when you have done that, come down again. We've got to find a place for *this*, as well.'

He glanced towards the limp figure in the chair. Wharton followed his glance, shrugged his shoulders, and then wheeled round and left the room. Jessica, who had stood by silently during this conversation, looked uneasy.

'This is getting a bit deeper than I bargained for,' she muttered.

'You didn't bargain for anything, my dear,' retorted Mr Clitheroe. 'You're not in a position to. If you're feeling worried, why not drink your cocktail?' He pointed, with a smile, to the full glass.

'No, thanks!' she retorted, now smiling also. 'That's a Jowle Street side-car. I think I'll mix myself another kind!'

As she did so, Mr Clitheroe watched her silently, while the hall grew fretful with shuffling noises. The noises shuffled and bumped upstairs. Then they ceased.

Wharton returned.

'And where, *this* one?' he asked, jerking his head towards the limp figure in the chair.

'Third floor front,' replied Mr Clitheroe.

'Bit of a way up, isn't it?' frowned Wharton. 'Why so high?'

'Because I say so,' snapped Mr Clitheroe, with sudden acidity. 'Don't waste time!'

Wharton growled, but obeyed. The diminutive Flitt assisted him. Once again the hall became alive with lugubrious movement. Once more the attractive woman and the unattractive old man waited in silence.

'And what's *my* next job?' demanded Jessica suddenly.

'To stand by, my dear,' answered Mr Clitheroe. 'To keep yourself in readiness. And to remain meanwhile the sweet pure creature you have ever been!'

'You know, one day,' said Jessica, 'you'll be so funny you'll make someone laugh.'

She turned and left him. He listened to the rustle of her silk as she departed. How different, that seductive rustle, from the bumping sounds—and how far more dangerous!

Dangerous to all, at least, saving Mr Clitheroe. Perhaps it was this soothing reflection that caused him to retain, almost unconsciously, his faint smile as he quietly paced the carpet, thinking . . . thinking . . .

But the smile vanished when he suddenly looked up from the carpet and saw Mahdi, the Indian, standing in the study doorway.

20

Wheels Within Wheels

It is a strange fact, which may one day be explained by historians or psychologists, that although civilisation travels westwards round the world and looks back over a conquered East, the East retains a compelling hold over the West and never allows the West to feel comfortable in its victories. Out of the silence that is away from factories, and out of the simplicity of primitive ideas arises a sense of ultimate power, and it is this sense that disturbs us when, temporarily detached from the civilised scheme that bears and encourages us along, we encounter the East alone and meet its mystic eye. It is the mysticism of the deathless and of the eternal, confounding our attempts to create and to slay. Just as Frankenstein was devoured by the monster he had made, so is man devoured by the things he destroys. A friend has no power over us, but the fellow we kill can return every night to torment us.

It was not only the mysticism of the East, however, that caused Mr Clitheroe to regard the appearance of Mahdi in the study doorway with acute discomfort. Until this moment he had been master in his own house—or, more correctly speaking, in the house of Mr Jack Hobart, now lying insensible on a little bed in the third floor front. He had bent other wills to his own. He had played with other moods. He had pulled the strings, and the puppets had danced. But now his quiet assurance left him, and as he stared back at the Indian, his keen eyes dulled a little.

That optical dullness was, nevertheless, the only outward sign he gave of his psychological transformation.

'Well?' he barked at last.

Then the Indian moved into the room and closed the door. It was as though he had been waiting for the establishment of his dominance by making the other speak first.

'Is it well?' he asked, after the door was closed.

'Of course, it's well!' retorted Mr Clitheroe testily. 'There was no necessity for you to use your latch-key.'

'As ever, over-confident,' answered Mahdi, his voice as well as his face expressionless. 'It is very far from well, Mr Clitheroe.'

'What do you mean?' demanded Mr Clitheroe, still striving angrily to conceal the disturbance within him. 'What do *you* know about it?' Mahdi raised his eyebrows slightly. 'I mean, about this particular business? I don't interfere with your department, Mahdi. Why do you poke your nose into mine?'

Mahdi thought for a moment, then replied:

'There is one of your English firms, Mr Clitheroe, where the directors start as waiters. When they become directors they cease to wait, but as they have been through every department they can tell others how to run every department, or they can run the department themselves if those others fail to run it well. Do you understand that? Or no?'

'Oh, I expect I understand,' grunted the old man; 'but

it doesn't alter the fact that you're wasting time here, and creating an unnecessary disturbance.'

'Who are disturbed?'

'Those who are working in my department!'

'And—you?'

'I? Oh, yes! You see, I am interested in my department, and I know it *can't* be run properly if it is upset!'

'I, too, share that knowledge, Mr Clitheroe. But if the waiter lays his table badly, he is bound to be upset one way or the other at last. First the director upsets him in the hope that he will learn to lay the table well. Failing that—' Mahdi shrugged his shoulders lightly. 'Well, Mr Clitheroe, then the director upsets him by dismissing him altogether.'

'You will pardon me,' remarked Mr Clitheroe, 'if I object to being classified as a waiter!'

'It is not a good simile,' admitted the Indian. 'The waiter, you see, can get another job.'

'Meaning, exactly?'

'That you would not get another job, Mr Clitheroe.'

'Oh-o! Wouldn't I?' retorted the old man, with spirit. 'You forget that, in a sense, I am a director too, and that I know how our particular business is run!'

'If you think that would help you, you prove that your knowledge is not complete,' answered Mahdi, and his eyes were now full upon Mr Clitheroe. 'It is because you possess such knowledge as you do possess that you would not get another job. Not, at least, on this earth.'

'I see,' said Mr Clitheroe. 'A threat!'

'Call it, rather, a fact.'

'Very well. I will. A fact that may have the quality of a boomerang, Mr Mahdi, eh? You can't frighten me. Besides,' he added, suddenly blazing with challenge, 'where is your proof that I am not running my department satisfactorily?'

'If you had crossed the road before I came here, you would have found it at No. 29,' answered Mahdi. 'You stare? Yes, of course, you stare. That proves, I think, your ignorance.'

'Of what am I ignorant?'

'Of a tramp who has taken up his residence at No. 29, which is immediately opposite No. 26, and who might have stayed there if I had not just made it clear to him that his presence is not wanted. Let me anticipate a question you would like to ask, but refrain from asking, since it might display further ignorance on your part. Why should your department worry about a tramp in the house across the road? I will tell you. Because there are windows in all houses, Mr Clitheroe, and people can see through windows. Something may happen here soon which should not be seen through a window. Something has already happened here that should not have been seen. Shortly before I came, a cart delivered something here. Suppose our tramp saw that?'

Mr Clitheroe looked anxious, though he strove to cover his anxiety in a blaze of indignation.

'Mahdi, you are an old woman!' he cried. 'Have you yourself been upset, eh? What is there in a cart delivering a package? Don't be damned ridiculous!'

'No fact by itself would have any significance,' responded the Indian calmly; 'but every fact is significant because there is nothing single in creation. Even the two greatest earthly facts, birth and death, would not exist without each other, or have any meaning. A cart delivering a package, if nothing came before and nothing after, would mean nothing. But if you see the cart delivering the package after, say, a pretty girl has left the house crying, there begins to be a sum. One, two.

Then, later, you may see—an Indian? One, two, three. Then later, you may hear a muffled cry. One, two, three, four. So the total grows. If it gets high, it forces itself upon your attention. A cart delivering a package. Nothing. A pretty girl leaving a house crying? Nothing. An Indian? Nothing. A cry? What, even of that? It may have been a cat. But all four? Your numbness to life is disturbed. You become interested, curious. And what of five and six, and seven? We do not stop at four *here*, Mr Clitheroe. You may commit a murder in daylight, in a crowd, if every incident attaching to the murder is an everyday incident, even to the death itself. Something ordinary and expected by the numb mind of man. No one will detect you. No one will murder you in revenge. But it is impossible to plan a murder along a string of perfectly normal and unnoticeable incidents. So we must work out our sum, and the numbers must not be seen. Your department failed because a case possessing the measurements of a coffin was delivered to your house without being made to look like a wash-stand or a grand piano. And because it was delivered too early in the evening. Are there to be any more failures?'

'Heavens above!' burst out Mr Clitheroe. 'And would a constable think nothing of a grand piano delivered at midnight?'

Mahdi smiled, and admitted the point.

'By taking me literally, you score,' he confessed 'My intention was not to create new construction, but to criticise that already in existence. I point out the flaws, and leave it to the department to remedy them, and to guard against the repetition.'

'Is there any means by which I can guard against a repetition of your visits?' demanded Mr Clitheroe, exasperated.

'Yes—one,' answered Mahdi, and his smooth voice hardened noticeably. 'You can make the visits unnecessary. You would not have received the first of them if it had not been necessary. When you contribute to the fund again, Mr Clitheroe, my visits will cease.'

'Bah! You've had thousands from me!'

'But not lately.'

'Doesn't one get any breathing space?'

'Do you pay *your* servants if they stop work?'

Something snapped inside Mr Clitheroe.

'Servants?' he cried, jumping up. 'How much longer am I to submit to that term?'

'As long as you remain one,' replied Mahdi. 'And as long as my own service lasts.'

Mr Clitheroe found his eye resting on the untouched cocktail. The second 'Jowle Street side-car' that had not been drunk. He motioned towards it.

'Well, have a drink,' he said. 'We won't quarrel. I'll mix myself another.'

The Indian inclined his head, and moved to the glass. Picking it up, he raised it.

'To the fund,' he said.

And, turning the glass upside down, poured the contents on to the carpet.

'What did you do that for?' exclaimed Mr Clitheroe, flushing.

'A habit of caution, to which I have many times owed my life,' answered Mahdi. 'I drink my own wine and I smoke my own cigarettes. You will excuse me.' He laid the empty glass down again. 'And now, to finish our business. Repeat your plans to me.'

'I'm damned if I will,' snapped Mr Clitheroe, still game.

Mahdi glanced at the clock.

'In four minutes I must go,' he said. 'Perhaps, when I go, you will no longer have any plans? Well, it saves much trouble. And a few years, to an old man—what are they?'

He slipped a knife from his coat, and toyed with it.

'Two can play at that game,' said Mr Clitheroe.

'So?' smiled Mahdi.

The knife sailed swiftly through the air, missed Mr Clitheroe's ear by half an inch, and embedded itself in the wall behind him.

'I have another,' said Mahdi.

Mr Clitheroe took a deep breath. He tried one more argument.

'Have you heard the fable of the golden goose?' he inquired.

'Oh, yes,' smiled Mahdi, 'but it does not apply. The golden, goose, I remember, was still obediently laying its eggs when its owner killed it. Besides'—the smile expanded—'you are not golden. Come, Mr Clitheroe. You forget facts. Let me tell you not a fable but a truth. Ten days ago a certain person whom you do not know and have no concern with was visited at Avignon. Four badges had been issued to him, and it was found that only three remained. One had been lost. There is a river at Avignon. The Rhône. It is pretty from the Blue Train as you go by the Riviera. The person I am telling you of did not find it so pretty. He was found in it next morning.'

'Very interesting,' commented Mr Clitheroe.

'And that was mere *carelessness*,' added Mahdi, his smile vanishing. 'That was not *insurrection*. Well, Mr Clitheroe, time passes, and there is much to do. Am I to hear your plans?'

Mr Clitheroe turned and walked to the wall. He pulled out the knife embedded in it. Then he walked back to Mahdi, and handed him the knife.

'I am a man of neat habits, Mr Mahdi,' he said, 'and you have ruined my wall and my carpet. In anxiety for my ceiling I will tell you my plans. But one of these days, perhaps, I shall plan to give *you* a drink of the Rhône, and you will find a river less easy than a cocktail to pour upon a carpet . . . Now, listen!'

Five minutes later Mr Clitheroe stopped speaking. The Indian had not spoken at all, and he did not speak now as he turned towards the door.

'Well, isn't it good?' exclaimed Mr Clitheroe indignantly.

'It will be good when you have carried it out,' replied Mahdi. 'See that you do.' He paused before adding, 'But why not use the cupboard under the stairs? Must you be told of everything?'

Then Mahdi slipped quietly out of No. 26 Jowle Street. And a girl, watching from No. 29, slipped out after him.

21

Little Hymns of Hate

Mr Clitheroe listened till he heard the front door close. Then he mixed himself a stiff drink. Then he pressed a bell.

'Wharton,' he said, when that individual presented himself in response to the bell, 'you are a fool!'

'Which means that you have just been called a fool,' replied Wharton, 'and that, at the first opportunity, I shall call Flitt a fool, and that, at his first opportunity, he will kick the cat.'

'Exactly,' nodded Mr Clitheroe. His drink had done him good. 'You have my full permission to pass the epithet on to Flitt. How was Mahdi allowed to slip in here without my being informed of the fact?'

'He has a latch-key,' Wharton pointed out.

'And you have all had my instructions to listen for his latch-key!' retorted the old man.

'Mr Clitheroe,' said Wharton, 'do you think you'd have gained anything if you'd had a few seconds warning? I have found that Mahdi is always pleasantest when he hasn't been thwarted. He is safest when he has his own way. He loves giving people surprises. Surprises—provided he is not surprised—are food and drink to him. The only way to deal with Mahdi is to feed his vanity, and to feed his vanity, and to feed his vanity, until—'

'Yes?'

'Until you've got him where you want him.'

'Ah! And where's that?'

'Just a matter of aim,' answered Wharton. 'Through the heart or the lungs or the stomach.'

Mr Clitheroe smiled.

'I note a certain similarity of thought, Wharton,' he observed.

'The fool is complimented,' Wharton smiled back.

'Yes, but he won't be complimented any more if he continues to talk of dangerous subjects. Where's Miss Drayton?'

'I got her to relieve me on the third floor before I came down.'

'Good. And the patient?'

'Still enjoying his forty thousand winks.'

'Where's Flitt?'

'By the front door, with a guilty conscience. And the cat is by Flitt. I think that completes us.'

'The cat always is by Flitt! What they can see in each other beats me. I can only imagine that Flitt has feline blood in him.'

'I've always regarded him as belonging more to the rodent species.'

'That would make his association with a cat more astonishing still. Well, see that Flitt keeps by the front door, and that Miss Drayton keeps on the third floor. You and I are going out.'

'Charmed,' murmured Wharton.

'You needn't be. We're not going up a lane together holding hands. I'm going one way, and you're going another.'

'Which is your way?'

'My way lies in the direction of the revolver that soundeth not,' answered Mr Clitheroe.

'And that hurteth not,' added Wharton. 'Don't forget that. It's most important to *me*!'

'Don't worry. I'll make Baines demonstrate on himself before he hands it over. If he lives after committing suicide, *you'll* live after I've winged you. The world is full of horrible things, Wharton, but no one need fear a blank cartridge.'

'Thanks. And which is *my* way?'

'Across the road.'

Wharton looked surprised.

'What for?' he asked.

'You'll have two jobs there,' replied Mr Clitheroe. 'The first is to make sure that the house is empty.'

'But we know it's empty.'

'Damn it, we don't! We only *think* it's empty. Some confounded tramp got in, Wharton, and Mahdi's been making a pretty song about it. And he was quite right,' he added grudgingly. 'That's the confounded part of it!'

Wharton whistled softly.

'Well, I'll soon clear the tramp out,' he muttered. 'We certainly don't want a chap like that around.'

'Mahdi's cleared him out,' said Mr Clitheroe. 'Or imagines he has. But, for once, we'll check Mahdi's work, eh, as he's so fond of checking ours. If the ragamuffin's still hanging about *we'll* get the blame for it, don't you worry!'

Wharton nodded.

'Right,' he said. 'And what's the other job?'

'The cupboard under the stairs.'

'What—going to use it?' exclaimed Wharton.

'This habit of raising your voice at emotional moments is growing on you, Wharton,' snapped the old man. 'For heaven's sake, keep your voice down! I'm not sure that I'm going to use it, but I may. Mahdi seems to think it's a better idea than our temporary coffin—'

'Look here!' interrupted Wharton. 'What's the game! If you imagine you're going to stick me down that hole—'

'*Will* you be quiet and listen, you lunatic?' demanded Mr Clitheroe angrily. 'Of course, you won't be stuck down that hole. The coffin was to have been *your* little temporary home, but now we're switching over to our patient upstairs, the cupboard across the way may be more effective for him. We won't need *him* afterwards, will we?'

'Switching over?' repeated Wharton. 'I suppose it doesn't occur to you that I don't know what the devil you're talking about?'

'This is what I'm talking about,' said Mr Clitheroe. 'Now listen, and don't interrupt.'

Wharton listened, with a frown that increased as the new plan was unfolded. At the conclusion of Mr Clitheroe's recital he shook his head.

'I don't like it,' he commented bluntly. 'Not a bit.'

'Unfortunately that won't alter the case,' answered the old man.

'It's taking a big risk.'

'It's impossible not to take a risk.'

'But this is an unnecessary risk!'

'On the contrary, Wharton. Hobart, alive, is a greater risk than he is dead. He has to be dealt with in either condition.'

168

'Well, *I'm* not the boss here—unfortunately. What you say goes, and I'm to take it that Mahdi approves. In that case, I may as well save my breath. Only don't forget that I've warned you. And don't forget that, if there's any trouble, I'm not in it—'

'If there's any trouble, Wharton,' interrupted Mr Clitheroe, 'you will be in it if necessary right up to the gallows. And now that is settled, suppose you get on with your job?'

Then abruptly, the old man left the room. Wharton gazed after him balefully. A second or two later he left the room himself and went upstairs. As he went, he heard the front door close.

Jessica Drayton met him on the third landing, and her greeting was ungracious.

'Am I to stay here all night?' she demanded. 'I thought you were never coming!'

'Afraid you'll stay here a bit longer,' he responded. 'Headquarter orders. I've got to go out.'

'God, we'll have earned our bit when it comes!' she exclaimed irritably. 'Where are you going?'

'Across the road.'

'What for?'

'To find a tramp, and to open up the way to hell.'

'I suppose you couldn't speak plainly?'

'No, my dear. It isn't the fashion in this house. And yet I might,' he added, looking at her suddenly, 'for a little reward.'

'I'm not selling anything,' she retorted; 'and slaps are gratis. I'm not sure that I want your information, either. I don't like this business, and the sooner I'm out of it the better.'

'Same here,' admitted Wharton. 'After this we might get

out of it together. But meanwhile, apparently, there's no choice. That cursed old man has got us, and that thrice cursed Indian has got *him*. So keep your eye on the patient, Jessica, and see he doesn't wake up till I return. I won't be long.'

'Where's Clitheroe? Downstairs?'

'No. He's gone out too.'

'Oh! Where's *he* gone to?'

'To get the gun.'

'Then if there's any trouble, who have I got left to call upon?'

'Flitt and his feline.'

'They'll be immensely useful! I think I could manage better without them. Still, even Flitt and the feline may serve to help the proprieties. If Mr Hobart wakes up and becomes amorous, I shall call the cat to be a witness to my chastity.'

She turned and re-entered the bedroom in which Jack Hobart lay. Wharton looked after her, frowning vaguely. Then he went down the stairs again, and interviewed Flitt by the front door.

'I'm going out, Ted,' he said. 'See there's no trouble till I come back.'

'Easy,' replied Flitt witheringly. 'It'll wait for yer.'

'If Miss Drayton calls, go up to her at once.'

'I got ears.'

'If the Indian returns before Mr Clitheroe does or I do, be sure to tip us the wink when we come in.'

'Corse, I got no brains, 'ave I?'

'None. And don't go poking around for any more drink,' concluded Wharton. 'You're bound to meet a sticky end some time or other, Flitt, but there's no need to anticipate it.'

He opened the front door and went into the street. Ted

Flitt waited until he was sure it was quite closed, and then spat at it. Then he slid a little panel aside, and stared out.

'Gone across the road, Lizzie,' he reported to his cat. 'What's that for?'

He continued to stare.

'Gone inter No. 29, Lizzie,' he reported again. 'What's that for?'

Then he left the peep-hole and went into the study. It was easy to guess what that was for. He came out smelling of it.

Inside No. 29, Wharton paused. The house was soundless, and to a less conscientious man the quietude would have saved a tedious search. Silence is no proof if you are looking for an Indian, but the average tramp is noisy; you can even hear him breathing. Still, Wharton was too worried to take any chances, and he searched the house from top to bottom. It was satisfactorily empty. Only cheese crumbs told of a recent presence.

Job No. 1 completed, he turned to Job No. 2. The cupboard under the stairs. The cupboard door was not locked, and for a moment this worried him, till he recollected that he had forgotten to lock it when he had last used it, although he had not forgotten to replace the boards. That had been some four months ago. An old man, with empty pockets, had been found in the canal shortly afterwards . . . What a fool he had been not to lock it.

'Still, who'd know?' he asked himself, as he knelt down at the entrance and felt the flat boards that formed the cupboard's flooring. 'The floor doesn't give anything away!'

Deftly, he removed the boards immediately in front of him, storing them away against an inner wall. Now he was not kneeling before flat boards, but before a yawning black pit. The blackness gleamed up at him as through a veil. He dropped a fragment of loosened wood into the pit. A moment later there came a little *plop* from the depths, and the blackness shivered. All at once Wharton shivered, also, and drew back.

Then he gave a little cry. Something had slipped from his pocket, and he made a frantic grab at it. Just in the nick of time he caught it, and he gulped almost hysterically in his relief. The thing he had caught was a little button, half-green and half-red, attached to a safety pin that dug into his hand as he clasped it.

He did not notice the pain of the prick, so great was his joy in saving the button from the black well below him. It was only when he opened his hand and saw blood on the palm that he realised the puncture.

'Damn the pin!' he muttered. 'I must fix it!'

He would have done so there and then but for a rat. The rat darted out of a hole, and he stuffed the button quickly in his breast pocket as he jumped back. The rat blundered into him in its unintelligent, lightning scurry. 'Get off, you brute!' cried Wharton. He slammed the cupboard door and locked it. He thought no more about the button.

But for the rat, Wharton would have remedied the defect in the safety pin, and the button would not have slid out of his pocket several hours later into the hands of Ben, and many things yet to be related would not have occurred. Our belief in human power is rudely shaken by the thought that our biggest moments may be due to the most insignificant causes. A piece of banana skin may lead to the birth of a genius. A rat may open the door to horror.

Wharton left No. 29 with relief, and returned to No. 26. He found Flitt and the cat still at their post, the former fragrant with his recent default.

'Clitheroe back yet?' asked Wharton curtly.

'No,' answered Flitt thickly, 'an' I wouldn't blub if he *never* came back!'

'Shut up!' snarled Wharton.

'An' Lizzie agrees with me,' said Flitt. 'Don't yer, Lizz?'

Wharton seized him by the collar and shook him. Out of the corner of his angry eye he caught a glint of green. He turned. Jessica was on the stairs.

'Thank goodness, you've come back!' she exclaimed, almost resentfully. 'Come upstairs!'

Wharton dropped the diminutive man he was shaking, and ran to the staircase. A moment later both he and the woman had disappeared.

'One day, Lizzie,' observed Flitt, picking himself up, 'I'll get them *all*.'

Ted Flitt looked very unpleasant at that moment. Lizzie turned her head away, as though she didn't know him, and licked her paw.

22

The Friendly Surface

The last thing Jack Hobart saw before losing consciousness was a woman's face, and the same woman's face was the first thing he saw when consciousness began to return to him.

Everything else was different. He was no longer in a study. There was no massive desk with a high back. Before the window was a dressing-table, while the window itself was in another position . . . But the woman's face—yes, the woman's face still moved vaguely within the confused arena of his vision, now bending over him, now a thousand miles distant, now here, now there. And since the face was the only familiar thing in a very queer world, he tried to hold on to it—to keep his eyes fixed on it—to use it as an anchor to hold him steady in the shifting sand. Odd that he should not feel more grateful to the face! It was helping him back to reality, assisting him to fight the demons of instability, and he ought to be filled with gratitude! Certainly it was beautiful enough. Yes, the beauty alone should have made him glad. Yet there was something wrong with it, something sinister. He was afraid of it even while its sight comforted him. Probably this was just an aftermath of his nightmare, a sort of clinging horror that hung around everything till he had gathered enough strength and sense to fight it off . . .

Then, abruptly, Hobart remembered. He knew now what was wrong with the face. Beneath the surface of beauty there lay some dark purpose of which he, Jack Hobart, had been the victim. He had not fallen ill. He had not suddenly fainted. He had been drugged by a cocktail mixed by this woman, and afterwards he must have been carried to this room. By her? Of course not! By the old man? The old man could hardly have managed it, either. No, Hobart had been carried by others who shared the dark purpose and who were also arraigned against him in this dismal house of which, ironically, he was the owner!

'Careful—careful!' he whispered to himself. Subtlety was needed here. 'You have not come to yet, Jack Hobart! You are still unconscious! Remember—still unconscious! When you do come to, you must have your full wits and your full strength!'

So he closed his eyes again, and fought his confusion quietly, in the darkness. But he did not need his eyes to know when the woman who had duped him through her beauty was close to him. He could hear the rustle of her dress, and inhale the fragrance of her scent and hair. He could even sense her aura as she bent over him and peered into his face.

Now he felt her fingers on his temple. Now he heard her voice.

'Poor fellow!' she murmured.

Poor fellow?

Why this sympathy? That was wrong! She should have

175

murmured, 'Damned fool!' Steady, Hobart, steady! Perhaps he had not heard correctly? His mind was beginning to go round again.

'Oh—the *brute*!'

Again, her soft murmur, this time with fierce indignation in it. And, again, the words did not seem to fit the situation. Brute? Who was a brute? She could not think *him* a brute, for he had committed no brutal act in her presence. The brutality had been committed by others . . . Was she condemning others?

Once more he felt her fingers on his brow. He fought against the pleasure of her touch. He fought in vain. Without knowing it, he opened his eyes, to be certain that the fingers were real, and he found the woman's eyes on his. They shone with relief. Impossible to continue his deception now.

'Thank God!' she exclaimed. 'No, don't talk for a moment! I thought you were never coming to!'

He closed his eyes again. He found that he couldn't think while they were open.

'That's better!' he heard her say. 'Lie still. I'll get some eau de cologne.'

He obeyed her. It was beyond him not to. Temporarily, he told himself. As soon as this weariness had passed off his brain would be active once more, and he would get everything straight. Meanwhile, the eau de cologne was wonderfully comforting . . . What colour were her eyes? . . . Her hair was auburn, of course. And she had long lashes, and marvellous, very red lips, and a dazzling white throat . . . in a moment he would simply *have* to re-open his eyes to see all these things again . . .

'You've been drugged,' said the woman. 'Do you know it?'

He opened his eyes, and stared at her. He felt ridiculously impotent. She was telling him that he had been drugged, when she herself had drugged him!

'Yes, I know what you're thinking,' she answered, as though he had spoken his thought. 'You are thinking that *I* drugged you. Well, I did!' She paused for an instant, gravely. 'But I didn't know I was doing it.'

'Didn't know it?' murmured Hobart.

'Of course, I didn't know it!' she responded, almost indignantly. 'Why should I drug you? Tell me that?'

'There seems no reason,' he said.

'There *was* no reason! I can only assume that my father intended to drug you, and that he had already put the drug in the angostura. I've tested it since. If I hadn't known what my own cocktail ought to have tasted like, I'd have shared your own fate, Mr Hobart. How are you feeling now?'

He shook his head.

'I still don't understand,' he said. 'Do you mean to say it was your father who intended to give me the dope?'

'Do *you* mean to say,' she retorted, frowning, 'that you still think I intended to give you the dope?'

'I haven't the faintest idea what I mean, Miss Clitheroe,' answered Hobart, 'or what anything means. But I can tell you this. I'm going to know before I'm many minutes older! If what you say is correct, your father—forgive me—must be mad!'

'I've already implied that I rather share your theory,' she responded; 'but it won't help things to go round and round the mulberry bush! You're not quite yourself again yet, I can see. Why not try and get a little proper sleep? Then you'll be all right.'

He sat bolt upright at the suggestion, and told himself, lying hard, that he did not feel dizzy.

'Sleep?' he exclaimed, 'Sleep again, when I've just woken up? Say, do you really think I'm quite such a baby as all that?'

'Very well,' she shot back. 'Show you're a big, sensible man, and walk out of this room! I suppose you know what you'll meet?'

'What? The British Army?'

'No. My father's army! He's got a fixed idea in his head that—now you must forgive *me*—you're an impostor, and he's told the servants that you are. Why, you wouldn't get as far as the next floor—'

'Oh, what floor am I on then?'

'The top floor. They carried you here. Exactly what my father's idea is I don't know, but I can tell you what *my* idea is. It's just this. You're not safe if I leave you. So the question is, shall I leave you or not? You can choose.'

Hobart looked at her closely. Was she genuine, or was she double-crossing him? Her story seemed fairly plausible. Obviously Mr Clitheroe was unbalanced, and obviously he was ill-disposed towards him; he might have designed to drug him and keep him a prisoner. Moreover, Hobart recalled that the woman had murmured expressions of sympathy while she had believed him to be still unconscious. Still . . .

'How could *you* protect me—better than I could protect myself?' he demanded.

'I'm not at all sure that I can protect you,' she answered. 'That's your own phrase. But I am sure you won't be able to protect yourself if it comes to a scrap. It would be three to one, and my father has a revolver.'

'Then where do you come in, anyway?'

'I come in this way. By pretending to side with my father I have established myself as your gaoler. As long as I am your gaoler you ought to be secure.'

'I see! And I'm just to stay here, like a good little boy, until tomorrow!'

'Yes.'

'And tomorrow?'

'Tomorrow, if you can't get away, I'll get the police to help us, and if necessary, I shall get my father certified. I'm not urging anything, Mr Hobart,' she added. 'You don't look to me like a man who cares to act on anybody's advice but his own.' In that, she read him aright. 'I'm just giving you the facts, and now the decision is up to you. Shall I go—or shall I stay?'

Again Hobart studied her, trying hard not to appear to be doing so. This was not easy, because she was returning his gaze fully; moreover, she was the sort of woman who was difficult to deceive. Her beauty was the beauty of experience, her glances were not the glances of an ingenuous novice. Yes, something in her expression troubled him constantly, and he could not say, in his clouded state, whether it were something inherent—some hardness of nature that even her beauty could not totally eradicate—or whether it were a reflection of his own distrust of her. A distrust that must be obvious to any intelligent or sensitive nature even if it were not openly expressed . . .

A disturbing idea darted into his brain . . . Those murmured words he had overheard while feigning unconsciousness! They were arguments in her favour. But suppose she had detected his deception? He recalled that he had opened his eyes previously for a few seconds, and if she

179

had observed this and had utilised her knowledge, she might have murmured her sympathy with the special object of disarming him! In that case, would it not be best to double-cross her, as she would be double-crossing him? Indeed, of what possible benefit could it be to him to tell her that he still doubted her, thereby weakening her friendship if she were really his friend, or strengthening her enmity if she were really his enemy?

'Yes, I must pretend to believe her, whether I actually do or not,' he told himself.

And, that being so, he could postpone his final decision as to his belief until his clearing mind, coupled with ensuing facts, helped the decision to materialise. His external attitude, meanwhile, would be the same in either case.

'Miss Clitheroe, I capitulate,' he said, finding dissimulation surprisingly easy once he had accepted it as his policy. 'For the moment I am in your hands, so please be sure you're kind to me!'

She smiled, and her smile would have rendered a weaker man quite helpless. But Jack Hobart was not weak. He was merely, as he put it, 'temporarily indisposed', with sufficient sense to realise the indisposition.

'You've decided to trust me, then?' she asked.

'Sure, I have,' he replied.

'Well, here's a chance to prove it,' she said. 'I'm going to pour out a glass of water and see whether you'll drink it.'

'Oh, I'll drink it,' he answered. 'I need it like blazes! I'll even shut my eyes while you pour it out, if you like, while you drop in the sugar!'

He closed his eyes, as still smiling, she turned to the wash-stand. But afterwards he watched her through slits while she poured the water out into a glass, and, apart from that first instant she was not out of his sight for a moment. Jack Hobart did not intend to go to sleep a second time.

'Thanks,' he said, as he took the glass from her hand. It was a perfectly manicured hand, the only blemish in Hobart's opinion being the marked reddening of the nails. 'Here's to our new understanding!'

He drank half the water, and then laid the glass down beside him.

'And now what?' he inquired.

'I suggest sleep.'

'You suggested that before.'

'A good thing bears repetition.'

'No, thanks, marm!'

'But you need rest—'

'A doctor in Sydney once told me I needed a tonic. I poured the stuff away and got well without it. What I need tonight, Miss Clitheroe, is to keep *awake*. And, you bet, I'm going to!'

'The new understanding isn't beginning too well!'

'Don't worry! A difference in policy doesn't necessarily imply a difference in interest. My policy is to keep awake, that's all. Why, there may be a chance to slip away before tomorrow if we're lucky and watch out for it. Besides—'

'Besides—what?' she asked, as he paused.

'There's *you*,' he answered, looking at her fully again.

'So the good-looking Australian is afraid of me!' she observed, with a faint smile.

'I reckon your own good looks might scare any man,' he replied, responding to her smile. 'But I'm not afraid of you. I'm afraid *for* you.'

'That needs explaining.'

'I wish all things in life were as easy to explain. Why,

suppose things go wrong here? Suppose they find out that you're double-crossing them? A lot of use to you I'll be if I'm dreaming of kangaroos!'

She sighed. Then, suddenly, she rose.

'Well, if your mind's fixed, I won't try and alter it,' she said. 'But *I've* got a policy too. I'm going down to reconnoitre. You approve of *that*, I hope?'

'I think a little scouting would be a fine idea.' He nodded, readily. 'See you don't get into any trouble, though.'

'I promise,' she answered. 'You won't mind if I lock you in, will you? I've got to do that—for appearances.'

A moment later she was gone.

As soon as the door had closed Jack Hobart sprang to his feet and ran to it. He heard the key click in the lock, and frowned. He *did* mind, very much. He wanted to charge down the stairs like a raging bull, hitting things.

On the other side of the door, the woman listened also, and learned by his breathing of his proximity.

'When he gets his full strength back he'll be able to bash that door down if he wants to,' she reflected. 'I can't manage this alone!'

She hurried downstairs.

23

Midnight

'Well, what's the trouble?' asked Wharton, as they mounted the stairs.

'There's going to be the hell of a lot of trouble,' replied Jessica. 'It's my opinion the old man's losing his head!'

'All the more reason for keeping ours, my dear,' said Wharton. 'Spin the yarn. Is our friend upstairs coming out of the dope?'

'He's come out.'

'The devil he has!'

'And he refuses to lie quiet.'

'That's one against you, my dear. You should have made the stuff stronger. What's happened?'

'We've been double-crossing each other like blazes, that's what's happened—and we both know it!'

'That's another against you! Losing your art—or your nerve?'

'We'll *all* lose our nerve if this goes on much longer!' she flashed back.

They had reached the second floor, and were pausing

outside a door. 'Come inside. We've got to discuss things. Where's Clitheroe?'

'Not back yet.'

'Well, he ought to be. Personally, I'd like a round table conference. I'm not squeamish, God knows, but that chap upstairs is getting on my mind!'

'I believe you *are* losing your nerve,' commented Wharton, studying her. 'What's he been doing to get on your mind? You're not falling for him, are you?'

'Don't be a damned idiot!' she retorted. 'I don't fall for anybody! Just the same, I wish he hadn't turned up.'

'No good wishing at this stage of the game,' frowned Wharton. 'He *has* turned up, and—according to the old man—he's likely to upset everything if he's not dealt with. He seems that sort.'

'Dealt with?'

'Yes—dealt with. If Clitheroe chooses drastic methods, we'll have to back him up.'

'Suppose we don't back him up?'

'I've thought of that too. But it's too late, my dear, to go back. Mahdi's using pressure, and if there's the slightest slip we'll all be in the gravy. Why waste time talking about it? Tell me something more about our patient. What did you do when he came to?'

'I did the obvious,' she answered. 'Pretended to be sympathetic, and all that. While he pretended to believe me.'

'I see. Vamp stuff. But how do you know he's only pretending?'

'He watched me while I poured him out a glass of water, and the moment I was out of the room he was off the bed like lightning, listening at the door,'

'That's not proof positive,' said 'Wharton.

'Add a woman's instinct,' she retorted, 'and the proof's *quite* positive. I'm supposed to be doing spy work on his behalf at the moment. Pathetic, isn't it? And if I don't return soon, with some plausible story, he'll have the door down, or start bellowing out of the window. Listen!' She started violently. 'What's that?'

A door had closed somewhere. Wharton growled at her. 'That's downstairs, not upstairs!' he exclaimed nervily. 'For old Harry's sake, don't lose your wool! I expect it's only Clitheroe returning.'

They waited in silence. Footsteps sounded on the stairs. In a few moments Clitheroe poked in his head.

He was carrying a parcel, and he looked warm and annoyed. As he stared at the two inmates of the room, his annoyance increased.

'Why are you both here?' he demanded raspingly. 'Flitt's downstairs, and one of you ought to be upstairs!'

'We're discussing the situation,' answered Wharton. 'The patient's come to, and we're deciding what to do with him.'

'Come to?' cried the old man, his eyes blazing. 'Come to? And nobody with him—'

'Oh, don't get excited,' interrupted Jessica, no less warmly. 'The door's locked. He's safe for the moment.'

'You fools!' snapped Mr Clitheroe. 'That kind of fellow is never safe for any moment! *I'll* go up to him, and if he makes trouble I'll try him with a dose of this!'

He opened the parcel, and stared at it, gasping. His companions stared also. Revealed was a substantial piece of cheese.

'What on earth—!' murmured Wharton. 'I say—is this some new gadget?'

The old man did not reply. He continued to stare at the

cheese. Then he swung round with an exclamation, and made for the door. As he did so, a figure came loping up the stairs.

''E's gone in, sir!' panted the figure. 'I seen 'im!'

'What—to twenty-nine?' cried Mr Clitheroe.

'Yes, sir! I watched, as you told me, and back 'e comes, like a flash—'

Mr Clitheroe interrupted with another angry exclamation, and turned to Wharton.

'That tramp fellow,' he said shortly.

'What!' exclaimed Wharton, in astonishment. Then added defensively: 'He wasn't there when I searched the place, that I'll swear to!'

But the accusation he anticipated was not made.

'I know he wasn't there,' said Mr Clitheroe. 'The fellow barged into me just now in the street—and tried to put me off with a silly lie. But we guessed the lie, didn't we, Ted? We guessed he'd go back to No. 29, and we watched for him, and we've *caught* him—eh, Ted? Well, now we'll give him the fright of his life, and make him wish he'd never been born!' On the point of departure he paused. 'Still, I'll leave nothing to chance this time. Jessica, ring up Dakers. Tell him to stand by in the next street with his taxi. We may want it, if our friend is slippery. We may want Dakers to drive him home and stow him in his attic. Yes, let Dakers come along, Jessica—it's time he earned a little of his pay.'

Then Mr Clitheroe went out into the passage.

'Meanwhile, what about our other darling upstairs?' Jessica called after him.

But Clitheroe did not hear. Wharton laughed.

'*I'll* go up and deal with the Australian,' he said. 'You go and do your telephoning.'

'Be careful the Australian doesn't turn the tables and deal with *you*!' retorted Jessica.

'Don't worry,' smiled Wharton. 'This isn't a test match!'

He went upstairs. Jack Hobart heard him coming, and waited by the door with clenched fists. He recognised the footsteps as masculine, and guessed that his recent companion had either been overruled or sought aid. The latter he divined. A moment later Wharton's voice, calling through the door, broke the tension.

'I understand you're awake,' called Wharton.

Hobart did not reply.

'If I'd been with you, you'd have gone to sleep again pretty quick,' continued Wharton. 'Your last gaoler was a bit too sympathetic.'

Hobart wondered.

'Like me to come in and tuck you up?' asked Wharton.

'Love it,' answered Hobart. 'I'm just longing for some real comfort.'

'Well, you can go on longing,' grinned Wharton. 'Because I'm not coming in. I'm going to stay outside. All night. With a revolver. Got that?'

'It sounds most convincing,' responded Hobart.

'Good!' said Wharton. 'It'll *be* just as convincing as it sounds unless you return to your little bed and stay there till morning. At the slightest noise, I *shall* come in.'

Hobart heard a chair being placed outside the door. He visualised his new gaoler squatting down on it. Quietly he returned to the little bed, and sat down.

As the seconds slipped by, his problem classified into a single question. How was he to get out of the room?

Every room is built with a minimum of two openings, a door and a window. The door being useless as a means of

187

egress, Hobart fixed his eyes on the window, speculating on its possibilities.

He could run to the window, thrust it wide and shout. He ruminated over the probable results. The door behind him would fly open and a bullet would speed across the room . . . Would it? . . . Yes, it would. 'For, obviously,' argued Hobart, 'I have walked into a madhouse!' The simple rules of logic did not appear to apply to events in No. 26 Jowle Street.

But the window might offer other aids to escape. Suddenly rising from the little bed, he tiptoed very softly across the room. There was a ledge outside the window. If one got on to the ledge, and upright, one could grasp a protuberance from which one might swing on to the roof. And, once on the roof . . .

He stood by the window for several minutes, studying it and the lie of the land. Suddenly he drew aside. The door of No. 29 was opening, and a man was coming out.

'By Jove, it's that damned old skunk!' he muttered. 'What's he been doing over there?'

The old man crossed the road. He disappeared from the watcher's sight as he drew up to the front door of No. 26, the window ledge protruding and blotting him out. A few moments later, a new matter claimed Hobart's attention. A face had appeared momentarily at a window opposite. At the window of the second floor front.

'Holy smoke!' thought Hobart. 'It's that queer old tramp! Now, what's *he* up to?'

He continued to watch. Odd fragments of some queer nocturnal drama were moving before him—fragments it was impossible for him to piece together. Did they have any concern with his own predicament?

'I wonder!' he reflected. 'P'r'aps I've walked into something bigger than I imagined! P'r'aps more than just the safety of Mr Jack Hobart is involved.'

This theory gained colour when the next fragment came before his eyes. A woman emerged from somewhere below the window ledge. It was his original gaoler. The woman who had drugged him. He caught a glimpse of her green dress beneath her furs as she emerged from the spot where the old man had disappeared. Obviously, from the front door. She looked along the road, ran quickly to the nearest corner, and, beckoned. A taxi-cab appeared. Then she turned and came back, reaching the door of No. 29 at the same moment that the taxi-cab reached it. She inserted a latch-key and went into No. 29. The taxi-cab waited. So did the watcher.

'Gone to sleep?' asked a voice from the door.

Hobart tiptoed back to the bed.

'Or just sulky?' went on the voice.

'Thought I wasn't to talk,' answered Hobart, from the bed.

'Oh—you're being obedient,' said Wharton, outside. 'Well, keep it up.'

Hobart waited a while. Then he tiptoed to the window again. The taxi-cab was moving away.

Ten minutes went by. Nothing happened. Hobart decided on his policy.

'I'll give that fellow an hour to fall asleep,' he thought. 'Then I'll open the window and get out of it, if it's my last act on earth!'

Back on the little bed once more, he lay down to count the minutes. But it was Hobart himself who fell asleep first. The drug was still hanging about him. When he awoke, he sat up with a guilty start. A church clock in the distance was chiming midnight.

'What a fool!' he thought. 'Have I been off as long as all that?'

The chimes echoed away into the surrounding silence, and died in it. Hobart turned towards the door. He heard soft, regular breathing. Quickly he ran to the door, and turned the handle, taking a full minute to do so. The door was still locked.

'Damn!' he muttered, while the quiet, regular breathing continued tantalisingly on the other side of the wood. 'If only I could get to him now, just as he is, and make him see stars! Well, the window it will have to be!'

He stole to the window, and quietly opened it.

24

Across the Roof

It has already been implied that Jack Hobart did not like running away. It was equally distasteful to him to call in outside aid when he had once begun to get his teeth into a job. He possessed the colonial's spirit of independence, an independence born of independent forefathers who had snapped their fingers at security and crossed great seas to enlarge their cramped souls in adventure; and the idea of shouting for help, after he had gained the ledge outside the window, only came into his mind to be dismissed.

He had been cheated and drugged and outwitted. These things had happened in his own house! Well, before he left the house he was going to get his own back, and he was going to find out what the big idea was. The discovery would lose its savour if he permitted it to be made by any outside person.

Jack Hobart wasn't especially interested in seeing Mr Clitheroe in handcuffs. He wanted to punch his nose.

But there were other reasons why Hobart did not call down into the street. Item, there was nobody in the street to call to. Item, by calling down he would immediately draw attention to himself and render his personal safety more precarious than ever. Item, even if he were successful in attracting the attention of a policeman or a passer-by, the story he had to tell would seem less plausible than the story Mr Clitheroe would assuredly tell in return. Hobart had no friends he could appeal to; he could supply no address to establish his respectability. Thus, Mr Clitheroe would have little difficulty in convincing the law that Jack Hobart was a burglar and in getting him locked up for the night. That would be a very poor conclusion to the adventure.

He seized the projection above him, leapt lightly from the ledge, and hoisted himself up. He found himself on a dark slope. The ceiling of the room he had just left had sloped, and he was now on the outer side of the ceiling. He groped around with his hands for something solid to grasp.

The comparative smoothness of the roof was interrupted by a small excrescence of brick. 'Good!' he thought, and gripped it. It came away as he did so. Letting it go, he swung his arm in a frantic effort to find some other anchorage, for he had trusted too much of his weight to the small projection and was now falling backwards. A chimney pot saved him from a sudden descent to the street below. His arm wound round and encircled it, while a loose brick and a couple of tiles slipped down the slope and over the edge. It made Hobart feel a little sick to realise how narrowly he had missed being in their company.

He heard the impact of the falling debris on the pavement. He waited for a few seconds, partly to learn whether the disturbance had been heard by others, and partly to regain his composure. Then, satisfied that the accident was not going to militate against his chances of success, he continued to climb along the slope, groping for projections that were firm and solid while he sought his objective.

His objective was a skylight.

There was no skylight in the immediate vicinity. This meant that he must climb up to the ridge of the sloping roof and search on the opposite side. He continued his way up the watershed. Now he was only a few inches from the ridge, and in a moment his eyes would peep over. But suddenly he stopped dead. Two other eyes, appearing from the opposite side, had peeped over first, and were staring into his.

It was a very nasty moment. The eyes that stared at Hobert's were luminously green. Then, as the darkness beyond separated itself from the darkness of the owner of the eyes, forming a little outline, two black ears materialised on either side of a smooth black head.

'By Jove, I owe you something for that!' muttered Hobart.

His momentary indignation was quickly followed by a happier emotion.

'Yes, but where have you come from?' he asked the luminous green eyes. 'Through an open window, eh? That's what I'm looking for!'

It wasn't certain that the cat had come through an open window. Exactly how cats get on roofs has never been discovered by man. They probably have their own methods, and if they really want a roof they will undoubtedly find one. Still, just as a human being will follow an easy path to a mild diversion, so a cat may pass through an open window to its natural flooring. In any case, this particular cat no longer loomed as a sinister circumstance. It increased the possibility of the skylight by fifty per cent.

Perhaps the cat objected to the abrupt beneficence with which it now became invested. It gave Hobart one more unpleasant moment by emitting a sudden yowl. 'Say, stop that!' whispered Hobart. 'Want to wake everybody?' The cat turned in response, showed a poker tail, and disappeared down the opposite slope again.

Hobart lost no time in following. He reached the ridge, and passed over the Himalayas into the mysteries of Tibet. A little patch of yellow winked up at him from half-way down the descending slope. Now the black form of the cat blotted it out. Now the black form passed beyond, and the yellow patch glowed again.

'Skylight!' thought Hobart, rejoicing.

But the cat had not paused, and when Hobart reached the skylight he gathered the reason. The skylight was closed. All he could do was to put his face close to it and peer through.

He peered through into a little passage. It was the passage, he divined correctly, outside the room, in which he had been a captive. And on an old wooden chair outside the door of the room—a door which Hobart had only seen previously from the insider—sat a man.

Hobart studied the man. It was his male gaoler obviously. Measuring him for future reference, he deduced that the fellow was similar in height and build to himself. There was also a certain facial resemblance, although Hobart was not very proud to own this fact. The fellow was asleep. A candle, at last gasp, flickered on a cheap, high chest. Electric light in No. 26 Jowle Street evidently ended at the second floor.

'By God, if I could get through this skylight, you'd sleep on for a bit longer!' thought Hobart.

Wood had divided them before. Now it was glass. Life was terribly tantalising.

The yellow patch became suddenly black. The tantalising vision vanished like a bad dream. The candle had flickered out.

Well, that was that. Now where was the cat? Hobart continued his cautious descent of the roof, and discovered that the slope was much longer at the back of the house than it had been at the front. It seemed to descend to the second floor. Reaching the end of it at last, he peered over the edge to see whether there was any possible continuation of his route. When his eyes grew accustomed to the new vista they were trying to penetrate, a vague railing grew out of the darkness beneath him. At first it looked like the mere shadow of a railing but as it materialised slowly it became the solid railing of a balcony. As it only protruded a very little way out from the wall, it appeared to belong one of those useless structures just too small for a chair and just too large for a window-box.

Something brushed against him.

'I wish you'd give me a bit of warning when you're coming!' he grumbled to the cat.

But again the cat proved his friend rather than his enemy. It jumped down on to the railing, turned housewards, and vanished.

'Eureka! *There's* the open window!' thought Hobart.

He turned over on his stomach, and gingerly lowered his legs downwards and outwards into the inky abyss. They met nothing. He endured an unpleasant moment when he had to decide whether to draw back to the roof or risk leaving it without the choice of returning should he want to; but he took the risk, and when his fingers were beginning to slip from the ledge they gripped and his straightened arms could stretch no straighter, the tip of a toe touched iron and told him that he had won a further stage of his hazardous journey.

Now he was on the railing, tipping forward gratefully towards the wall. Before his knees was the opening he sought. Dropping carefully to the diminutive balcony floor, he peered in through the open window. All was stillness and silence and blackness . . .

No! Something moved in the room! Slowly . . . softly . . .

'One day,' thought Hobart, 'I shall kill that cat!' He entered the pitch-dark room, and stood still for an instant listening for sounds that were not feline. He heard none. The hope that he was in the room alone with the cat was emphasised by all this passivity. Had any person been in the room as Hobart had entered through the window, he must have been seen by that person—a dim form leaping through—and there would have been an immediate attack on the intruder. But Hobart had not been attacked. He had not been seen! So far, then, so good!

He began to grope around. In a passage above him a sleeping man stirred.

'Now, let me get my bearings,' thought Hobart. 'This is a tall, rather narrow house, and I started from a top room at the front. Say there are three floors. Yes, I think I remember the windows from outside. From the front room of the top, the third floor, I climb out over the roof, and turn to the back of the house. The roof slopes a long way down at the back. Either there is no back room on the top third floor, or it is a very small one, with no window. A cupboard room, perhaps, or a little room with a small window at the side. It doesn't matter, anyway. I get down as far as the second floor, I am on the second floor *now*. I am in a back room on the second floor, and my sleeping gaoler is still above me, while between the two flights which separate me from the front door, I may meet three other people—the old man, the woman—damn her!—and that apology of a fellow who hangs around the front hall. Well, I'm ready to meet them. I hope I meet them all—though, for preference, one at a time. And remember, Jack Hobart, there's no need to be gentle when you *do* meet them! You're in your own house, and it's a real rough house . . . Now—where's the confounded door?'

As he moved towards it, his foot struck something on the ground. Something low and flat. He stooped and felt it. Yes, low and flat . . . and long . . .

'Odd bit of furniture, this,' he reflected. 'Sort of a chest, eh? Lid a bit loose too.'

He raised the lid. He stooped lower. The cat, hunting perhaps for mice, crept close, sharing his curiosity. Together, they peered down into the invisible.

Then someone leapt from the darkness beside Hobart, and something crashed on his head. As he reeled into oblivion, he made a frantic grasp, and wrestled momentarily with a startled feline. But his fingers grew limp, the feline shot out of the window in a mad frenzy, and the old man who had emerged so galvanically from a corner stared down at Hobart's form as it crumpled into the chest.

'Eh!—what was that?' muttered the gaoler on the floor above.

The gaoler blinked about him vaguely. The passage was dark. He cursed himself. He groped for matches, after much fumbling managed to relight the stump of candle.

'Hallo, you in there!' he called through the door.

197

Receiving no reply, he suddenly unlocked the door and looked in. The room was empty. The candle, helpless against the draught, died its second and final death.

He ran to the open window. He stared out. Across the road, on the doorstep of No. 29, a ragged man was standing.

25

Nadine Goes In

Saving for the depressing illumination from the lamp-post at the corner, Jowle Street was in utter darkness when Nadine returned to it. No light glimmered from any window. But that was not proof that it slept.

Two hours had passed since she had scribbled her hurried note and had left No. 29 with the Indian, and much had happened in that time. Nadine herself had been fully occupied. But more was to occur before the night was through, and, as though gifted with prescience, the girl paused for an instant and shivered. The instant passed, however, and her nerves were steady again when, after a rapid glance at No. 26, she turned towards No. 29 and approached the front door.

Reaching it, she listened. No sound came from within. Softly she tapped on the worn wood. On the other side of the wood, only a few feet distant, a sailor lay, but he did not hear her tapping. Her hand went to the bell, hesitated, and came away again.

She turned her head, and glanced once more at the house opposite. Then, swiftly, she left the doorstep and slipped into the side alley where, earlier, the sailor had slipped and bumped into a cat. The girl was spared this little shock, but disappointment awaited her at the end of the alley. A window she had hoped might be open was closed and latched.

She returned along the alley and, making no more effort to enter No. 29, directed her attention towards No. 26. Now she stood on the doorstep of that unpleasant house, and her psychology changed. No longer hesitating, she rang the bell, and a little man sitting on a stool ten inches away from her hand raised his drooping head with a sudden start.

'What a night!' he thought, and put an ugly eye to a slit.

He saw nothing. The person he wanted to see was too close to the slit to give the ugly eye any satisfaction. So he tried speech, since vision failed.

''Oo's there?' he called, in a worried undertone.

'Let me in at once,' replied Nadine, also in an undertone, but sharply. 'Don't waste time.'

''Oo *are* you?' retorted the little man doggedly.

'Does the name Mahdi signify anything to you?' asked Nadine. 'And the colours red and green?'

Evidently they did, but the door did not open. The little man left it abruptly, and was replaced a few seconds later by another man twice his age. The new warden of the door repeated the original request for information.

'Who is it?' came the demand, this time with spirit.

'My name won't mean anything to you,' Nadine responded with equal spirit; 'but I can show you something that will. How much longer am I to be kept standing here? Suppose somebody passes by? I was told I should meet fools here, but I hardly thought the folly would begin on the doorstep!'

'Perhaps our definition of the word "folly" differs,' said the voice on the other side of the door. 'To me is not folly to hesitate before opening the door to strangers at two or three a.m. What have you got to show me that *will* mean something to me, and so prove my folly?'

'Can you see through a wooden door?'

'No—but through a slit!'

There was a tiny click as the panel was slipped aside. The old man's eye appeared at the top of the slit, and a more brilliant eye—the eye of an electric torch—appeared at the bottom of the slit. The torch sent its ray through to the porch, like a miniature searchlight.

'Hold up this interesting thing?' said the old man. 'There is light enough now to see it.'

'How do you know I can hold it up?' demanded Nadine.

'If you cannot, our conversation is ended, and you can go away and knock up some other fool,' answered the old man.

'Perhaps you're not quite such a fool after all,' said Nadine, and held up the thing. 'Now are you satisfied?'

In the little ray of light gleamed a small coloured object. The colours comprising it were red and green.

'A little closer,' commanded the old man's voice.

Nadine advanced the small object closer to the source of the ray. Several seconds passed while it was scrutinised.

'It is a little larger than I should have imagined,' commented the scrutiniser, at last.

'Of course it is a little larger,' retorted Nadine, impatiently. 'I am surprised that its size does not impress you more. It is Mahdi's.'

'Mahdi's!'

'Yes. And now, if you do not let me in at once, you will soon see a larger one still.'

The door opened. Nadine slipped inside. Then the door closed quickly behind her, and the electric torch was switched out.

'You are covered,' came the old man's voice through the darkness. 'I can shoot you without a sound at any instant that I choose. Don't move. Beside me is a dear fellow who would die for me, if necessary. Wouldn't you, Ted? He has a knife. And on the stairs is another trusted one who, by pressing a little button which his finger is now touching, can electrocute you where you stand. Not bad for fools, eh? And now let us get down to serious business.'

'I *mean* to get down to serious business,' returned Nadine. 'Switch on your light and take the badge I shall hold out to you. You will find Mahdi's mark on the back of it. Then shoot me and knife me, and electrocute me. Not bad for fools? My friend, you are running the risk of being the biggest fool I have ever met! I am here to keep you from your folly, and to do the work that Mahdi should have done himself. He admits it. Now then. Switch on your light, and be quick.'

The light appeared. Her words and her imperious tone seemed to be having some effect. Again the badge appeared in the torch's ray, and the old man took it. He examined it closely. Then he handed it back.

'Where is Mahdi?' he inquired.

'Mahdi is with someone even more important than himself.'

'Oh?'

'If he were not, he would be here.'

'I see. And who is this more important one?'

'Has Mahdi ever mentioned a name?'

'No.'

'Then I shall not.'

'As you like. I take it you are Mahdi's deputy?'

'Hardly that.'

'Who, then?'

'A deputy implies an inferior.'

'Really! You speak as though you were the more important one yourself!'

'I am sufficiently important for your obedience. Be satisfied with that. Now then. Waste no more time. Show me your arrangements.'

The old man hesitated. He made one last gesture of caution.

'Is there anything else you can do to prove your right to be here?' he asked. 'If, as your attitude suggests, my sagacity is on trial, you must forgive my insistence on proving it.'

'How will this do, then? There was a man watching this house from a window opposite—'

'I got rid of him,' interrupted the old man quickly.

'You did not get rid of him,' retorted Nadine. 'He was still there soon after midnight. Mahdi and I got rid of him. Does that knowledge prove my credentials?'

The old man looked worried. Then he shrugged his shoulders. His resistance had been overcome.

'Damn that slippery fellow!' he muttered. 'If ever I get hold of him I'll make him howl! Well, well! It seems I'm bound to accept you. What do you want me to do?'

'I've told you.'

'Tell me more explicitly.'

'I am here to supervise your plans.'

'But Mahdi knows them, and approves of them.' Suddenly the old man added, with a momentary return of his suspicion: 'Didn't he tell you of the plans?'

'Of course!'

'Then you know them!'

'Naturally.'

'And in that case, there is no need to repeat them. Walls have ears, eh? I take it, of course, that you approve of the scheme? You haven't come here, at this hour, with an alternative, I hope?'

'I approve of the scheme,' replied Nadine; 'but I am not satisfied that you will be able to carry it out.'

'Why?' demanded, the old man.

'Because, so far, you have bungled. I want to see your preparations with my own eyes—'

'Listen to her!' burst out the old man indignantly. 'She comes in my house, Ted, and she expects me to take her all over the place as though I were a—' He broke off, and veered round to her again. 'P'r'aps you'd like to see our *prisoner* with your own eyes?'

'Prisoner?'

'Yes, yes!'

Nadine was silent for a moment. Then, her voice harder than ever, she answered:

'I certainly intend to see the prisoner with my own eyes. Seeing is believing, my friend. Where is—the prisoner?'

'He is upstairs,' said the old man grimly. 'Come! I will take you to him.'

The torch was glowing now. He turned towards the stairs, and invited the girl to follow.

'At the top?' queried Nadine casually.

'He was at the top,' answered the old man; 'but after he tried to escape I put him in a safer place.'

'Where?'

'Heavens above, how you plague one with questions! I

am going to show you where. Didn't you say yourself that seeing was believing? Stay by the door, Ted. Wharton, you go on ahead of us.' The man on the stair ascended and disappeared. 'Now, young lady, you will see a pretty sight.'

They mounted the stairs in silence. When they reached the second floor, the old man stopped and pushed open a door.

'In here,' he instructed shortly.

They entered. The torch flashed on a long box on the floor.

'There,' said the old man. 'There is our prisoner.'

Nadine stared down at the box. The lid was closed. She stifled a shudder. Her voice was still calm as she commented:

'A box may be empty.'

'This one doesn't happen to be.'

'Still, prove it!'

'This time, I decline.'

They regarded each other. Wharton, in the background, moved a step closer. A long box with a brilliant circle of light on the lid, two faces dimly illuminated above the box, and a shadowy figure approaching quietly . . .

'What is the reason for your refusal?'

'Perhaps an old man of my experience rebels against supervision—'

'Aren't we all supervised?'

'. . . By a charming girl who, however charming, is barely a quarter of his age.'

'I think you have another reason,' said Nadine, after a short pause. 'You imagine I am afraid to look on the dead?'

'I did not say he was dead.'

'Is he?'

'Not yet.'

'Why not?' She marvelled at her cool and callous tone.

'Sometimes,' answered the old man dryly, 'one postpones the final coup until the moment of actual necessity.'

'That may be wise,' said Nadine. 'But the necessity will arise in this case?'

'I fear it will!'

'When?'

The old man did not respond. His eyes were fixed upon the girl, and he was studying her expression closely.

'Oh—well, the exact time does not matter,' she exclaimed suddenly, and the expression he was studying betrayed no sympathy. 'Where is your telephone?'

Wharton shot a quick glance at the old man, but the old man was too intent on Nadine to notice him.

'What do you want the telephone for?' he asked.

'I must telephone to Mahdi.'

'Why?'

'To tell him that your prisoner is safe.'

'Is that necessary?'

'Absolutely. He is waiting.'

'Very well,' nodded the old man. 'We will go down. The telephone is below. You will stay here, Wharton, and see that the lid of that interesting box does not fly open. Come, young lady!'

He stood in the doorway, and she passed out. They began to descend the stairs.

'Shall I telephone for you?' suggested the old man, halfway down.

'No, I must speak to him personally,' returned the girl. 'He must be convinced by my voice that I am here.'

'As you like,' said the old man.

They reached the hall.

'In here,' said the old man, pushing a door wide.

The girl entered. As she did so, the light was switched on. Across the room, on a little bracket, was the telephone, and by the telephone sat Mahdi.

26

Mahdi Takes Control

If the sight of Mahdi seated by the telephone provided a shock for Mr Clitheroe, it provided an even bigger shock for Nadine, but the girl showed the greater command of herself. With a tiny shrug she controlled her emotion. Mr Clitheroe, on the other hand, burst into immediate invective.

'What the devil!' he cried. 'Is my house to be turned into a Jack-in-the-box? Am I to have no say what happens here?'

Mahdi ignored him. His eyes were upon the girl.

'You have chosen to deceive me,' he said, in a voice that was sinister through its very lack of expression.

'Appearances are against me, Mahdi,' responded the girl.

'Appearances only?'

'Yes. But you don't look in the mood for explanation and I am not in the mood to plead.'

'Explanations,' repeated Mahdi softly. His white teeth seemed to expand over the word. 'No, I do not think I am in the mood for explanations, Nadine. They would take too long. You would have to explain why, when we left the house across the way, you begged me to take you to a night club when my desire was that you should go straight home. You would have to explain why you were—so kind to me, till you induced me to dance with you against my better judgment. And why you fainted. It was, I grant, well done. And why, at one moment—' He paused, and something darted into his eye for an instant. 'You clung to me tightly.' He became expressionless again. 'And why you then begged that I should put you in a taxi and send you home. And why you did not go home—but came *here*! Unless all this was to secure the little red and green badge that doubtless gave you entrance, there will have to be very much explanation, Nadine—and, as I have said, I have not time for it.'

'Yet I could explain, Mahdi,' insisted Nadine doggedly.

'Well, perhaps you shall be given your chance to do so,' answered the Indian. 'But not now. Not here. And not to me,' Now he turned to Mr Clitheroe, addressing him for the first time. 'You have some place where we can keep her for tonight?'

'Don't worry about that,' snapped Mr Clitheroe venomously. 'She shall be kept here! But, perhaps, *I* am in a mood for explanations,'

'I hope so—but to give them, Mr Clitheroe, not to hear them,' murmured the Indian. 'I will attend to you in a little while. First, however, the girl. Where do you propose to put her?'

Mr Clitheroe swallowed. He was very white.

'My friend,' he said, in a rasping voice, 'you think you can do what you like with me! Suppose you are wrong?'

'We will talk about that, too, in a little while,' answered Mahdi, without moving an eyelid. 'I still wait.'

But Nadine did not. She was out of the room in a flash,

slamming the door behind her. She heard an oath, while she raced across the hall. Before her was the front door, and for once it looked friendly. She stretched out her hand for the handle.

Then two arms wound themselves round her legs, and she felt herself falling. The arms tightened, forcing her feet together. Ted Flitt was performing his one effective accomplishment.

'Let me go!' she gasped.

'Not 'arf!' grunted the human octopus as it dragged her down.

'I'll give you ten pounds—twenty!'

This time the human octopus did not deign to reply. He merely gripped harder. She lost her balance and tottered to the ground, while a fierce face suddenly appeared above her, a face framed in agitated white hair.

'Hold her, Ted,' said the owner of the fierce face. 'By God, she's dangerous!'

The words sounded ironically in her ears. Pinioned by her feet, half-stunned by her fall, and surrounded by three determined men, it was difficult at that moment to conceive that she formed a source of danger to anyone. But the three determined men were taking no chances. A handkerchief descended over her eyes. When she attempted to cry out a gag was forced into her mouth. Then she was lifted from the ground, and consciousness slipped away as she was borne through the darkness . . .

'And now, Mr Clitheroe,' said Mahdi, when they were back in the room, 'we will think about you.'

'And also about yourself,' replied Mr Clitheroe. 'I warn you, Mahdi, there's going to be trouble if I have any more of your dictation.'

'And about myself,' nodded the Indian calmly. 'Let us think about myself first. Being the more important, it should be so. Now, Mr Clitheroe—what about myself?'

'Oh, drop that tone!' exclaimed the old man. 'You've no right to it! Didn't the girl fool you?'

'And you, also.'

'Yes, but that was the result of your own folly! A chit of a girl dupes you, and yet you can still come here and act as though you never made errors, and were qualified to sit in judgment on those who have—'

'You admit you have made errors, then?'

'Of course I've made errors! My greatest error has been standing so much from you, Mr Mahdi.'

'Yet, if I had not returned here just now—like a Jack-in-the-box, I think you said?—and if I had not been in a mood to profit by my error and not to hide it from myself, as you try to hide your errors from yourself, the girl would have completed her deception and, under pretext of telephoning to me, would have telephoned to the police.'

'Idiot!' retorted Mr Clitheroe. 'Do you s'pose I wasn't on to it? I wouldn't have let her telephone.'

'You *couldn't* have let her telephone,' answered Mahdi. 'I have cut the telephone wires.'

Now the old man's eyes blazed furiously.

'Cut my telephone wires?' he cried, pale with anger. Only when he was expressing violent indignation could he feel entirely free from the other's influence. 'Without consulting me?'

'In future, Mr Clitheroe, I do not consult you.'

'Oh! Don't you? Well, I don't consult you, either! And let me remind you, sir, that you are in a house where *I* rule, and—since you have chosen to cut my telephone wires—you are not in a position to communicate with anybody outside this house unless I permit you to. Wharton and Flitt will obey me, not you, and I can get rid of you in two seconds if I want to. *For ever*, Mahdi! Just by pressing a button!'

'You will never get rid of me, Mr Clitheroe,' answered the Indian, 'because I am bigger than you are. But do you know what would happen even if you did get rid of me?'

'For one thing, I should keep all I make!'

'Oh, no, Mr Clitheroe. You would not keep all you make. Nor would you get anything when you were making nothing. I am bigger than you, but there is someone who is bigger than I, and that someone is watching both of us, and Wharton, and Flitt. If you killed me, as you would like to, or if Wharton killed you, as he would like to, or if Flitt killed Wharton, as he would like to, the one who is bigger than us all would allow none to survive. We survive while we function, and we function while we form a complete and flawless organisation. There are plenty of other organisations if ours ceases to exist. We are a mere incident, Mr Clitheroe, to the brain that runs us. The only way for us to survive, if we fail in our part, is to kill that brain, and the brain is far too big for that. Only the trusted and the chosen know in whose head the biggest brain works. *You* do not know it, Mr Clitheroe.'

'But *you* do?' came the sneering question.

'Perhaps.'

A sudden idea flashed into the old man's mind. Not too wisely, he voiced it.

'Suppose you and I worked together, Mahdi,' he said, 'and became that biggest brain?'

'How could we do that?'

'If—say—some accident happened to the biggest brain! If the biggest brain itself ceased to exist!'

As a rule, Mahdi's face was expressionless. Expressionless, at least, to western comprehensions. But now it lost its mask, and became so wholly contemptuous that Mr Clitheroe winced as though he had been struck.

'If there were any chance that I should use my knowledge against the bigger brain,' replied the Indian, 'do you suppose I would possess that knowledge? You talk like a child, Mr Clitheroe. It is time you learned your limitations. Indeed, I am here to tell you of them. From this moment you take your orders from me, and at the first sign of disobedience there will be an end of you. While your success is a mere incident to the bigger brain we have been talking of, and means most to you, your failure will not be tolerated. Do you understand?' Mr Clitheroe did not reply. 'Or shall I make the position clearer? *I can!*'

'Damn you!' muttered Mr Clitheroe with sudden sulky impotence. 'Have it your own way.'

Mahdi smiled. Superficially, for a moment, he looked almost pleasant.

'The child is wise,' he said sarcastically. 'There is some hope for him. Now, listen. I shall soon leave you. It is, I regret, inevitable. But I shall return before you have any further visitors, and I shall be in the house while you are receiving these further visitors in the manner we have decided on.'

'Does this mean you will join in the reception of the visitors?' asked Mr Clitheroe, just managing to control himself.

'Oh, no.'

'Or interfere?'

'I will interfere only if it becomes a necessity,'

'And who will judge of that?'

'I, naturally.'

'Very well, Mr Mahdi,' snapped the old man, glowering. 'It seems I have no choice. I am grateful, at any rate, for the small mercy of your preliminary absence. You are not the companion I love best in all the world!'

'On my side,' answered Mahdi, 'I shall sadly miss your ingenuous charm, Mr Clitheroe.'

He rose, and walked towards the door. Mr Clitheroe rose also.

'I wonder what would happen if I *really* killed you, Mahdi,' said the old man.

'You would not be at the funeral,' smiled Mahdi.

'Then I must let someone else kill you,' replied Mr Clitheroe, 'or I shall miss a pleasure.'

Ted Flitt let the Indian out, and not for the first time, spat after him.

'Yes; why not Ted Flitt?' mused Mr Clitheroe, watching.

27

When Morning Came—

The dark hours crept by, the hours of temporary oblivion. On a hard wooden floor outside a bottomless cupboard an out-of-work sailor slept. Near a front door with a sliding panel a stunted bloke whose nose was almost as crooked as his character strove not to sleep. In a study an old man nodded. By an oblong chest a big man dozed. And elsewhere, at other points in the enveloping blackness of night, lay others who were to awaken to a day of varying emotions.

But two people of our acquaintance did not sleep. One was Mahdi. The other was Mr Eustace Moberley Hope. Business and pleasure kept these two from their respective beds.

The clocks chimed three, and four; then five, and six. The towers of churches grew gradually distinct. The tower of the church nearest to Jowle Street, however, remained almost obliterated. Although the hue of the concealing curtain changed from black to grey, there was no other indication that the night was being slain.

Few people passed through Jowle Street. None from

choice. A milkman took it in his round. A postman trudged its length. From one or two doors, as the morning advanced, depressed people emerged, and went to work, or to look for work. But, for the most part, the residents of Jowle Street stayed inside, as though they had lost their heart for movement and adventure. A town can take it out of you. So can a street.

The milkman, the postman, a shabby youth delivering papers, five residents and a cart provided the only signs of movement in the gloomy, foggy thoroughfare until five minutes to ten. Then another figure slipped into Jowle Street, a dark, lithe figure, like a shadow in the mist. At No. 26 it vanished. Jowle Street was empty again.

But not for long. A second figure, more portly, turned into the street, trudging along with even, measured steps. A constable, this time, whose mind was very far away from the horror through which he unconsciously walked. He was absorbed in the homely occupation of a cross-word puzzle, and he was trying to capture nothing more forbidding than a vegetable of seven letters ending in 'i'.

Unlike the figure that had preceded him, he did not pause at No. 26. The house meant nothing to him. He trudged on, seeking his vegetable, and vanished beyond. And, as he vanished, a third figure appeared.

The third figure did pause at No. 26. It was a girl. She paused and stared at the front door, and afterwards, still hesitating, glanced up and down the road. Then, as though suddenly afraid of her hesitation, she ran quickly up the low steps and rang.

Other visitors had been kept waiting on that doorstep. She was not. The door opened almost immediately, and an old man peered at her.

'I'm glad you've come, Miss Sherwin,' said the old man. 'I was afraid you might not.'

'Even after your letter?' demanded the girl.

'Yes, even after my letter,' replied the old man. 'Everyone is not as wise as you. Let us go into my study and talk there.'

'The quicker the better,' she answered. 'I want to get this over.'

'So do I,' nodded the old man, as they crossed the hall to the study door. 'So do I. And if I could have got it over when you called last night I would have done so. But the—the people we have to meet were not here then, and, in the circumstances—'

'The people we have to meet?' interposed the girl. 'Who are those?'

Her voice was terribly anxious. Her eyes, when you peered into them, betrayed a sleepless night. The old man smiled sympathetically at her.

'You will know very soon, Miss Sherwin,' he said. 'But let us take things in their proper sequence. It will be best. We must enter into this matter with clear minds. No confusion. Don't you agree?'

'Oh, please stop talking like that!' she exclaimed. They were now in the study, and she sank into a chair. 'Tell me at once what you meant by your letter. Why is Douglas—Mr Randall—in danger, and how can my coming here prevent it?'

'You will learn that, also, very soon. But please answer one or two questions of my own first. You have not spoken to Mr Randall about this?'

'You told me particularly not to.'

'We do not always do what we are told.'

'But you said it would increase his danger if I spoke to him—or to anybody! It was difficult, though. Last night he took me to a dance, and when he saw how worried I was—naturally I couldn't help showing that—he kept on questioning me. In the end I made him take me home. I couldn't stand any more. And I haven't slept a wink.'

'Poor child!' murmured the old man. 'And you have no idea at all what this danger is?'

'I'm waiting for you to tell me, Mr Clitheroe.'

'No suspicion of any kind? Not from any other source?'

'None.'

Mr Clitheroe nodded. He seemed relieved. The front door bell rang.

'Ah!' he exclaimed. 'Here is another visitor.'

The girl jumped to her feet, all nerves.

'Who is it?' she exclaimed.

'Excuse me a second,' he said. 'I will let him in.'

He left the room, and the girl waited with her hand at her breast. Voices sounded in the hall. Suddenly she started.

'Douglas!' she cried,

A young man entered. He looked as anxious as she, and no less astonished.

'Doris!' he exclaimed, stopping short. 'Why, how—?'

He turned to the old man behind him, and his voice was almost threatening.

'Why didn't you tell me Miss Sherwin would be here?' he demanded.

'Be patient, be patient, my dear young people!' responded Mr Clitheroe reprovingly. 'Here am I, in a terribly difficult position, doing my best for your happiness, and you both jump down my throat as though I were some—some malefactor! Sit down again, Miss Sherwin, I beg. And you sit down, too, Mr Randall. Then I will tell you the whole story, and I think you will agree that I have acted for the best. One moment.'

He ran back to the door and looked into the hall. The young man and the girl watched him, then glanced at each other.

'We had better not raise our voices,' said Mr Clitheroe, returning into the room and closing the door. 'If what I am about to tell you angers you, or excites you—as it may— try and keep calm, I beg. You can do so by remembering that the trouble will have been completely dealt with by the time you leave. At least,' he added, with a little frown, 'that is my intention and my hope.'

'But what is the trouble?' demanded the young man. 'What *is* this danger that threatens Miss Sherwin? And why all this secrecy?'

'Threatens *me*?' cried the girl. 'I thought it threatened *you!*'

'It threatens both of you,' interposed Mr Clitheroe, 'since when people are engaged the happiness of one involves the happiness of the other. Is that not so? And may I once more remind you of the necessity for keeping control of ourselves and for lowering our voices? I don't know whether you noticed a rather unpleasant little fellow in the hall? He is not supposed to be there, but I caught a glimpse of him as I went to the front door just now—' He paused, and looked towards the door, then made a sudden dart and opened it. As he did so, Ted Flitt scurried away. 'There! What did I tell you?' muttered Mr Clitheroe, as he closed the door again with a frown. 'Now I hope you are satisfied that we must keep hold of ourselves.'

As the door closed behind him, Ted Flitt grinned. The

grin vanished, however, as a voice addressed him from out of the shadows.

'Do not smile yet, Mr Flitt,' said the voice smoothly. 'This is only the beginning. There is a long way to go yet.'

'Dam that Indian!' thought Mr Flitt. 'I'd send 'im a longer way if I knew 'ow!'

Meanwhile, in the study, Mr Clitheroe continued with his discourse.

'In order to explain the letters I wrote to each of you,' he was saying, 'I must go back quite a number of years. I am a stranger to you, but I knew your father well, Mr Randall, and at one time we were actually in partnership together. That was when you were quite a small boy, and when I was nearly appointed your guardian.'

'My guardian!' exclaimed Douglas.

'Yes. But, unfortunately, there was a—a misunderstanding concerning the matter of profits, and—well, it ended our association. I imagined I was entitled to a larger share than actually fell to me, but I preferred not to push the point. Perhaps you should not be ungrateful to me for that, Mr Randall, since you are at this moment enjoying the full fruits of your late father's business.'

'Look here, sir!' interposed Douglas. 'Are you insinuating that my father—'

'I am insinuating nothing,' retorted Mr Clitheroe. 'I am simply explaining a position that bears upon the present situation. Otherwise I would not dig up the past. There would be no object in it. I am explaining to you, Mr Randall, how I enter into the present situation, and how a rascal who is attempting to blackmail you came to approach me first.'

His two listeners stared at him unbelievingly. They seemed incapable of speech.

'I see you do not like the word blackmail,' remarked the old man. 'Nor do I. It is a horrid word. But sometimes it has to be dealt with. And when this rascal wrote to me, imagining that I was actually your guardian, Mr Randall, what was I to do? He thought I was your guardian because he had been employed in your father's business at the! time I was in it, and he knew of what was on the carpet—but he was dismissed for theft before your father and I quarrelled. So now, like a bad penny, he turns up again, having apparently raked up something reflecting on your honour, Mr Randall—or purporting, shall we say, to reflect on your honour—and demands money from *me*—from *me*, Mr Randall to keep him quiet.'

'Where is the lying beast?' asked Douglas, pale with indignation. 'Let me deal with him.'

'I intend that you shall,' answered Mr Clitheroe, with a grim smile, 'but let me finish my story first. There isn't much more. When he first approached me I could have turned him straight on to you, if I had chosen—'

'Yes, why didn't you?' demanded Douglas hotly.

'Because it occurred to me that the matter could be settled much more quietly at my house than at yours or Miss Sherwin's,' said Mr Clitheroe, 'and I was willing to undergo that inconvenience for the sake of my old partner's son. Of course, if you wish, I can drop right out of it,' he added. 'You can both go home, and our friend will follow you and create his scandal right under the noses of your families and friends. I thought, however, that—with my assistance—we might deal with him more effectively here. Was I right, or wrong?'

'You were right, Mr Clitheroe!' exclaimed Doris gratefully. 'Please forgive me for my doubts when I first came in.'

221

'Not at all!' he protested. 'Not at all! Your doubts were perfectly natural. And the only reason I couldn't explain matters more fully to you before was because I hesitated to put anything definite in writing. I indicated the danger, and trusted—rightly, as matters have turned out—to your good sense to take a hint.'

'Yes, but what I want to know is this,' interposed Douglas, growing more indignant every moment. His hot temper was being roused to fever point. 'What has the skunk got against me? There's nothing he *could* have! You believe that, don't you, Doris?' he cried, turning to her swiftly.

'Of course, she believes it,' said Mr Clitheroe soothingly, and moving to the cupboard under his desk, 'and of course I believe it. The trouble is that the world isn't so kind, and that, as our "skunk"—most satisfactory term that, eh?—as our "skunk" well knows, mud sticks. Now, I suggest a little drink before we proceed any farther—to reinforce ourselves for the next step, eh, Mr Randall?'

Douglas hesitated, and Doris looked at him warningly.

'Just a small tot,' urged the old man, already producing the decanter. 'The next step is not going to be an easy one, and our "skunk"—yes, the term is admirable—is an ugly customer. This will help you to deal with him.'

He held out the glass. Douglas took it with a short laugh.

'He's right, Doris,' he said. 'This'll make me twice my size!'

He drained the glass. The effect was not cooling.

'Now then, I'm ready for him,' declared Douglas. 'By Jove, sir, that was good! Just right. Well, when's he coming?'

'Be careful, dear!' warned Doris.

'He's the one that's got to be careful,' responded Douglas. 'Thinks he can come along and upset the universe with his dirty yarns! Well, he's going to find out his mistake. When is he coming, Mr Clitheroe? I want to meet him now. *Now!*'

'He is waiting to meet you now,' answered Mr Clitheroe quietly.

'Do you mean he's here, in the house, at this moment?'

'Yes.'

'What—is it that miserable little toad you chased in the hall—?'

'No, not him. That miserable little toad—really, your terms are most happy—that miserable little toad is merely one of—one of the brotherhood. The unbrotherly brotherhood. He has come along with the skunk to see there's fair play. He didn't quite trust me, you see. And—well, perhaps he had no cause to, eh?'

Mr Clitheroe chuckled. He seemed to be enjoying himself. Douglas laughed also.

'You bet,' he agreed. 'But where *is* the skunk, then?'

'Upstairs.'

'Good! We'll go up now. At least, you and I will. Come along.'

Mr Clitheroe glanced at the girl. She was paler than ever, and her eyes were full of apprehension. .

'Well—do you stay here, my dear?' he inquired. 'Or—do you think—it might be wiser if you came up with us?'

'You stay here, Doris!' ordered Douglas. 'Mr Clitheroe, can I pour myself out one more small dose? Just a small one? Don't worry, I know what I'm doing.'

He did not wait for permission. Mr Clitheroe continued to look at Doris.

'He may need you, to restrain him,' murmured the old man. 'Really, I'm getting a little alarmed.'

223

'Of course, I'm coming up with you,' said the girl definitely. 'I wouldn't dream of staying away.'

'Very wise, very wise,' nodded Mr Clitheroe. 'Quite apart from anything else, it will be much happier in the end if you, also, hear what our friend upstairs has to say.' He turned to the young man. 'Well, Mr Randall, we're ready. I wouldn't touch any more of that, if I were you.'

'I'm not going to,' responded Douglas, having now worked himself up to the necessary degree of courage. Normally, he was not overburdened with it. 'I know when to stop. Come along, come along!'

He was first out of the room. Doris followed quickly, and laid a restraining hand on his arm. She had entered the house in fear. Now she was terrified.

'Douglas!' she whispered in his ear. 'Let's go away!'

'Go away!' exclaimed Douglas thickly. 'Before we've dealt with this blackguard.'

'Yes. I'm afraid.'

'Well, I'm not.'

'Please! Please!'

Douglas frowned, and shook her arm off.

'But you heard what Mr Clitheroe said,' he cried.

'And he was damn right! If we don't settle this now, we'll never settle it. He'll follow us home. He'll kick up all the mud he can invent, and we'll have him on our heels all our lives.'

'But who's going to believe him, Douglas?'

'Everybody.'

'Except me,' she whispered, taking his arm again.

Douglas hesitated. A momentary doubt flashed through his brain. Was she right? . . .

Standing in the kitchen doorway, Ted Flitt felt himself

224

projected forward. He did not see the arm that projected him, quietly and firmly, but he guessed its colour. As though a will stronger than his own had entered into him, he walked forward after that preliminary propulsion till he came within the vision of the young man hesitating by the staircase. And there he stood, smiling evilly, and fulfilling the design of the stronger will.

For, on seeing Ted Flitt, Douglas Randall hesitated no longer. The sight inflamed him, recreating his spasmodic ferocity.

'Hallo—there's the toad, isn't it?' he cried. 'We'll deal with him later, eh?'

Mr Clitheroe nodded and, as Flitt retreated from sight—drawn back once more by the stronger will, the design of which had now been accomplished—the old man moved to the stairs and invited Douglas to follow him.

A few seconds later Mahdi stood in the hall alone, listening to the sound of ascending footsteps.

28

The Performance

While Mahdi listened to the receding footsteps from the hall below, Wharton listened to the same footsteps from the second floor front above; but in his case the footsteps grew louder and louder instead of softer and softer, and his mouth tightened grimly as he toyed with a revolver in his hand.

'God, I'll be glad when this damned game's over!' he muttered. 'S'pose it don't go according to plan?'

But the plan had been decided on and there was no turning back now. Wavering, indeed, might spell defeat. So when the door opened Wharton quickly banished all outward sign of uncertainty and greeted his visitors with a grin of sneering assurance.

'Ah! So we've arrived!' he exclaimed impertinently. 'Good! We've wasted enough time as it is.'

'I agree to that,' replied Mr Clitheroe, playing his part as convincingly as his accomplice was playing his. 'The sooner we get down to business the better. Mr Randall, this is our skunk.' As Wharton raised his eyebrows the old man turned back to him and continued: 'Yes, that is our name for you, and we think it rather an appropriate name. You don't mind, I hope? This is Mr Randall, and this is Miss Sherwin, his fiancée. And, now the introductions are over, what is the next step?'

'The next step is ten thousand pounds,' answered Wharton, coolly.

'No, it's *this*!' cried Douglas, who had remained silent during these preliminaries with difficulty.

He raised his fist, but Doris seized his arm. Wharton's revolver was pointing towards her heart.

'Now, just stop talking, all of you,' said Wharton, 'and listen. Believe me, it'll save a lot of time, and you can reckon I *mean* to save it! You can also reckon that this little affair I've got in my hand will go off the moment I want it to—'

'You fool!' interrupted Mr Clitheroe. 'If you use your pea-shooter it'll be heard all over the street.'

'Oh, no, it won't,' retorted Wharton, suddenly discovering that he was rather enjoying himself. He was acting under orders, but there was some amusement in the fact that he had to appear to be hectoring the very persons whose orders he was carrying out. 'Oh, no, it won't, Mr Clitheroe! My little pea-shooter, as you call it, is one of those dumb little fellers. No one would hear a sound. It just does its work quietly, and says nothing about it. So, you see, you'd better do *your* work quietly, too. Now then! Get over by the window, you old fossil. And you get there, too, Mr Douglas Randall.' As the men obeyed, the one with feigned, the other with genuine anger, he addressed Doris who was standing motionless. '*You* needn't go so far away, my dear,' he said. 'I don't mind company, if it's the right kind.'

'You bounder!' Douglas blurted out. 'Why didn't you warn me he had a gun, Mr Clitheroe?'

'I didn't know,' murmured Mr Clitheroe apologetically, 'or I'd have brought one up myself.'

'Of course he didn't know,' sneered Wharton. 'Do you think I'm quite green? D'you think I don't know how and when to play my cards? This little silent friend of mine is one of the cards and now we've got that fixed we'll get down to the game. Oh, but there's just one thing I'd like to add first. This little silent gun of mine isn't the only one inside this pretty building. There are others about, and I've plenty of friends in the vicinity. If, by chance, any accident *did* happen to me, it wouldn't help you in the least. On the contrary, it would only increase your difficulties, for then there'd be my death to hush up, as well as sundry other little matters I'm now going to talk about, and the ten thousand pounds I mentioned a moment ago would jump up to twenty or thirty.'

'Are you serious?' asked Mr Clitheroe.

'Dead serious, to use an appropriate phrase,' responded Wharton, with a wink. 'I'll be more trouble to you dead than alive.'

'But isn't there some law that excuses the murder of a blackmailer?' suggested Mr Clitheroe.

'There may be,' agreed Wharton; 'but one's got to go through a lot of danger and mud to reach it. And, if Mr Randall *does* get hold of my little friend here'—he wagged his revolver—'and saves his own skin afterwards, it won't save Miss Sherwin's skin. You see, my friends have made a little oath for my security at this interview. An eye for an eye, a tooth for a tooth—and a life for a life. The life required to pay for my life would be Miss Sherwin's. So that's that, everybody, and now how about that ten thousand pounds?'

'Yes, but what are you to receive ten thousand pounds for?' burst out Mr Clitheroe, who had appointed himself as spokesman.

'For not spreading certain unpleasant news,' answered Wharton, 'concerning our young friend here, Mr Randall.'

Then Douglas found his tongue.

'News? What news, you dirty hound?' he exclaimed.

'A lady is present,' coughed Wharton.

'She wants to hear,' said the lady faintly.

'Very well, then,' sighed Wharton, and shrugging his shoulders, he laid the revolver down on a little table beside him. He did so, apparently, so that his hands might be free to bring a letter-case out of his pocket.

Mr Clitheroe eyed the revolver. The little table was on Wharton's left. Doris was on his right. Near the table was a cupboard door, and for an instant Mr Clitheroe shot a glance at that, also . . .

'I have a statement here,' said Wharton, still fumbling with his letter-case, 'which is signed by five witnesses. Each witness can be produced, if necessary, and each is ready to come forward—'

'For how much apiece?' inquired Mr Clitheroe smoothly.

He was advancing towards the little table, and paused to put the question. Wharton did not glance at him. His eyes were fixed on those of Douglas.

'*I* work for money, but they would work for love,' replied Wharton cynically. 'Sheer love of the truth.'

Mr Clitheroe advanced a step or two nearer the little table.

'Yes, for sheer love of the truth, Mr Randall,' went on

Wharton. 'They are not here at this moment, unfortunately, because they all live at—Eastbourne. By the way, have you ever been to Eastbourne, Mr Randall?'

'Who hasn't?' retorted Douglas.

Mr Clitheroe's hand went forward quietly, and descended on the revolver on the little table.

'Well, *I* hadn't, until three months ago,' answered Wharton. 'Did you happen to be there, about that time? I see from your expression that you *did* happen to be there. And were you with him, Miss Sherwin?' he inquired, now turning to the girl. 'I have an idea that you were not.'

Mr Clitheroe's hand came away from the little table. The revolver was in it.

'Do you suppose I follow him wherever he goes?' she retorted hotly. 'Douglas! What does he mean?'

'No, you were in Le Touquet, Miss Sherwin. Mr Randall joined you later. But not before he had exhausted certain very pleasant possibilities in Eastbourne, and had sown some agreeable if awkward memories there—'

'You're lying!' shouted Douglas.

Mr Clitheroe began to retreat quietly from the little table towards the window. Outside, the fog was thickening. Perhaps he owed the success of his manoeuvring in the room.

'I have five people who will prove I am not lying,' answered Wharton, 'and who can prove to you, Miss Sherwin, as well as to others, that the facts written out on this sheet of paper are accurate.' He was still looking at the girl, and all at once his eyes kindled greedily, and he smiled. 'I can well understand how sorry Mr Randall would be to lose your affection.'

'Don't be impudent!' she flared.

Mr Clitheroe reached the window. He laid the revolver down on a chair. The chair was between him and Douglas.

'Really, Miss Sherwin, you tempt me to be more impudent still,' replied Wharton, with a leer. 'When one looks at you, one understands how easy it is for men to fall. Whether in Eastbourne or in London—'

'Here,' cried Douglas. 'Stop looking at her like that—'

As though to emphasise the picture, Mr Clitheroe switched on a light. The faces of Wharton and Doris became illuminated in the surrounding dimness. His was red and inflamed with sudden ugly desire. Hers was white.

'Why shouldn't I look at her,' said Wharton, continuing to do so. 'Why shouldn't I? Beauty above money, eh? Yes suppose I reduce the ten thousand pounds to nine—for a kiss?'

Before she could retreat, he suddenly threw his arms around her. She gave a frightened gasp, and struggled, to free herself. Douglas's eyes fell upon the revolver, so invitingly within his reach . . .

What happened during the ensuing moments Douglas never rightly knew. Impotence, fear and anger swept over him, and the drink that seemed temporarily to have dulled his brain now fanned the fierce flame. He seized the revolver and fired. No sound came out of the muzzle, but the man at whom he fired gave a stifled shout and fell to the ground. The girl, now free, tottered and swayed.

'Catch her—she's fainting!' rasped Mr Clitheroe.

Douglas did not move. He stood dazed.

'Quick, fool! She'll fall!' came Mr Clitheroe's sharp command again.

Douglas lurched forward. He got to her somehow, and she lay inert in his arms. Meanwhile, the old man was glancing out of the window, through a little gap in the curtains . . . a little overlooked gap . . .

A face peered at him through the little gap. A face across the way. No, not a complete face. Just the upper part, including the eyes. Mr Clitheroe's own eyes became momentarily transfixed. For an instant he seemed on the point of losing his admirable composure. An instant later, however, he had swiftly closed the curtains, and his voice came softly and swiftly across the room to the agonised young man who was holding his unconscious fiancée in his arms.

'Listen! Do as I tell you!' said Mr Clitheroe. 'You have killed a man, and we are surrounded by that man's friends. The danger is obvious. Take Miss Sherwin quickly into the room at the back—just across the passage—and wait there. Quickly! Quickly! Don't leave until I come for you. No, no—better still, I'll send my daughter to you. Luckily she is in the house. When my daughter comes, then you can leave Miss Sherwin with her and return here. But not before, remember! Miss Sherwin will be in danger if she is left alone.'

He crossed to the door and opened it. Stunned, bewildered, and with his nerves shattered, Douglas obeyed, carrying the girl out of the room, across the small landing, and into the room opposite.

'I am going to lock you in here for a few seconds,' muttered Mr Clitheroe. 'It will be safest—for Miss Sherwin, remember! We must think of her safety above all things.'

The young man made no protest. Initiative, a quality in which he was never too prolific, had departed from him. He was vaguely conscious of the old man's withdrawal from the room, and he heard, dully, the sound of the key being turned in the lock . . .

Back in the front room, Mr Clitheroe's manner changed.

'Quick!' he barked, to the figure on the floor. 'Get up!'

Wharton sprang to his feet.

'Worked all right, eh?' chuckled Wharton hoarsely.

'Damn it, no!' retorted Mr Clitheroe. 'That blasted tramp's seen us!'

'What!' gasped Wharton.

'Seen us! Seen us! *Seen us!*' hissed Mr Clitheroe. 'Go across and settle him!'

'Hell, I will!' exclaimed Wharton.

In spite of his urgent hurry, however, Wharton paused at the door.

'Can you manage alone?' he asked, with a look towards the cupboard.

'Yes, yes!' answered Mr Clitheroe. 'I've got to, haven't I? Get on with it!'

Wharton disappeared. The old man scowled after him, then turned to the cupboard, and brought out a key. A couple of seconds later he had opened the cupboard, and a figure stared unseeingly at him. The figure was sitting on the ground, propped up against one of the walls. Scarcely less grim than the figure was the old man's callous acceptance of its presence.

Wharton had gone, yet here, surely, was Wharton again. The figure was of the same height and the same build, and was dressed in almost identical clothing.

'I reckon you didn't help yourself when you poked your nose into other people's business!' muttered Mr Clitheroe vengefully. 'There's no chance of *your* ever seeing Australia again, my friend.'

He caught hold of the figure and, with surprising strength, dragged it out. He dragged it to the spot where Wharton had fallen, and arranged it in a similar position. Then he went out into the passage, and just managed to prevent himself from jumping. Mahdi stood regarding him.

'Go back!' ordered Mahdi quietly.

Mr Clitheroe retreated into the room without a word. The Indian followed him and closed the door.

'And still you bungle,' said Mahdi.

'If you refer to the tramp, I refuse to admit that I've bungled any more than you have,' retorted the old man.

'Do not argue,' answered the Indian. 'You continue to bungle.'

'How?'

'What did you tell Wharton to do?'

'I told him to settle the fellow.'

'And what did you mean by "settle"?'

'It ought to be clear enough.'

'That is your weakness. "Ought to be." I have altered your instruction—or, as you may claim, defined it. Wharton has now gone to kill the tramp.'

'I see,' sneered Mr Clitheroe. 'What's a murder more or less to you, Mahdi? You see that you get no responsibility for them!'

'I did not know that you had a tender heart, Mr Clitheroe.'

'Damn it, who's tender? But there's such a thing as wisdom, isn't there? Two murders in one night might take some getting away with.'

'Two!'

'Have you forgotten *this* fellow?'

Mr Clitheroe pointed to the Australian on the ground. The Indian smiled.

'Oh, no! I have not forgotten Mr Hobart! But it is not yet decided that Mr Hobart is to be killed.'

'You decided we were to stick him down the well.'

'But now the *tramp* is going down the well.' Mahdi smiled again. 'We must think of the traffic congestion.'

'I suppose that means you've changed your plan again!' exclaimed Mr Clitheroe. 'Or, rather,' he added savagely, '*my* plan?'

'It is necessary to be elastic when those who carry out plans make continual mistakes,' the Indian pointed out. 'With a patience that has its limit, Mr Clitheroe, I have several times changed your plan to remedy your own defects. And so, now, I say that Mr Hobart will not, after all, go down the well.'

'Where will he go, then, after I have done with him?'

'Back into the nice, long box where he has spent most of the night.'

'And then?'

'The van will call for the box. The box of books, you understand.'

'Yes, yes. And where will the van go?'

Mahdi paused for an instant. His eyes grew cold and steely.

'That is nothing to do with you, Mr Clitheroe,' he answered. 'If, for once, I take a murder off your hands, you should be grateful. But be sure of this. Mr Hobart will not trouble you any further. He will pay the price of his interference in another place, and before another judge. And so—' His white teeth suddenly snapped together, and a look darted into his eyes that even made Mr Clitheroe shiver. 'And so will—*that girl*!'

'Ah, that girl!' murmured the old man. 'Yes, she will certainly have to be dealt with. I can well imagine, Mahdi,' he added maliciously, 'that you will want to settle with the fair lady yourself!' He shrugged his shoulders. 'Well, she is waiting for you in her temporary prison, and Mr Hobart will be waiting for you in the nice, long box, so you can call for your captives when you want them, and take 'em to the end of hell, as far as I care. Meanwhile, *may* I get on with *my* business?'

'It is necessary that you do,' replied Mahdi.

And, his own immediate business accomplished, he slipped quickly from the room.

Mr Clitheroe took a deep breath, then darted out after him. The Indian had vanished. His absence was a relief, though not the abrupt manner of it. Mahdi's comings and goings were always unnerving. Moving to the top flight of stairs, Mr Clitheroe ascended. He found Jessica waiting for him in the attic room.

'Well?' she asked, turning quickly as he entered. 'Has everything gone all right, or are we in an unholy mess?'

'Everything has gone all right!' snapped the old man. 'And now it's your turn to see that things *continue* to go right. Come along down.'

'Politeness doesn't cost anything,' she snapped back. 'But perhaps Mahdi has been getting on your nerves?'

'Be quiet! I don't want any comments. Our young fools are in the back room, and you're to go in and look after Miss Sherwin.'

'While you finish your conversation, with the other young fool?'

'Exactly.'

'And what happens after that?'

'We send 'em home.'

'Together?'

Mr Clitheroe considered. 'Yes, I think so,' he said, after

a pause. 'Probably, when I've finished my chat with the boy, I'll have the girl in and then we can send them off in a taxi with a friendly pat.' He did not smile at his own cynicism. 'But be ready for anything. With Mahdi around, there's no knowing where all this is going to end.'

'Who else is around?'

'What do you mean?'

'Where's Wharton?'

Mr Clitheroe had been waiting for that. He swallowed. 'Wharton is across the way.'

'What's he doing across the way?'

'Killing a tramp.'

Jessica stared at him. He stared back. The same thought was chasing through both minds. Was this tramp killable?

'That man's a boomerang!' exclaimed Jessica.

'Forget him!' barked Mr Clitheroe. 'He's boomed his last by now, at any rate. Oh, come along! What are we standing here for?'

'Because I want to know the whole position,' she retorted. 'Where's Flitt?'

'At the door.'

'And the damned spy who calls herself Nadine?'

'Still locked up.'

'Well, things seem water-tight. But, as you say, we've got to be ready for anything—and it isn't only Mahdi we've got to look out for. Carry on, Daddy. My God, won't I be glad when I've seen the last of you!'

They descended the stairs. They reached the door of the room in which Douglas and Doris were locked.

'No need for me to go in,' muttered Mr Clitheroe, as he turned the key. 'Send the boy in to me—I'll be waiting in the front room for him.'

237

'With pleasure—if he's not too good looking,' answered Jessica sarcastically.

They separated. The old man re-entered the front room where the unconscious Australian still lay. He glanced unsympathetically at the helpless figure, then raised his eyes to the window at the other end of the room.

'Wharton's a damn time,' he muttered. 'Why the devil isn't he back?'

29

The Terms of Silence

The door opened behind Mr Clitheroe, and he turned. Douglas Randall stood in the doorway.

The boy was spiritless, beaten. The terror of his position and the enormity of the act he believed he had committed—was not the evidence of the act still on the floor?—had carried him into a condition he had only previously experienced in nightmare, and he was incapable of dealing with it. Added to his own terror was his terror for his fiancée. Numb and helpless, he was at the mercy of any stronger will that cared to direct him. And Mr Clitheroe, watching him, was well aware of this.

'Come in, Mr Randall,' the old man said, 'and close the door behind you.'

The boy obeyed.

'This is a terrible business,' Mr Clitheroe went on, scarcely troubling to assume the sympathy he did not feel. Douglas was deadened to the finer shades of acting. 'Have you thought out yet what you're going to do?'

The boy shook his head.

'Then let me try and help you, Mr Randall, by telling you the precise position. I'll not mince words. I'll give you the exact facts. And I know the facts, because—in your interests—I've been ascertaining them while you've been waiting in the next room. The first fact is that you have killed the leader of a rascally gang. The second is that the members of the rascally gang are mighty angry about it. I've been interviewing one or two of them below. And the third is that, unless they receive what they term "compensation" of a very substantial nature, they will retaliate.'

Mr Clitheroe paused, to let the final word sink in. Douglas gripped the back of a chair, but said nothing.

'Of course, we could go to the police,' resumed Mr Clitheroe. 'That, in other circumstances, would be the obvious course. But would that assist you? You must decide. If you go to the police you must confess to the murder—'

'Is it murder to kill a rat like that?' interrupted Douglas, finding his voice at last. It was a high and emotional voice, and Mr Clitheroe raised a finger warningly.

'A little softer—be advised—a little softer,' he murmured, thereby killing the boy's tiny flicker of spirit. 'A rat? Yes, certainly. And rats are best out of the way. But one cannot anticipate the decision of a judge and jury in a criminal court'—Douglas shuddered, as it was intended he should— 'and before you proved he was a rat you and Miss Sherwin would be dragged through a pretty shattering experience.'

'Why Miss Sherwin?' muttered Douglas.

Mr Clitheroe regarded him almost pityingly as he responded. 'Because, quite apart from Miss Sherwin's interest in you, she could not be kept out of it. The motive for the murder'—he insisted on using the word—'would be discussed, and also the reason for the interview at which the murder took place. There is no possible way in which Miss Sherwin could be kept out of it. And what happens to you, Mr Randall, is only one side of the question. What happens to Miss Sherwin is the other side. Unless compensation is paid, I am afraid there will be a second murder, of which Miss Sherwin herself will be the victim.'

'Then I've *got* to go to the police!' exclaimed Douglas.

'And so expedite the carrying out of the threat?' asked the old man. 'Believe me, Mr Randall, these fellows mean business, and if you go to the police you will deprive both Miss Sherwin and yourself of your only chances of security.'

'What do you suggest I ought to do, then?' said Douglas.

'Well, you could pay the compensation.'

'How much would that be?'

'They have asked for twenty thousand pounds; but I might beat them down a little.'

'Twenty thousand—'

'Yes, it is outrageous. But fortunately you have it. You have considerably more. It may be a small price to pay, after all, for your fiancée's safety—and your happiness.'

'Her safety, yes! But where would the happiness be?'

Mr Clitheroe shrugged his shoulders.

'If I were in your shoes—engaged to a charming girl—I would hardly ask that question, Mr Randall,' observed the old man, with a touch of irony.

'But—that! *That!*' gasped Douglas, suddenly pointing to the figure on the ground.

'That could be dealt with—if we decided to make a bold bid for the happiness.'

'Dealt with?'

'I said so.'

'How?'

Mr Clitheroe paused; then explained:

'Listen to me attentively, Mr Randall,' he said. 'And remember that, in what I am about to say, I have no personal interest. I merely say it as your friend. My only personal gain, if you agree to my proposal, will be that my home would not be associated with a murder trial and I should escape interviewers and sight-seers—and for this small benefit I should be taking a distinct personal risk. Now then. Do you remember a long wooden case in the room you have just come from?'

'I—I think I do.'

'Did anything strike you about it?'

'No.'

'Does it—*now*?' The young man stared, as an incredulous idea began to form in his muddled mind. 'Yes, I see, it does. That case, Mr Randall, was delivered to me recently from a second-hand bookseller in Charing Cross Road. I bought a large number of old encyclopædias and volumes, and his van delivered them in that somewhat unpleasant-looking box. I thought at the time that the box bore an odd resemblance to a coffin. What do *you* think?'

'I don't know what you mean!' muttered Douglas.

'But surely you do?' protested the old man. 'Why make me say things that might be more happily understood between us? However, if you insist . . . I had intended to have the box chopped up for firewood. I could however, re-sell the old books to our rascals downstairs, and they could cart it away—with its contents—to some distant spot.' He glanced down at the figure on the ground. '*Now* do you know what I mean, Mr Randall!'

Douglas nodded and swallowed.

'Would they—do it?' he managed to ask.

'They have already agreed to do it,' answered Mr Clitheroe, 'provided they get their compensation. Believe me, I have been fully occupied since I saw you last, and I have learned exactly how the land lies. It will not help them to have this made public, and they are quite willing to help you to keep it quiet—for a price.'

'Yes, but look here!' exclaimed Douglas, while perspiration stood on his brow. In response to another warning gesture by Mr Clitheroe, he went on in a lower voice, 'Look here! If—if they take the—if they take him away in the case, what will they do with him?'

Mr Clitheroe smiled sourly.

'That, surely, need not concern you?' he suggested.

'I don't know about it. They may hold it over me.'

'Yes, they may hold it over you, and they may follow their present claim with further claims.'

'Well, then—'

'But are you in a position to dictate? Isn't it better, at the moment, to take the one and only chance you have? Of course, if you think otherwise, then you must go ahead and allow the matter to become public. You will be tried for murder, and Miss Sherwin will go in terror of her life.'

'God!' groaned the boy. 'Let me think—let me think!'

'I have even provided for your thought,' answered Mr Clitheroe. 'When they demanded their absurd sum—twenty thousand pounds—I told them that it was hardly likely that you carried so much about with you in your pocket. I implied that you would need a little time, and suggested that you should be given till this evening to decide—and to make your arrangements. At nine o'clock they will send the van for the case. They will take away the case—and its contents—if by that time you have agreed to their demands and have returned here with the money, or with some form of security covering the amount. I believe,' went on Mr Clitheroe smoothly, 'they will come down to fifteen thousand. I suggest that you regard that as the figure, and stick to it. After all, unless I am wrongly informed, you possess well over a hundred thousand, so you will have plenty left—'

'For them to bleed me of later on?'

'Perhaps. I hope not. If they press you again, we may find some way of dealing with them that is impossible at the moment. Meanwhile, at least, we shall have secured Miss Sherwin's safety. So, what do you say?'

'I seem to have no alternative,' muttered Douglas. 'But for God's sake let me get out of this house now. Can't you see, I'm not able to think yet—I'm not able to think—'

'Naturally not, naturally not!' nodded Mr Clitheroe. 'But, am I to expect you back?'

'Yes, yes!'

'Good! Then let us now take the first step towards the security you need by—er—disposing of our—of our friend here. It will obviously not do to let him remain on my floor any longer. Will you help me to—er—convey him into the next room? Let me think. Yes. My daughter had better take Miss Sherwin upstairs while the removal is in progress—'

The lack of sympathy in the old man's attitude suddenly smote the other's clouded brain.

'By God, sir!' he burst out. 'Aren't you damned callous?'

Mr Clitheroe realised his lapse, and converted it to his own advantage. Instead of showing the sympathy that was wanted of him, he suddenly stiffened.

'You seem to forget, Mr Randall,' he said coldly, 'that after all, I am assisting a man who potentially is wanted by the police. Do you really expect me to shower affection on you?' Douglas stared. 'Let my acts speak of my friendship,' said Mr Clitheroe, 'and forgive me if my attitude reflects a certain conventional distaste for murder. Now then, will you help me?'

Douglas crumpled. He had no more fight in him. He removed his haunted eyes from Mr Clitheroe to the even less appetising sight on the carpet. And, as he did so, the front door bell rang below.

'Who the devil's that?' exclaimed Mr Clitheroe sharply. He hastened to the window and peered down. He grunted in annoyance. The roof of the porch obscured the visitor from view.

30

Ben Gets In

Doorsteps have been neglected by the historian. He has dilated on the varying atmosphere of towns and of streets, of houses and rooms and cupboards, but he has passed over the doorstep as though, indeed, no significance lay beneath its superficial transitory mission. *You*, however, do more than pass over a doorstep. You pause upon it. You wait upon it. You hope, or fear, or yawn, or grow tense upon it. In the little interim between arrival and departure you may pass through a lifetime of emotion or remain as static as a stone.

Ben, on the doorstep of No. 26 Jowle Street, passed through a lifetime of emotion. True he was outwardly static. His attitude, judged physically, was statuesque in its denial of the laws of movement, but beneath the unpolished surface of the statue terrific things were happening, and he was enduring the whole gamut of vivid and ghastly experience.

Now the door was being opened by a mad old man, and the mad old man had a carving knife. 'Come in!' said the mad old man.

'Wot's that for?' asked Ben, his eyes glued to the knife.

'For you, darling,' answered the mad old man. And he stuck the knife into Ben's chest, and Ben died with a swish like a pricked balloon, and while he was wondering which way he was going the old man beckoned to an Indian, and they pulled his wishbone . . .

Now the door was being opened by an enormous policeman. The policeman seized him and handcuffed him and hissed, 'Come and be hanged!' And he went and was hanged . . .

Now the door was being opened by a three-headed giant. That, of course, was simply ridiculous, but then, you may have gathered by now, Ben was simply ridiculous. Otherwise would he still have been in Jowle Street, seeking entrance through its most forbidding portal? The three-headed giant gave a roar and ate him up three times, once with each head. Ben listened to his bones crackling . . .

Now it was the man he had murdered who opened the door. Why not? This man had already arisen from one death. Why should he not get up after another? Anyhow, here he was, with wounds all over him, opening the door to Ben. And Ben murdered him again. And he bounced up again. Ben killed him seventeen times and then gave up with a sob . . .

And now the door was beginning to open slowly all by itself. Slowly—very slowly. And no one was behind it. Only black, yawning space. 'Gawd—it's really 'appenin' this time!' gasped Ben. He closed his eyes and rushed into the space, and banged his head against the door. It hadn't been really happening. The door was still closed.

But something else was really happening. As though in response to the thud of Ben's head—for the contact of his head with the wood of the door had also really happened—a little shutter was being cautiously raised, and an eye was appearing at an aperture. Ben stared back at the eye balefully. Thus bulls have stared, angry and impotent, at the scurvy tricks of matadors.

''Oo's there?' asked the owner of the eye.

Ben did not answer. For one reason, he was still speechless from his bump. For another, Fate chose to play a card—and Fate had decided, perhaps while Adam was courting Eve, that Ben should one day enter No. 26 Jowle Street. The card Fate played was held, appropriately, in Ben's own hand. It was the little red and green button. The hand that held it was raised in the abortive attempt to prevent, by pressure, the birth of a bump, and it so happened that the button was revealed at the same time between two of the fingers. Then, swiftly and astonishingly, the door did actually open.

Ted Flitt, who opened the door, had been scarcely less agitated than the person he opened the door to. Events were getting beyond him, and although his was a minor part—saving in one particular, shortly to be revealed—he was weighed down by his responsibilities and agitated as to his capacity to carry them out. He had seen his betters 'put through it'. He had been 'put through it' himself. There were indeed so many things he had been told he must do, and so many he had been told he mustn't do, that confusion reigned in his mind; and, when confronted with the need for a quick decision, he could not always remember which was which. Wherefore Ted Flitt had returned to first principles when he had seen the red and green badge through the slit, and, throwing over subtleties, had opened the front door in obedience to the accepted sign.

Ben, this time, did not rush through. 'Let's get this straight,' he thought to himself. 'Is it, or ain't it?'

You can't be sure of anything immediately after a bump. But, of course, the stars and the comets and the lights and the pits keep running round and round in a circle, like, whereas this present blackness before him was stationary. He tested it by putting his finger through it. The finger pierced nothingness. 'It ain't,' he decided. 'It *is*!'

And, suddenly confronted with this stupendous fact, for Reality *is* stupendous just after you have mislaid it, he lost his head and shot in with the speed of a cannon ball.

Then another stupendous fact confronted him. Stupendous in character, if not in size. He found himself gripping the throat of, surely, himself!

''Strewth!' he thought. 'I'm committin' suicide!' For an instant he really believed he was. He'd once heard a spiritualist say that, just before you died, you sometimes bulged out of yourself and looked back. The next instant, however, he decided that he couldn't be. You cannot commit suicide without getting hurt, and he didn't feel hurt. Not around his throat, at least, and his astonishment had suspended all physical sensations higher up.

'Yus, but if it ain't me,' came his next thought, 'why don't 'e squeak?'

The reason for this was quite simple. When a certain tightness exists around your throat, you can't squeak.

Then other thoughts rushed helter-skelter into Ben's mind, while he still held on to the throat. He held on to the throat because he realised that, in some queer manner, he had gained a physical advantage over whoever this fellow was, and he couldn't afford to throw the advantage away. He had to retain it while the thoughts raced through him.

This was one thought. The fellow he was holding was, if not himself, like himself. This was another thought. The fellow was terrified. 'Lummy, 'e's frightender than me!' reflected Ben. 'Ain't we a cupple?' And, others: ''Ow long are we goin' ter stand like this?' 'Wot 'appens if some'un comes dahn them stairs?' ''Ow much more 'ave yer got ter press ter mike a chap die?' 'Is 'e goin' ter be any good ter me dead?'

And then, suddenly, Ben's mind stumbled into a more practical channel of thought. He realised that, dead, this fellow would be quite useless to him, whereas alive he might prove invaluable. For here, at last, was something weaker than himself. Something more pliable, more contemptible! Something he could *use*! He saw himself amazingly as a killer, with a killer's power. The Past and the Present shouted in his favour. And through the shouting, gradually increasing in volume, came another thought, a thought without which all else was insignificant: Where is she? Where is she? *Where is she?* . . .

He heard himself hissing the question. He, Ben, hissing! 'Quick, yer measly devil! *Where is she?*'

The measly devil tried to gesticulate.

'Yer dead if yer don't answer!'

The measly devil tried to.

'Wot—yer *won't?*'

Now the measly devil managed to waggle a portion of anatomy towards a passage in the rear. It was enough for Ben. In a trice they were both speeding along the passage, for which evolution Ben altered his grip to the back of his guide's neck. At the end of the passage they halted.

'Go hon!' ordered Ben.

''Ow can I?' almost sobbed Ted Flitt.

Perhaps after all he couldn't! Ben considered the point. The passage twisted downwards, and it is difficult to twist down a passage unless your neck is entirely your own. On the other hand, the sudden emotion of finding that your neck has been given back to you may endanger the neck of the donor. No, Ted Flitt's neck could not be given back to him unless some other equally vital portion of anatomy were yielded in exchange.

So Ben studied Flitt for another portion of anatomy that would permit progress without power. And, all at once, his eyes came to rest on a portion of hip.

''Allo!' thought Ben. 'Wot a mug!'

Yes, he was a mug! He ought to have noticed that significant bulge at Flitt's hip before. And as he noticed it now he was almost too late, for Flitt gave a sudden twirl and swung one of his arms downwards. Ben was just too quick for him. 'No, yer don't!' he muttered. And, reaching the hip an instant before its rightful owner, he whipped out the ill-concealed revolver.

'Now I gotcha proper!' barked Ben, digging the revolver into Flitt's back. 'Quick march, or yer a gorner!'

Then Ted Flitt gave up. With a whimper he obeyed, and began leading his captor down the twisting passage towards the basement.

'No tricks!' said Ben.

''Oo's playin' tricks!' answered Flitt.

'You ain't,' Ben told him.

Then he told him something else.

'Listen, yer blinkin' termarter pip,' he said, 'and that's puttin' yer too big! If I ain't' seein' that gal in less'n twenty ticks, yer goin' ter 'ave a 'ole in you wot a train could go through, see?'

251

Flitt saw. A tick has never been precisely measured, but it is certain that fewer than twenty elapsed between Ben's threat and their arrival at a door. The door was in a dark alcove. Terrified and flustered, Flitt brought a large key from his pocket and unlocked the door. A black, unlit chamber lay beyond.

'Git a light!' ordered Ben.

Conscious of an increased pressure in his back, Flitt fumbled with a box of matches, and struck a match. As the little flame spurted, the cellar grew into being.

'Candle or somethink,' said Ben curtly.

A candle was lit. It stood on one of two wooden chairs that formed the entire furnishing of the cellar. On the other chair, bound and gagged, was Nadine.

Joy and anger combined tumultuously within Ben's soul and gave him a sensation of sickness. For a moment his authority wavered, and Flitt leapt round from the candle.

'Git on the grahnd!' roared Ben, ducking just in time. 'Or yer marked fer six foot below it.'

Once more the revolver covered Flitt, but this time it was his misshapen nose that came into the range of further accident. He flopped to the ground like a blancmange yielding to a heat wave, and lay there flat. Ben ran to the girl.

'Gawd, wot 'ave they done ter yer, miss?' he mumbled, and as he addressed her he found himself fighting weakness again. The sight of her helplessness and her incongruous beauty—for what had beauty to do with this dank, candle-lit cellar?—invaded his conquering spirit and made him feel all weak like.

But he wasn't going to risk being caught any more. While he ungagged and unbound her, he kept one eye ever ready for the figure on the ground, and at the slightest movement he swung round to it with a picturesque epithet. By the time the girl was free, 'tomato pip' had become a compliment.

Nadine did not speak during the unbinding. When her hands were free she helped. Possibly her own heart was a little unsteady, too. But when the rope slipped finally from her, she stood for an instant looking at Ben, and he passed through another of those rare moments that humble one and give one back one's tottering belief. Surely if Creation could evolve such a look as this, there must be something good in it?

There was no time for prolongment of the moment. Every second was vital.

'Quick, miss!' muttered Ben. 'We gotter git out of 'ere!'

She hesitated.

'No time ter lose, miss,' he urged.

'The man—is he safe?' she whispered.

'You fust, 'im arter,' muttered Ben.

Then he too hesitated. A door had closed softly in the hall above.

If some archaeologist of the future discovers Ben's brains and regards them as typical of our time, it is not likely that we shall stand very high in history, yet there are moments when we all surpass ourselves, and Ben surpassed himself now. Lurching towards the sprawled-out Flitt, he whispered fiercely in his ear:

'Git hup and take orf yer coat.'

Flitt's ear was used to ferocity, but he had never heard anything so definitely ferocious as this before. He leapt up as though an explosion had just occurred beneath him, and his coat was off in a trice. Passing his revolver to Nadine, Ben whipped off his own coat. Then, during a surprisingly few seconds for what they contained, an exchange of certain clothing was made, and the episode concluded with the binding and gagging of the unhappy ex-gaoler.

'I'll bet this is the on'y time on Gawd's earth,' was Ben's fiercely whispered parting shot, as he prepared to lock the cellar door, 'that anybody was glad ter 'ave a fice like your'n!'

The key clicked in the lock. As it did so, a shadow passed into the sphere of dim light at the turn of the basement stairs, and materialised into the Indian.

31

Outside the Cellar Door

The intelligence that had inspired Ben to change clothing with Ted Flitt ceased to exist at the sight of Mahdi. Of all things that had terrified Ben during the past hours it was the Indian who had terrified him most, and the Oriental's appearance now on the basement stairs utterly extinguished the sailor's brain. But fortunately a precisely opposite effect was produced on Nadine. On her the Indian acted as a sudden stimulant, whipping her finally out of her numbness and supplying her with the wit and vitality to carry Ben's intelligence on. Thus, she answered Mahdi's dawning question before it was asked.

'Yes, I'm beaten, Mahdi,' she murmured. 'My gaoler was cleverer than I took him to be.'

'So?' said Mahdi. 'Then how do you come to be outside the cellar?'

'I'd already got outside the cellar in my attempt to escape.'

'I see.' Mahdi's voice was thoughtful, and his eyes now turned towards Ben, who luckily bathed in shadows. 'But I might also ask how the clever gaoler permitted your attempt to escape?'

Again Nadine stepped into the breach. She was giving Ben time to recover.

'There may have been someone who nearly proved even cleverer than the gaoler,' she exclaimed.

Something in her tone, or a quick thought inspired by her words, caused the Indian to bring his eyes swiftly back to the girl's face. Ben, struggling hard to find his lost brain, felt as though a scorching heat had been blessedly removed from his forehead.

'You refer to a tramp?' inquired Mahdi.

Nadine shrugged her shoulders. 'Perhaps,' she said.

'Where is he?' demanded Mahdi.

And then Ben found his brain. It was half-way to the moon. A moment later and it would have been all the way to the moon, and Ben would have followed it, but he was just in time to catch hold of it with one hand, and to jerk the other hand towards the cellar door. Mentally speaking, Ben was in several pieces and several places.

The Indian looked at the hand that was jerking towards the cellar door. Then he looked at the cellar door.

'In there, Mr Flitt?'

Ben nodded. He had been speechless through terror before. Now he was speechless through triumph. He was duping the Indian! Actually duping him . . .

Mahdi moved a step forward. Then he paused, and once more Ben felt his forehead scorching and his brain moving moonwards.

'What will the clever gaoler do if his prisoner makes a dash?' he inquired.

For a peripatetic brain Ben's was not doing so badly. From a very long way off it directed Ben to produce his pistol and to point it towards the girl's breast. And then it asked him, suddenly close, why he had not produced the pistol before, why he had concealed it behind his back, and why he was not now pointing it at the Indian instead of the girl. A quick swing round—bing!—pop him off! . . . Yes, why not? Quick swing round—bing!—pop him off! And then a bunk up the stairs, and across to the front door . . . What was the order? . . . Swing round—bing—pop—bunk . . . Swing round—bing—

The Indian was moving forward again. 'Where's 'e goin'?' thought Ben. He couldn't make sure whether the Indian were moving towards him or the cellar, or exactly midway between the two. It must be the cellar! He had called him 'Mr Flitt'! Well, that proved it, didn't it? Swing round—bing—pop—no! 'Arf a mo'! Wait till he got by! That was the ticket. Then, when he had got by, and was at the cellar door, with his back turned . . . swing round bing—pop—bunk . . .

It is probable that if some statistician or surveyor of foreheads could have measured the perspiration on Ben's brow at this moment, the density would have constituted a record; although the record was destined to be broken twice more on the same spot before Ben's brow returned to its normal texture. As the Indian drew nearer and nearer, the brain behind the brow separated and became a thousand brains, each shrieking, each thinking differently, each swimming about impotently and blubbing for its mother. The Indian grew large and small, as seemed his habit at poignant moments. The whites of his eyes revolved like Catherine wheels. Time revolved with him. Was it yesterday, or today, or tomorrow? And through it all, like the throb of an engine or the beat of a pulse, ran the ceaseless, meaningless rhythm: round— bing—pop—bunk . . . round—bing—pop—bunk . . .

Then reality came hurtling back. The Indian had passed and was at the cellar door. At the cellar door! Beyond Ben! With his back to Ben! At the mercy of Ben!

With violently trembling fingers—'yer see, yer ain't quite yerself,' Ben reflected in one of those timeless instants not recorded by clocks—the dazed fellow began to swing the pistol round towards the Indian. The Indian turned the cellar key. The pistol continued to swing round. The Indian began to push the cellar door open. The pistol swung round more. It was a slow-motion swing. Now the muzzle pointed directly towards the Indian's back . . .

And then a hand closed over Ben's. If it had closed over suddenly, Mahdi would have been dead the next instant; and Ben would have qualified at the same moment for a lunatic asylum. But it closed over quietly, softly, yet with a strange firmness. Something cool, something infinitely steadying, pervaded Ben. For the first time he experienced the full executive quality of the girl he was humbly trying to serve . . .

Now the cellar door was wide open, and Mahdi was peering in. A bound and gagged figure peered back at him from a dark corner. And, all at once, Ben realised— or thought he realised—the reason why he had not been allowed to shoot Mahdi in the back. When Mahdi stepped into the cellar to investigate that bound and gagged figure more closely, it would be simple to spring forward and close the door behind him. And to relock it! And to solve the Indian problem!

But Indian problems are not so easily solved. For some reason of his own, Mahdi did not step into the cellar to make a closer investigation of the bound and gagged figure. Satisfied, with what he saw, he suddenly stepped back into the passage and relocked the door himself. Then he put the key into his pocket, and turned once more towards the two who were watching him.

To Ben's relief, and also amazement, he found that his pistol was now pointing towards Nadine again. He did not remember returning it to this position . . .

'Listen, Mr Flitt,' came the Indian's quiet voice. It would have sounded pleasanter if the 'Mr' had been omitted. The 'Mr' sounded contemptuous and ironical—but then, a fellow like Mahdi would surely feel contempt for a fellow like Flitt? 'You are, like everybody else in this house, a fool, but you have performed one service which has been fruitlessly attempted by all the other fools. You have caught the biggest fool of all.'

Ben's brain began to spin again. He felt his identity slipping from him. He couldn't be quite sure whether he was in the cellar or outside it. Meanwhile, the voice of Mahdi went on:

'Yes, the man locked in there is the most perfect fool I have ever met. He has no brains. He has no strength. He has no motive. Yet—like your fool at Poker—he has beaten us at every turn, and might have continued to beat us had he still been at large. Yes, I admit that, Nadine. It is no disgrace. A drunken fellow across a track may derail the millionaire express. A fragment of grit may upset a solar system. Without any qualification—without any purpose'—he paused for a moment, in subconscious response to a quickly suppressed question in Nadine's eyes—'this fellow has hung on like a barnacle! He has even killed a man, Nadine. Killed a man with four times his strength—who was sent to kill *him*.'

Nadine stood very still. Ben lowered his eyes. He couldn't keep up with this.

'Without a purpose,' repeated the Indian, suddenly musing. 'Without a purpose? The instinct of self-preservation is strong, and that, of course, is a purpose of sorts. But self-preservation alone should have dismissed him the first time I saw him . . . Yes—I wonder!'

His eyes searched Nadine's ruthlessly. Without removing them, he now addressed Ben again. He had an uncanny trick of pitching his voice in any direction he desired.

'This lady, Mr Flitt, has not been without a purpose. She, too, has menaced us. But before I have done with her I shall find out what her purpose is. Yes, Mr Flitt, I shall make that my special object. And, since the cellar now has a new occupant, I shall take her to another prison, where the voice of one who controls us all, Mr Flitt, will question her in his own particular fashion.'

'One who controls you all?' asked Nadine quietly. 'Who is that?'

'You will learn. You shall be dealt with by no less, Nadine! I hope you will see it as an honour when I convey you from here into his presence.'

'You're going to take me to him, then?'

'I have said so.'

'When?'

'There will be no delay. Be sure, the meeting is mutually required. Meanwhile, Mr Flitt, you will continue to carry out instructions here, to ensure that *another* required meeting will also take place—'

'What other meeting?' demanded Nadine.

'Why should I tell you?' smiled Mahdi.

'Well, I don't want to be told,' retorted Nadine. 'It is a proof, after all, that you still fear me, Mahdi.'

The smile on Mahdi's face remained.

'A simple trick to draw, the information,' he said. 'But the child shall be satisfied. For perhaps she must be *convinced* that she is no longer to be feared? Only as a loved one could she bite. Oh, yes, Nadine, I too have been a fool. But the truly wise admit their folly—and rend the causes of it . . . What is the matter, Mr Flitt? Do not alter the position of your revolver. Pray keep her covered! . . .'

'And is all this chatter of yours *another* simple trick,' asked Nadine, a touch of deliberate scorn in her voice, 'to divert us from the information you were going to give me?'

'No. You shall have the information. It will not help you. A long box will leave this house tonight. The long box will be conveyed to the place where, also, I am going to convey you, Nadine, and the long box will contain the person with whom this further meeting is desired. You may yourself meet this person,' he added reflectively. 'You may be able to help in the explaining of him—should he unwisely refuse to do the explaining himself.' He paused. 'And now, I think, it is time for us to go. Unless, perhaps, you want any more information?'

'You might tell me one more thing,' said Nadine, 'if you're in the mood.'

'Ask quickly!'

'What is going to happen to—the biggest fool of all?'

She glanced towards the cellar. She was asking the question for Ben's guidance, and he hung on to the answer.

'The biggest fool of all,' repeated Mahdi, softly. 'So—you think of him? Well, Nadine, so do I. Believe me, he shall not be forgotten. When the biggest fool and I next meet, he will learn the price of folly!'

He held up his hand for silence. The hall above had become alive with faint sounds. Footsteps crossing the floor—low, uneasy voices—the front door closing . . .

'And there go two more fools,' murmured Mahdi grimly.

'Yes and what will *their* folly cost?' inquired Nadine, with contempt.

'Shall we say fifteen thousand pounds—to start with?' replied Mahdi. 'You see how little I fear her, Mr Flitt. I tell, her everything! Now, come!'

He seized her wrist with sudden ferocity, but his eyes still smiled. The movement, coupled with its cynical denial of significance, chilled Ben. Beneath his smooth exterior, the man was a savage, a bursting volcano! And a single bullet could extinguish him!

Again, Ben's fingers itched almost uncontrollably. Why did he hesitate? Why?

And then, in a sudden illuminating flash, he knew. The girl was willing the reason into him. If Mahdi were dead, how would she learn the whereabouts of the one who controlled them all?

32

The Conversation in the Hall

So Ben did not shoot Mahdi. Instead, he stood silent and inactive while Mahdi produced a long gleaming knife and invited Nadine to ascend the stairs ahead of him. He watched Nadine obey. He watched Mahdi slip behind her as she did so, the point of his long knife within an inch of her back. He watched till they reached the bend and vanished round it, and he was alone again.

Then revulsion set in. Revulsion and panic. No longer assisted by the steadying influence of Nadine, he visualised her walking to her death, and he lost his head. For some reason, she wanted to meet 'the one who controlled them all'. But why should she be allowed to endanger herself further? With a gulp Ben rushed to the stairs and began clambering up. But just before the bend he stopped short. Mr Clitheroe's voice arrested him.

'Hallo—what's all this?' barked the old man's voice.

The Indian's responded unemotionally: 'I am taking away one of our prisoners.'

'Where to?'

'That does not concern you.'

'By God, haven't you ever heard of the word co-operation?'

'I prefer the word obedience. What of our other prisoner? You have him safe?'

'Of course!' snapped Clitheroe. 'You'll die worrying!'

'Where is he?'

'Suppose I answered that it didn't concern you?'

'I would repeat the question.'

'Before this girl?'

There was a short silence before Mahdi's voice sounded again. It was as cold as steel. It held Ben rigid on the stairs.

'The girl is finished. She goes with me. Now answer!'

'Well, well, have it your own way!' muttered Clitheroe. 'The other prisoner is safely tucked away into his little box. The little box is in the back room on the second floor. The door of the back room on the second floor is locked. And the key is on the outside. Does that satisfy you?'

'And the others?'

'The others? Still before the girl?'

'Have I not told you she is finished? My questions supply the proof of it. And must I ask each question twice, Mr Clitheroe?'

'I am glad I at least have the power to annoy you, Mr Mahdi! That is something! Maybe one of these days I shall annoy you even more. Meanwhile, you wish to know of the others. I will tell you. The two golden geese have just left. They have been efficiently frightened. The male goose will return this evening with the golden egg. And this evening, also, the little box, with its occupant, will be called for by the van which is to deliver it to—I suppose I am not even to be told that?'

'If I told you that, I would be telling you where I am taking my present prisoner—'

'Then they are to meet, these two?'

'An illuminating deduction, Mr Clitheroe!'

'But then I *am* illuminating, Mr Mahdi, and only you fail to perceive my light. Well, well, the meeting should be interesting, but if I am not to be present I must content myself by imagining it. And perhaps, after all, that is best. If you are going to be unkind to the young lady whose back you are pricking with your knife—'

'And whose heart you are covering, Mr Clitheroe, with your revolver?'

'Precisely! For a young lady whom we neither of us fear any longer we are taking unusual precautions, eh?' The old man's voice rose sarcastically as he made his point. 'As I said, Mr Mahdi, if you are going to be unkind to her and to our other prisoner, I am perfectly content to remain in ignorance of the fact. At the same time, if an incompetent individual like myself may offer advice, I advise you to be careful. The young lady, I can vouch from my own little encounter with her, is intelligent, and although she is saying nothing at this moment I imagine she is thinking a great deal. The gentleman in the box upstairs also is no fool, and may prove this to you when he comes round . . . but I see you are not interested in my little caution?'

'Have you anything more to tell me?'

'Oh, yes. I will be quite complete. Jessica, my alleged daughter, has asked to be released from any further part in our little business. I have refused to grant the release, and have told her she must remain in the house until the little business is over. She will obey me—'

'As you obey me.'

'And as *you* obey one greater than either of us, eh? I think only two more remain to speak of. Our little flea, Flitt, has been keeping guard on the cellar, and I assume he is still below. And Wharton—well, I don't know where Wharton is, because I haven't seen him yet since he returned from No. 29, though I did hear him ring while I was upstairs, and wondered why the devil he didn't use his key.'

'Wharton did not ring, Mr Clitheroe,' answered Mahdi. 'The man who rang was the man Wharton had been sent to kill.'

'What?' cried Clitheroe.

'The man who, in fact, killed Wharton.'

'*Killed Wharton!*'

'I have said so. Are you still satisfied, Mr Clitheroe, with the efficiency of yourself and your staff? And of your qualifications to give advice?'

Mr Clitheroe had no reply. Mahdi continued, in a toneless drone:

'When I crossed the road to find out why Wharton did not return, I found that he was incapable of returning. He was lying dead! And since it would not have helped us had he been found lying dead by anyone else I conveyed him to the cupboard under the stairs and started him on his journey to the canal. The wisdom of this was very soon proved. While I was in the cupboard, three people arrived, and it was only by closing the cupboard door that I escaped detection. Two of the people went upstairs. A policeman and our tramp. Meanwhile, I slipped out quickly, giving a shock, I fear, to the third person, who was drunk and who had stayed behind on the bottom step. He ran the moment he saw me, and I chased him to make sure that he would keep running. Then the policeman joined in the chase, and I was free to return and deal with the tramp.'

'You mean—the fellow had got in?' gasped Mr Clitheroe.

'I have already told you that,' responded Mahdi. 'How he got in I do not know, and it no longer matters. Flitt has atoned for whatever error he made, and he had control of the situation when I arrived. You see,' added the Indian sardonically, 'when credit is due, I award it.'

'Yes, yes—we all know how lavish you are with your praise,' muttered Mr Clitheroe, fighting back. 'So Flitt beat the tramp, eh? Well, that certainly earns him promotion—'

And then Nadine made her one and only remark during the conversation.

'Will he be promoted from the cellar to the second floor?' she asked.

Her voice was scornful and significant. Those who were with her heard the scorn, while the man who was below heard the significance. And heard, also, the sudden pounding of his heart. The second floor! The next job! That was what she was telling him! The second floor, where lay the long, wooden box . . .

'Yes but where *is* the tramp?' cried Mr Clitheroe, all at once.

'The tramp is in the cellar, bound and gagged,' answered Mahdi's voice. 'The key of the cellar is in my pocket. Do not worry about him. When I return I shall deal with the tramp. But now, it is time to go.'

The voices ceased. The sounds of movement drifted away towards the front door. Nadine, her obedience enforced by knife and bullet, was being conveyed out of the house. Within, a bewildered sailor remained to carry on her work.

What work? The sailor did not know. But he knew that he had been asked to attend to the trouble on the second floor—that the request had been wrapped up in the girl's one observation just before the conversation in the hall had concluded. He knew that she had divined his ears would be listening. And he knew that his main object was less to solve the mystery of this forbidding house and deal out justice to its occupants than to obey without question the will that sang with such strange music in his heart.

So, once again, he sat upon his impulse to rush into the hall and use his weapon. Instead, he crept up. Noiselessly, till his straining eyes beheld the backs of those who had just ceased talking there . . .

Three backs. At the open front door. The furthest two were Nadine's and Mahdi's.

Mahdi had hold of Nadine's arm, and no passer-by would have guessed that the grip, friendly enough in appearance, bore any threat. A threat, for instance, of swift injection. Behind them stood Mr Clitheroe watching their departure. He stepped out on to the porch, and then stood still again. Now was Ben's chance!

For although Ben might fool Mahdi in the darkness of the basement, he knew very well that he would have no chance of fooling Mr Clitheroe. Mr Clitheroe would interview him in a stronger light. He would force him to use his voice. Moreover, Ben divined that whereas Ted Flitt was a familiar figure to Mr Clitheroe, he may have been merely a passing one to Mahdi. Yes, clearly an encounter with Mr Clitheroe was to be avoided!

Wherefore Ben slithered with all the silence he could command round the top of the stairs, his eyes fastened meanwhile on the back of the old man who was standing a few inches beyond the doorway. Suddenly the old man raised his head. Ben found himself behind a coat suspended

268

from a hat rack. He did not remember getting there. He just found himself there. In sudden emergency Ben did not wait to think. He thought afterwards, and subsequent thought frequently failed to enlighten him.

He stayed behind the coat for nineteen years. Then he peeped round a sleeve. The old man was still standing in the doorway. He was still looking out into the street. There was no sign of any other back. Ben waited nineteen more years, then slithered away from the coat and dived silently towards the stairs.

If the staircase had been an ascending escalator, he could not have been up the first flight more quickly. He had an amazingly effective method of putting his head down and pushing with his legs. But the second flight was not so favourable to the process. As his head was still down, for he did not even come up to breathe, he failed to notice a soft wall until his head was boring into it. A soft wall that yielded a little at first, and then became rigid and indignant.

Ben raised his head to look at the wall. It was a woman's skirt. He raised his head higher. The woman who was wearing the skirt, in her turn, looked at the missile. It was the woman who had once offered Ben a cigarette which he had unwisely smoked.

Ben did not know from her expression whether she recognised him or not. All he could read in it, during his brief and hurried scrutiny, was the emotion of a woman who has been barged into. And, being filled with equal emotion, he did not stay to see any transition. Praying for vocal ability, as Samson prayed for strength, he twisted his throat into Flitt-like channels and gurgled:

'Sorry, miss!'

Then, he curved round the soft wall, lowered his head again, and completed his journey to the second floor.

Arrived there, he stopped. The stoppage was imposed upon him. A wooden door cannot be barged into as carelessly as a woman's skirt. Moreover, this wooden door was locked. But the key was on the outside, so the solution was at hand.

He caught hold of the key. Before turning it, he listened. Was the woman coming up after him? He heard nothing. He turned the key, opened the door, and dived into the room.

And, as he closed the door, he heard the key being turned again behind him.

33

The Long Wooden Box

Ben had been in some unenviable positions during the past twenty-four hours. He had been bullied. He had been shot at. He had been drugged. He had been abducted. He had been murderously attacked. He had been dropped down a hole in a cupboard. He had given himself up for murder. But numbness had not come to him. He could still feel the fingers of horror when they pressed him in any new part. And they pressed him in a new part now as he heard himself being locked in a dim back room with a long wooden box for company.

His first impulse was to fly to the window. He did not act upon the impulse for the reason that his legs refused to take him there. Instead, they gave way suddenly, and he sat down upon the box. Then movement returned, and he sprang half across the room.

The box was covered by a black cloth. A deliberate attempt, apparently, to introduce a funereal atmosphere. But at one end, where the cloth had been displaced by Ben's bound, white wood peeped out, and the funereal atmosphere was a trifle less apparent. 'Go on—you ain't *reely* a corfin!' thought Ben. The thought brought little consolation.

He counted a hundred and thirty-two, and then took a step towards the thing that was not really a coffin. Then he counted two hundred and six, and took another step. Then he counted one, dived forward, seized the black cloth, pulled it, and closed his eyes tight.

While his eyes were closed the lid of the box flew up and a skeleton jumped out and embraced him. With a gasp he opened his eyes, and the imagined skeleton vanished back into the box. The lid was still closed. Ben himself had vanished to the farthest wall, and he was trying to get through it. The bruise was developing on his forehead.

'I'll tell yer wot it is,' he informed himself seriously. 'Yer frightened.'

Now that he knew, he felt a little better. Apart, that was, from the bruise. The wall had not been kind to that.

'Yus, but 'oo *wouldn't* be frightened?' he went on. 'I don't believe the Prince o' Wales'd like it!'

That made him feel a little better still. He brought himself away from the wall and, with the Prince of Wales, began to return to the box. Because, of course, no matter if the Prince of Wales *didn't* like it, that wouldn't stop him from doing his duty. And Ben had his duty too.

'Why, yer silly idgit, yer *knoo* a box was 'ere,' he rounded on himself. 'That's wotcher come up for, ain't it?'

Yes, but he hadn't known that the door was going to be locked against him. He hadn't known that, while he was investigating the box, the door would be liable to fly open at any moment not of his own choosing and that the enemy might come pouring in on him! He visualised a dozen people pouring in upon him. Then, with a momentary return to logic, he realised that there could only be two. Flitt was locked in the cellar. Mahdi had gone—with the cellar key. The big chap was dead. And that only left the old man and the snaky woman.

'Yus, and, lummy, I got this!' thought Ben suddenly. The revolver! Clutched all this while, though forgotten, in his hand.

Of course, that explained why the enemy *didn't* come pouring in upon him. They knew they would be received with a bullet. So they preferred to wait until reinforcements arrived . . .

'Well, I gotter git *busy!*' muttered Ben. ''Cos when that blinkin' Injun does come back, 'e'll unlock the cellar door, and then there'll be four on 'em!'

Therefore, while instinct kept him away from the wooden box, simple logic drew him towards it again. He must open it and deal with the contents while there was yet time.

The lid of the box was quite easy to manipulate. It was not nailed or screwed down; it was secured at the front by a simple hook. Ben would have been better pleased if the hook had been less simple, for then the unpleasant shock he was anticipating would have been delayed, but the hook responded immediately to manipulation, and the next moment Ben discovered himself raising the lid.

As he did so he prayed for emptiness. The prayer was not answered. A figure lay stretched out in the box. He could just see it dimly.

Ben stared at the figure with glassy eyes. Then, as he recalled the last time he had seen the man—erect and virile, and genial despite his challenge—his eyes lost their glassiness and a new look entered into them. He forgot, for a few moments, his own troubles in the contemplation of another's.

'Gawd! Wot a crew!' he muttered.

He turned towards the door, his fingers tightening on his revolver, then turned back to the box and its occupant.

'So *this* is why yer didn't come aht of the 'ouse again, old cock!' he murmured. 'Wunner 'ow long yer've bin 'ere like this?'

Ben hated people who didn't move. They made him remember that one day he wouldn't move. But he had a job on, and he'd got to go through with it, so he poked his head sideways into the box and put an ear to the occupant's chest.

'Good!' he said, as he brought his head out again. ''E ain't a deader!'

Then what was the trouble?

'Suffercashun?'

But there were holes in the box. Both the top and the sides had been perforated. Besides, if you suffocated, you became a deader, didn't you?

'Dope! That's wot it is! Dope!' concluded Ben. 'Like wot they did ter me!'

Well, you came out of dope. That's right! Corse you did! Hadn't Ben? So, if Ben waited, *this* chap would come out of it too.

Wherefore, Ben waited. There was nothing else to do. He waited with one eye on the box and one eye on the door. The minutes slipped by.

'Ain't *anythin'* goin' ter 'appen?' he wondered presently.

A good deal was going to happen, but not just yet. He went on waiting. His bruise grew. His forehead throbbed. He began to feel faint.

'Corse, food don't matter,' he told himself.

Then, all at once, he stiffened. He had heard a soft movement outside the door.

The movement was not repeated. Had the person gone away, or was the person still there? Or hadn't it been a person? Or had the person been there all the while? Ben crept to the door and listened. The silence became horrible. He raised his hand to bang on the door and break the silence, but desisted. If somebody was outside it would be satisfactory to make them jump, but if nobody was outside it would bring somebody who might make Ben jump! Better let sleeping silences lie.

But what about the window? For the first time Ben's mind concentrated on that. He crossed to the window, and peered out. Little balcony. Big drop. He came away from the window.

Then followed another period of waiting. The minutes became hours. Ben fought against the forces that were weakening him. The forces of tension and terror and fatigue. Also of an injured forehead. He tried to think of something useful. He couldn't think of anything. Yes—one thing. A juicy chop, swimming in gravy.

'Wot 'appens,' he wondered, 'when yer git so 'ungry yer can't think any more?'

He believed he would soon know. Perhaps, then, you couldn't even think of chops? This one was slipping away from him. Floating off in the gravy. For now the gravy had become a river. A red river. Oi! None o' that! Good—here was the chop back again, all rich with brown outside. Brown! *Brown!* Not red, d'you hear? . . . Why didn't the chap wake up? Nice and brown. He ought to be out of it by now. And tender, so that when you put your teeth into it . . . Just dope, that's all. Corse, he wasn't dead. And when he came out of the dope, *he'd* know what to do . . . Yus, with some nice Brussel-sprouts and pertaters, and a chunk of cheese to end up with . . . cheese . . . something about cheese . . . cheese in a parcel . . .

Hallo! What was happening? . . . It was all dark . . . Ben sat up with a jerk, and, as he did so, something sat up beside him. A sort of solidified shadow of himself. He tried to shriek, found he couldn't, and clasped the solidified shadow. For an instant two weak men tried to hurt each other. Then one of them slid back into the box from which he had arisen, while the other tried hard not to sob.

''Ere—steady, lad!' thought Ben. ''Old on! 'E's comin' to.'

But why was it so dark? And why did he feel so terribly weak? And why was everything wobbling? Perhaps *he* had been doped, also—with fatigue! Perhaps this was what happened when you went on getting hungry till you couldn't any more.

He bent over the box. He felt that, whatever he had to do—and he had a muddled sensation that he had a lot to do—must be done quickly. Otherwise he would wobble off again. Meaning himself, Ben—not t'other chap. ''E's comin' and I'm goin'!' he explained to himself. The urgent question was whether they could meet in transit.

'Oi!' whispered Ben, into the depths.

'Who are you?' answered the depths.

'Chap yer spoke ter—'ouse across the road,' said Ben. 'I'm on yer side.'

'Is that why you went for me?' came up to him next.

'That don't matter,' replied Ben, trying to save time. 'Gal's gotter be saved.'

'Girl? How? Go on!'

276

Ben thought hard. How did one go on? He felt he had omitted something. Something important. What was it? Oh, of course!

''Ow are yer?' asked Ben.

'Groggy—but game!'

'Same 'ere—on'y more groggy.' Lummy, he *did* feel groggy! 'Fack is, mate, I'm done. Feel orl light like. Dunno wot I'm sayin' much. Oi! You still there?'

'Sure!' came the reassuring response.

'Comin' to, like?'

'Rather. I've been coming to for an hour—only I didn't want you to know.'

'Why not?'

'How did I know who you were? But go on! About this girl?'

''Oo?'

'Stick to it!'

'Yus, but somethin's bobbin' abart. I feel queer, that's a fack. Don't serpose yer got a chop on yer? I got a 'ole in me the size o' the Crystil Pallis . . . 'Ere—quick! I'm goin'.' A hand darted forward and steadied him. 'Wot's that? Well, ain't I told yer? We gotter save the gal?'

The occupant of the box was now sitting up again. His own mind was not clear, but it was clearing.

'Yes, yes, we *will* save the girl, never fear!' he whispered in Ben's ear. 'But you must tell me how we've got to set about it.'

Ben listened hard. He nodded. He understood.

'You mean the feller the boy shot,' he mumbled. 'Well, *I* killed 'im. The boy didn't. But that don't matter. That's jest blackmail, that is. Fifteen thahsand. That don't matter.' His eyes were closed, but suddenly he opened them, and stared desperately at the man who still held his arm to steady him. 'Gawd—they've took 'er away. Took 'er away! Doncher 'ear? Took 'er away! And they was goin' ter take *you* away in this 'ere box. Wot yer got ter do is ter git the pleece . . . git the pleece, and then—'

'Yes? And then?'

The voice sounded very far off.

''Oo? Oh . . . foller the box . . . that's it . . . foller the box . . .'

And then it suddenly grew very dark again, and everything in the whole world vanished with the exception of a golden-brown chop dripping with rich gravy and hanging inaccessibly from a star.

34

Into the Box

Presently even the chop vanished, and the darkness became absolute. Hunger, fatigue and a bruise wiped out Ben's Universe. In other Universes the queer business of life ran on, with its strange sense of significance and eternity, but Ben was oblivious to all function and emotion. He neither loved nor hated, rejoiced nor despaired, fulfilled nor desired. Nor was he teased by the faint reflections of these things. He was at peace.

His final peace, however, had not yet dawned. The Fates still wanted him to play with. Into the darkness, at last, came a vague disturbance. The darkness separated, then came together again, then separated again. What was carving it up and destroying its soothing nullity?

It wasn't light. No, the blackness remained black, despite this invasion upon it. Sound? Yes, that was it. Sound. The carving knife was sound . . .

The faintly-functioning form of Ben shifted uneasily. Then, after a pause, shifted again, and cocked an unwilling, faintly functioning ear.

The sound increased. The form of Ben began to function less faintly. Now it was almost sitting up, its two hands gripping the side of the wooden box towards which its head had drooped.

'Oi!' murmured Ben. It was his S.O.S. to his lagging brain.

The sounds continued to increase. They became recognisable. Footsteps. Voices . . . Voices. Footsteps . . .

'They're comin',' he gasped. ''Ere—*do* somethin'!'

Another exhortation to his brain. And the brain responded:

'Wot?'

Then it asked another question:

'Where's the other bloke?'

Now Ben's hand groped down into the box, to discover its emptiness. The other bloke had gone. Where? How? Out of the door? No, that was impossible. The door was locked on the outside. The window then? Yes, the window. The window was open, and the black smudge of the balcony gloomed beyond.

But why had he gone? In a flash that hurt him, Ben remembered. 'Follow the box . . . Follow the box!' Ben had told him to follow the box . . . To go and fetch the police and follow the box . . .

The box! *This* box! This box for which these approaching voices were coming! Yes, and suppose the other bloke had had an accident or something, and wasn't able to follow the box? Come to that, why did he have to follow the box? Ben couldn't remember. Something about . . . Something about . . .

Another flash came to Ben and hurt him more. Why, the girl, of course! This box was going to the place where the girl was! It was the sign-post to her.

The voices were now outside the door. The key was being softly turned.

'Gawd!' gasped Ben, and rolled into the box.

The lid was down before the door opened.

A light flashed for an instant. Ben glimpsed it through the perforations in the wood of his prison. Then came darkness again, and a voice.

'Gone,' said the voice. 'It was expected!'

It was the Indian's voice. It chilled Ben, stuffy though his prison was. It seemed, also, to chill others present.

'Through the window,' went on the voice. 'Your final folly, Mr Clitheroe. You know, of course, what this means?'

'I'll catch him!' came the old man's mutter.

The Indian's smooth drone replied to it.

'You will not catch him, Mr Clitheroe. It is written that you will never catch him. But one day *I* will catch him— yes, that, also, is written. And, meanwhile, he is at large, and is talking to policemen.'

'Yes, while *we* talk here!' cried Mr Clitheroe. 'Quick! Down to the front door, Flitt—'

'Stay where you are, Mr Flitt,' interposed Mahdi, 'and help with this box.'

'But—'

'Silence, incompetent! You have had the man for hours in this room, and you let him go! Are you *still* under the delusion that you have a brain?'

'I tell you, he had a revolver!' snapped the old man nervily. 'Flitt's revolver! Was I to risk my life? Or Jessica here? There were not enough of us to rush him—Flitt has been locked in the cellar until this moment, as you know— all because *you* went off with the key—and who'd have guessed that tramp could have got out of that window? Why, it seems impossible!'

'Still, he *did* get out,' answered Mahdi sternly, 'and at any moment now he will be back here with the police. We are fortunate to have even these few seconds. Do you insist on wasting them? Come! Act!'

'Oh, yes, by all means!' retorted the old man rebelliously. 'We are to help you escape with this damned box—'

'Do you want your damned box to be discovered here?'

'No! But what happens when *we* are discovered here, after you have gone?'

Very coldly came the Indian's response.

'It is because you need to ask that question—because you are not competent to find an answer yourself—that you will *not* be discovered here, Mr Clitheroe. When the police arrive, they will find the house empty.'

'Indeed! And where shall we be?'

'With me. All three of you. In the presence of one who will deal with you.'

'You mean—we're to accompany you?'

'So!'

'But suppose we refuse?' It was the woman's voice this time.

'You will not refuse,' answered Mahdi. 'You know the price you would pay. You will accompany me, and *at once*! And, now—the box!'

The next instant Mahdi's voice sounded again, closer. Ben tried to think of a prayer, and failed.

'Someone has opened it,' said Mahdi. 'The lid is unfastened.'

'Then prove *your* brains, Mahdi,' snapped the old man, 'by fastening it yourself before someone else pops out.'

'Without being sure first that the someone else is inside?'

'Now I'm fer 'eaven!' thought Ben.

But Mr Clitheroe delayed the journey. He dashed to the box and adjusted the hook. A pin point of light darted through one of the perforations and flashed for a moment on a portion of the occupant's coat. Then the pin point of light went out, and Mr Clitheroe reported:

'He's inside all right! Feel the weight of the thing.' He seized an end, lifted it, and dropped it with a thud. 'Satisfied, eh? Or now do *you* want to waste time? Come on, Ted! Let's get to it. We don't want the police to catch sight of the van outside.'

The case was lifted. Rivers of perspiration ran down the face of the huddled man inside it. He thought he had come to the end of ruthless experience. It occurred to him, now, that he had only just begun.

The journey down the stairs and out into the van was a jolting, jostling nightmare. At one moment he appeared to be standing erect in his dark little prison, at another on his head. He struck each side, he was shot into each corner. For the first time in his life he understood the meaning of packing-paper, and would have bartered his soul for it.

But, apart from the noise of his bumping—and that was only loud to him—no sound came from inside the case. If Ben made a sound of agony or of protest, the case might be examined, and if the case were examined he might not be allowed to remain in it. And, if he did not remain in it, he would never be able to find the girl again. 'Yer unsensible, see—unsensible,' he told himself. 'Doncher fergit!' A sharp nail did its best to induce the condition he was feigning, but merely succeeded in rendering the condition more desirable . . .

And now a new sound fell upon the sufferer's ears. The acoustics changed, and the noise of an engine dominated the world outside the wooden box. A final jerk upwards, that nearly broke Ben's neck, a sudden medley of anxious whispers—unpleasantly close—a closing door, and then movement superseded sound. The next stage of Ben's journey had begun.

35

Out of the Box

In darkness, Ben travelled through darkness. In company, he travelled alone. He had no knowledge of time or of direction, and he did not know whether he were passing through silent streets or populated thoroughfares, through roads with houses or lanes with trees. He could not differentiate between bumps and hills or jerks and corners. One mile might have been twenty, or twenty one.

But, although his mind was a useless, broken thing, he hung on to it. He must at least watch over the parts to give them a chance of reassembling. Oblivion—that was what he wanted. He wanted to die. Just where he was. After the next jerk. Quiet like, and no questions asked. But he mustn't die. He mustn't sleep. He mustn't even close his eyes, excepting when he felt nails coming. All the little life that remained in him must be preserved, to fling at the feet of a strange and haunting beauty.

For somewhere within that wooden case, secreted deeply in the crumpled, ridiculous form it contained, was the spark that burns despite all logic and lights the world.

One queer thought kept recurring during the journey. It provided the thinker with an odd imaginative comfort. 'Nice start they'd get,' ran the thought, 'if I was ter suddenly pop up through the lid!' Of course, there was no chance of his popping up through the lid. The wood was solid, and, although he did not know this, the box had now been roped. But it was a nice thing to think about, just the same. Nearly all the really nice things can only be thought about.

Then there was another thought, not quite so soothing. 'If that chap wot wos in 'ere fust 'adn't come rahnd afore they thort 'e would, p'r'aps we'd both be in 'ere!' The verdict, Ben decided, would have been: 'Death by squashing.'

Less soothing still was: 'Wot's goin' ter 'appen when we harrive?'

And then, all at once, they did arrive. The car stopped. It had reached its destination.

Where was the destination? A house? A forest? A barn? Ben wondered as, after a short respite, the uncomfortable business of moving began again, and he felt himself being lifted from the car. 'Well, there's one thing,' he reflected, seeking grains of comfort. 'I'm learnin' a bit abart me funeral!' But he wanted to learn other things, as well, so he listened hard for sounds he could identify.

Plod! Plod! Plod! Them was footsteps. Wishy-wishy-wishy! Whisperin' that was. Crunch! Crunch! Crunch! Gravel. Creak-creak! What was that? Bang! Door closin'. Then the creak must have been the door openin'. Growl! 'Allo! Somebody was cross! Oi—steady! Now they were setting the box down. 'Ere—ease a bit! Wotcher think's inside? Carpets . . .

It was a nasty jolt, that! It made Ben want to cry. The darkness grew darker, and he forgot about things for a bit. For quite a considerable bit. Then he came to with a jolt, tried to sit up, and bumped his head.

Voices sounded above him. He hung on to them. One was Mahdi's. The other was—No! Yes! *The girl's.*

There was no mistaking the girl's voice. It was music amid discord. Or, in Ben's own phraseology, 'like a bit of 'ome,' albeit a home that figured merely in Ben's most daring flights of fancy . . .

'No. I'll tell you nothing, Mahdi,' the girl was saying, 'until I'm face to face with the man you brought me here to see.'

'So!' responded Mahdi's voice. 'Still imperious, though helpless!'

'Yes, Mahdi. You see, although I *am* helpless, you're still afraid of me.'

'That ancient trick!'

'Why not call it by its right name, Mahdi? The truth?'

'The truth? That I am afraid of you?'

'If you are not afraid of me, why have you bound me? Why are you keeping me here? Or—is it, perhaps, your master who is afraid of me?'

A short silence followed. Ben visualised the speakers as clearly as though he were seeing them. The girl, bound, but calm, her eyes unwavering. The Indian, inscrutable, confident, scornful, concealing the strange fires within him. Then all at once the Indian laughed softly. His voice rang cynically through the space above the box.

'Listen, Nadine,' said the voice. 'I will tell you. Perhaps if you were free, I should be afraid of you. I should remember that you have tricked me with your smile, and one who tricks Mahdi is not to be dismissed lightly. But you can do me no harm now. Nor can others who, for a different reason, I might also have feared. The reason, in *their* case, is not skill, but incompetence. They are as helpless as you, and, though unbound, they too are locked in a garage—the garage adjoining this. If the walls were less thick, you might hear, still, the protests of three incompetent pawns.'

'Your master has many pawns, Mahdi?'

'The number of his pawns would surprise you, Nadine. And all are well paid until they cease to serve him. Then they become merely menaces who must be destroyed—together with the master's enemies.' The voice ceased for an instant, then continued, with quiet menace: 'They are to be destroyed *now*—with his enemies. *Do* you understand me, Nadine?'

There was another little silence. Ben's mind groped fruitlessly among his newly acquired knowledge. He was in a garage with Nadine and Mahdi. The other three—the old man, the snaky woman, and Ted Flitt—were in the adjoining garage. Everybody was locked in, and everybody was going to be destroyed. With the exception, one supposed, of Mahdi . . .

'When is this destruction to take place?' asked Nadine.

'In fifteen minutes,' answered the Indian.

'Here—in the garage?'

'In fifteen minutes, there will be no garage.'

'Gawd—a blinkin' bomb!'

He wondered whether, if he prayed like Samson, he would be granted strength to burst the lid of the box? Samson's story was the one bit of Bible he knew. He'd seen a picture of it in a packet of cigarettes. But even if God treated him as well as he had treated Samson, would it be any use? Ben couldn't see what use! No, better lie quiet for a bit longer . . .

'Tell me, Mahdi,' said the girl, and the steadiness of her

voice seemed to Ben like a miracle. He himself was one complete wobble. 'Am I to see your master in the next fifteen minutes, or is he to hide himself in fear of me until I am dead? He seems to be more like a frightened ant than a person.'

Then Mahdi laughed, and there was a note in his laughter that Ben did not recognise, and could not place. What did this laughter mean? It was soft, almost purring. There were scorn and triumph in it, and the quiet assurance of a cosmic vanity. For several seconds the sinister sound echoed through the garage. Then, abruptly, it ceased.

'I am the man,' said Mahdi.

Nadine did not lose her poise. She merely drew in a quick, sharp breath. She refused to placate the cosmic vanity.

'So—*you* are the master, Mahdi,' she replied slowly.

'Yes. I am the master, Nadine.'

'Do the others know?'

'They will never know. The pawns live and die in ignorance. It is my rule.'

'Then am I to feel honoured?'

'You *are* honoured—in the last moments of your life. It is a recognition, Nadine. Having dined with the master, and danced with the master, and played with the master, and fooled the master, you now receive the master's reward—the knowledge of his identity, which you sought. And now he asks why you sought it.'

'That should not baffle you,' answered the girl, after a moment's pause. 'Many have wished to know you.'

'And many have failed.'

'I have not.'

'No. And you are about to pay the price of your success. At last, we understand each other, Nadine.'

'Yes, Mahdi. We know each other now. I know you for the leader of one of the most contemptible organisations that have ever fattened on other people's weaknesses, and you know me for a more humble member of an organisation more reputable. I found *your* weakness, Mahdi!'

'True. But profit by it too late. You will have no chance now, Nadine, to tell what you have learned to your friends the police. For, I expect, the police were your friends?'

'Were?' retorted the girl. 'I'm not dead yet!'

'But I never saw you with any member of—how did you phrase it?—that reputable organisation.'

'Would you have trusted me, if you had?'

'So! You separated yourself from the police, to work for them? That was clever—and courageous, Yes, I should certainly have suspected you earlier, Nadine, if you had not taken that precaution. But what a pity I cannot reward you for your work. What a pity! And what a pity, Nadine, that you meddled in *my* work! . . . And there is another here who meddled in my work. With twelve minutes to spare, there is still time to hear what *he* has to say—if, indeed, he is in a position to say anything.' His voice drew nearer the box in which Ben lay. 'I am curious about this other meddler. Very curious.'

When concentrating on others, you may forget about yourself. Now, all at once, Ben ceased to forget. He realised he was a map, running with rivers of perspiration.

In a few seconds he would cease to be merely a listener in the desperate drama that was being enacted outside the box. He would re-enter the drama and participate in it. As the lid opened and reality replaced imagination, he would actually see the girl, and the cords that bound her. But, nearer to him, would be the face of Mahdi. Yes, immediately above him! A few short inches over him! Staring down at him! With what expression? Ferocious surprise? Livid hate? Or—worse—no expression at all? Just two pools of white, with central points of burning black, that scorched and scorched and scorched . . .

Little noises sounded around him. He tried, as once before, to identify them. A sort of scraping. Would that be a knife? A sort of snapping. That sounded like rope. A sort of slithering. Would that be a hand moving towards the fastening hook? A sort of clicking.

A few hours previously, Ben had been stung by his impotence into killing a man. But if he had been impotent then, how much more impotent was he now! His arms could not strike, his legs could not kick, his head could not butt. He was stiff and cramped. He was fatigued and famished. Such brain as he had was numb. And against him would be pitted a free, lithe creature, strong and supple, clear-minded, quick-witted, with a ruthless will that cowed and a ruthless blade that silenced. It wasn't fair—it wasn't fair! The moment was coming—the moment of test, for which all other moments had been endured—and it wasn't fair!

And now, perhaps, without knowing it, Ben prayed to God even as Samson did; and as he prayed, the miracle occurred. His cramped fingers touched something cold.

New perspiration swept over him. The perspiration of despairing hope. The cold thing was something he had forgotten, something he had been destined to forget for the impetus of re-discovery. It had entered the box with him in that frenzied instant at No. 26 Jowle Street. It had lain with him ever since, travelling with him, sliding with him, bumping with him. And now, here it was, touching his fingers, the answer to his voiceless prayers, the key to possible deliverance.

His fingers closed over it, while a hinge creaked above him. He shifted his position slightly. He worked the cold thing round till it was against his side, with its thinnest extremity pointing upwards. The lid of the box began to open.

Gradually the wooden roof disappeared. In its place grew a dark, oval silhouette, with two bright, burning points. For the fraction of an instant Ben stared upwards at the bright, burning points. They appeared to be trying to sap his feeble strength, to numb his will. But, just before they succeeded, just before he was pinned down, he managed to press the cold thing. There was a blinding crash . . .

Then Ben saw a strange vision. Two figures. The first was on the ground, quivering into immobility. The second was staring down at the first. The quivering figure on the ground was the Indian, of course. But who was the other figure?

'Gawd, it's me!' thought Ben.

Wasn't he in the box?

He tottered round. In a corner of the garage was another figure. The figure of a girl, tied to a chair, and hanging limply over her cords. Of three minds in that confined space, only Ben's functioned.

The sudden realisation of this filled the functioning mind with a sense of terrifying responsibility. *'Do something!'* throbbed the sense. That's right. Do something. Just take a breath, and do something.

Hallo! What was that? Somebody was sobbing! He started counting. It wasn't the girl. It wasn't the Indian.

'Lummy, it's me agine!' he thought, amazed. 'Wot am I blubbin' for?'

He tried to stop. He couldn't. A new theory dawned upon him.

'It ain't cryin',' he decided. 'It's laughin'. Somethin's funny!'

What was it? A chop? Yes, that was it! He was riding on a chop and winning the Derby! He could hear the crowd shouting and banging . . . He wrenched himself off the chop. His legs gave way, and he found himself on the Indian. He wrenched himself off the Indian.

That was it! The Indian! *That* was it! All his life he had been running away from Indians. They'd chased him and tried to kill him. They'd crept up creaking stairs, slithered from under beds, leapt out from cupboards. And now *he'd* killed one. There the Indian lay, still and quiet, never to move again. Never to creep, never to slither, never to leap! And he, Ben, had done it! He, Ben! He, Ben! He, Ben! Ha, ha, ha! Ha, ha, ha! Ha, ha—!

Yes, but why had he done it? Wasn't there a reason somewhere? If only he could stop feeling sick. And if only those people would stop shouting and banging, so that he could think! He was mounting the chop again. He was riding it through the spangled sky. 'If I can git ter God,' he thought, ''E'll tell me wot I did it for! 'E'll tell me wot I gotter do!'

He was very near now. Faster, faster! These shouting people mustn't stop him! Then a face appeared in the sky. It was not the face of God, for that is never revealed to us, but it was the nearest to it that Ben would ever know . . .

It brought Ben back from limitless space with a sickening sweep. It provided him with just sufficient sense to understand that his senses were nearly done for. He staggered round. The girl still hung limp over her cords.

And now, a queer, grotesque caution entered into him. He became like a man spending his last penny. The penny he was spending represented his final store of functioning capacity. It was just a question of economics. Could you buy a motor car with a penny?

The only way to do it was to be very still and very slow. Otherwise you would fall over and never get up again. Over there was a girl. You had to get to her somehow. On the ground was a knife. You had to get to that too, because you had to cut the girl's cords. And there was the shouting and the banging. That had to be attended to, also. The question was, which was the best order to do these things, in case you went wollop before you'd done them all?

He bent down towards the knife, very slowly. 'I've stopped cryin',' he thought. 'Good.' He was also pleased to find that he could think, but he must think very slowly and deliberately, just as he must act very slowly and deliberately. That penn'orth had to go a long way.

Soon, however, another thought became necessary.

'If I gits dahn too fur,' he wondered, 'can I git up agine?'

He decreased his pace, and then felt about the floor with his hand. He couldn't look at that moment. The floor was swaying.

His hand touched something. Not the knife, surely? He brought the thing up to his nose. It was a key.

And then, in a sense, history repeated itself. This key, which the Indian must have dropped when falling to the ground, completed the salvation which the revolver had commenced, and, like the revolver, had been delivered into his hands at the crucial moment. For the shouting, which he had deliberately attempted to ignore, now burst more coherently upon his ears, and one of the voices sounded vaguely familiar.

'Say, it's stout!' cried the voice. 'But we'll have it down!'

Thud! Thud! The banging continued.

It was the voice of that other bloke—the bloke who had first been in the box. He must have got out of the window somehow . . . he must have followed the box somehow . . . he must have brought help somehow . . .

Ben took the biggest breath he had ever taken in his life and, clutching the key, hurled himself towards the door. He must have reached it somehow. The key chattered into its hole, and turned . . .

The door swung open. Ben tottered back. People poured in.

'Gal,' said Ben stupidly. 'Hover there. And a bomb.'

Then he began to cry again.

36

And Life Goes On

The people who poured into the garage were Jack Hobart, Douglas Randall, a taximan, and four policemen.

The four policemen had been collected locally, after the taxi had tracked the pursued van to its lair and reinforcements had been deemed necessary—for Hobart now limped, and the taximan was seventy: but Hobart and Randall had met and formed the nucleus of the army as far back as Jowle Street. The former, recovering from the effects of a nasty descent from a second-floor window, had been leaving No. 26 by a dark side alley. The latter, himself suffering from a different kind of a shock received earlier in the day, was approaching with hush money for the murder of the very man he now saw before him. The meeting had been emotional. It required explanation. But since, at the same moment, a box was being carried from No. 26 to a waiting motor van, and Hobart suddenly recalled that he had been particularly instructed to follow this box, the explanation had had to wait until a taxi had been requisitioned for the pursuit.

It was in the taxi that Hobart and Randall resumed their emotions, exchanged stories and, putting two and two together, made a very ugly four.

These facts, briefly stated, may interest the reader who has stayed the course. They were, however, of no immediate interest to Ben. He, with considerably more taken out of him, had also stayed the course, and for a space he could not measure he was not interested in anything at all. Matters were now out of his hands. The girl had been saved. The gang of blackmailers had been rounded up. Above him was the great, silent night. He just lay on a patch of grass and stared up at it.

He did not know how he had got on the patch of grass. Somebody, presumably, had carried him there, it didn't matter. He did not know why there was a tiny warmth in his stomach. Somebody, presumably, had devised something for his stomach. It didn't matter. He did not know what tomorrow was going to bring. Whether it would be a long, long sleep, or a continuation of the strange, fretful business that preceded the long, long sleep. It didn't matter. Nothing mattered. Nothing.

Vague things happened about him. People moved. People whispered. People murmured . . .

'Everybody been got out?'

'The bomb—anyone found it?'

'S'pose we're far enough off?'

Silence. Only the night and the stars again. Then:

'What about the Indian?'

'No thanks! A bit too risky!'

'Yes, but anybody seen him?'

'Ain't he dead?'

One of the stars moved. It seemed to separate itself from

its neighbours and flash across the blackness.

'Oi—don't do that!' thought Ben. A dull sound answered him . . .

'*Boom!*'

Something descended near him, with a little, unnatural flop. It was a fragment of brick. A few seconds ago it had been a portion of a garage. Ben sat up suddenly.

''Ere—wot's 'appenin'?' he gasped.

He found himself staring into two soft eyes. The strength that had shot him up into a sitting position left him as suddenly as it had come. The owner of the eyes was speaking to him. What was she saying?

'Lie down again.' The voice was even softer than the eyes. 'Lie down. Everything's safe.'

He obeyed. The grass seemed warmer, somehow. And the stars seemed brighter. And the tension that held the world together seemed to be relaxing.

Ben lay very silent, staring up into the enigma of space and wondering what it all meant, while cool fingers touched his forehead. And then Ben ceased to wonder. For that is the greatest enigma of all. A woman's touch, even on a battered brow, can dispel the need of inquiry.

THE END